BLOODLINE
RISING

BLOODLINE RISING

KATY MORAN

CANDLEWICK PRESS

First U.S. edition 2011

Library of Congress Cataloging-in-Publication Data is available.

Library of Congress Catalog Card Number 2010046692

ISBN 978-0-7636-4508-3

10 11 12 13 14 15 16 BVG 10 9 8 7 6 5 4 3 2 1

Printed in Berryville, VA, U.S.A.

This book was typeset in Giovanni.

Candlewick Press
99 Dover Street
Somerville, Massachusetts 02144

visit us at www.candlewick.com

*For my sisters,
Victoria Clark and Laura Moran,
and for Will Llewellyn, who went
with me to Constantinople*

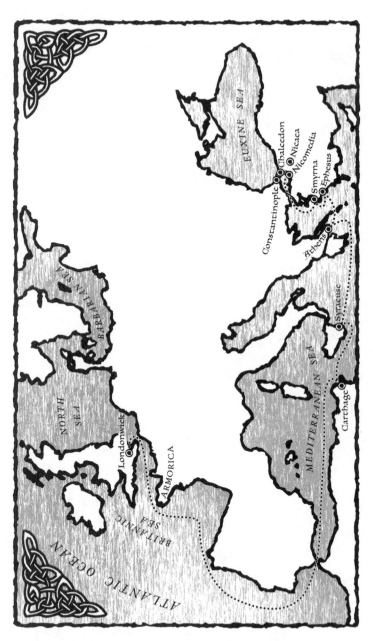

Cai's Journey from Constantinople

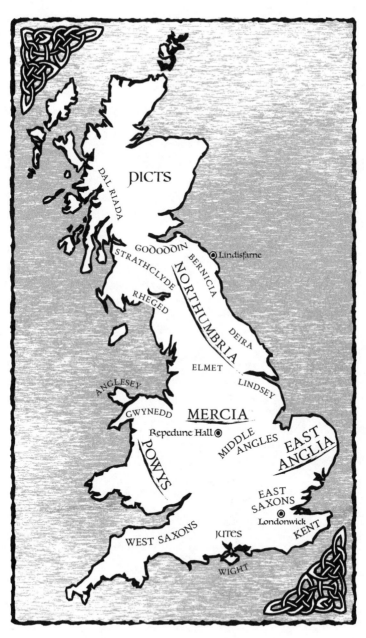

Cai's Britain c. AD 655

PART ONE

Constantinople

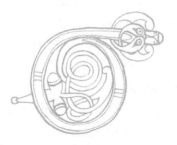

Prologue:
Constantinople, AD 643

The young man moved like a cat: quick, sure. His name was Essa; his eyes were blacker than well water, and they glittered with a strange, hard light. More than a handful of the harbor's pickpockets glanced his way and made other plans — swiftly. There was easier prey. Tall and rangy, Essa wore a sword in a dark, silver-wrought scabbard. Only a fool would have doubted that he was ready to use it, or the keen-edged dagger in his belt, or any one of the six knives hidden on his person.

"Come on, my honey." He stepped, light and fleet, from the wooden gangway onto the quay, then took the girl's hand and helped her ashore. She was with child — and near her time.

If Essa and his girl saw how folk stared at them, at their lean fairness, at the strange brightness of their hair — hers white, like the wing of a swan, his flame-red — they paid no heed. Caught up in the swirling throng, dazed by the crackle and hiss of the strange tongue spoken all around them, they wove through the crowd to the harbor wall.

"We did it, Lark. We got away." He held the girl as close as her swollen belly allowed.

Lark smiled, leaning back against the sun-warmed stones. "What are we going to do now?"

"Have a child, by the look of you."

She laughed. "Talk sense. The haul your mother gave us shan't last forever, and like as not, the folk in this place shall do everything they can to cheat us, just as they did in Carthage."

Essa closed his hand around the hilt of his sword and shrugged. "Ah, well, then, you shall have a child, and I'll fight for gold. This emperor of theirs must have an army somewhere. We'll find it."

Lark looked away, sighing. "We've coin enough to last awhile."

They turned as one, backs to the sea. Shielding their eyes with their hands, Essa and Lark gazed up at the soaring city walls ahead: the jumbled red rooftops and white buildings; the veins of greenery stretching down to the water — dusty gardens and tangled, overgrown orchards; the vast, domed church of rose-pink stone skeined with drifts of bluish smoke; and the huge sky above it all, dotted with wheeling seabirds, dashes of white against the brightness. *How many people must live in there,* Essa wondered, *seething all over one another like ants?* Among the jumble of wharves and ship masts, there were even rickety houses crammed onto piles stretching out over the water, where lines of ragged, faded washing flapped in the sea wind. Women — thumb-size at this distance — gathered around washing tubs, shrieking at the children who leaped off the pilings into the sea, narrowly missing the fishing skiffs that thronged the harbor.

Looking at it all, hardly able to believe the sheer size of this city, Essa felt a pang for the wide, flat marshes of his homeland, where the sky stretched on forever and a man could really breathe. *But there's no going back*, he thought. *We can never go back.*

"Do you think they'll be all right?" Lark said at last, and in her mind she saw those who had been left behind. So few had survived. "Do you think they'll forget us, in the end?"

Essa leaned down, breathing in the warm, salty smell of Lark's hair. "Fenrir will never forget," he said quietly. Then he smiled. "And Mother will tell Thorn about us, and Hild and Egric, and my father, and it shall all grow into a fireside tale."

Lark took his hand. "And what a tale. What a mess."

He laughed. "Ah, God, but we're away from it now. Are you ready?"

And in the years that came afterward, Essa would say he knew, even then, that there was no hope they could escape what had gone before. For a man's past is like his shadow; it follows him everywhere, always just a step behind.

They walked on, into the city.

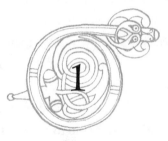

Constantinople, some years later

They are not quick enough to catch me. Jesu, but it's hot up here. A dusty heat haze hovers above the city, blurring the great dome of Santa Sofia. The sea beyond glitters like cloth-of-gold. A pearl of sweat slides from beneath my head scarf and down my cheek. Swallowing a bubble of laughter, I slip into the shadow of a church. From this rooftop, I can see all the way back down to the street market nibbling at the walls of the hippodrome. There they are: two city guardsmen pushing through the heaving crowd. It is like looking down on a carpet seething with moths.

Too slow, my friends, too slow.

The Greens and the Blues are racing at sundown, and already folk are spilling into the circus quarter from every street, square, and slum. Unlike me, they do not know which charioteer will be the faster tonight. A lot of them will lose money on it, some more than they can afford. *They should not be so free with their coin, then,* I think, but then am annoyed with myself. Why should I feel sorry for them? The choice is theirs.

I squat in the dust and bite the last pink, glassy pomegranate seeds from their bitter skin, watching the crowd flow around my two guardsmen. All this fuss for a mangy fruit. It is not often a stallholder sees me, and ill luck it was that the guards were only paces away. I shall have to be more careful. I laugh again — softly, though, for I can hear voices coming from the room below this rooftop — feel them, almost, shaking up through the sunbaked red tiles.

Time I was away. There is work to do.

Demosthenes is in the circus stables, leaning over the stall gate and murmuring something into the pricked-up ear of one of his horses — Helen, she's called. Demosthenes races a pair of grays, matched so well that they hardly take a step out of time. The other he calls Paris. Demosthenes reads too much; if I were a charioteer, I would not name my horses after a pair of doomed lovers.

Leaning into the shelter of a barrel stacked up by the far wall, I breathe in the warm, round stink of oats, straw, and horse dung. I watch Demos lean farther over the gate, rubbing Helen between her black-tipped ears as he whispers to her. He talks to Helen as if she were a woman rather than a horse. He loves her. He does not know I am here; I am good at not being seen. I smile, resting back against the sun-warmed barrel. Demosthenes the Great may love his horses, but it will not stop him from losing this race. *You are the greatest chariot rider this city has ever seen,* I think, *but you are really bad at dice.*

I step out of the shadows.

The charioteer turns to look at me. "You again, boy," he says. Demos is a slight man, not much taller than I am, with black hair that curls back from his forehead. But the muscles on his lean arms are knotted like leather cords and I know he is not a man to bait. His pride is wounded, for a start. That always makes them worse: madder than snakes in a barrel. "You're like a ghost, the way you creep around." Demos frowns. "How came you to be in here?"

I smile, fixing my eyes on his, and for a moment he looks as if he has lost his senses or cannot remember who he is nor why he's standing in this stable. "My master sent me to remind you," I say. "About the race."

Demos shakes his head, running his hands through his hair. "Tell the Emperor of Thieves not to fret — the Blues shan't win tonight, and my debt'll be paid off. Let me tell you one thing, brat: never play dice. Or not for money, at least." The charioteer stares at me, eyes narrowed. "What age are you, anyhow? Should you not be at home with your mother?"

But I don't have time to spare for foolish questions. "Hear this," I tell him. "If you win tonight, before sunrise the whole city shall know you've been fixing races for gold. But if you lose, as we agreed, no one will ever know of it. Do not forget."

Demos sighs, and the fine lines around his eyes seem to grow deeper. He looks so tired, and I know why. Once there was a churchman who spoke out against the True God, and I saw him borne through the streets by a great tangled throng of men and women — even some children younger than me. They were baying and screaming, tearing out his beard, gouging at his eyes. I remember my mother: *What manner of place is this, where they treat men like lumps of meat?* she cried. My shoulder ached by the time she had dragged Elflight and me home. This was before Tecca was born. Oh, but it hurts in my belly to think of Tecca, even now. We heard that when the mob had finished with the bishop, the corpse was missing an arm and that his tongue had been ripped out.

That's what shall happen to Demos if anyone finds out he fixes the races for coin, I think, and I can tell by the weariness in the charioteer's eyes that he knows this, too.

"I've chosen my path. I'll go where it takes me," Demos says, and his courage makes me feel ashamed; I'll never be like him. My path is the quickest road to riches, and may the devil take anyone who gets in my way. It is not an honorable choice, but this is the first time I have cared. Demos walks across the stable toward me, moving swift and catlike. "There's something about you, boy," he says. "I've been trying to catch at it for weeks. Who are you?"

Mary, Mother of God. It is time I was gone.

Out of the stables, back into the heaving marketplace of the hippodrome. The great bulk of Santa Sofia looks down on me as if in judgment; her walls glow pinkish in the dying light. Smoke from a thousand cook-fires blues the air, and I suck in the scent of grilled meat: chicken and tiny quails with sweet flesh nestling under the blackened skin, fish drawn silvery and flipping from the Sea of Marmara just this morning. I'm hungry, despite the pomegranate, but there's no time for my kind to fill our bellies while people swarm into the hippodrome for the race. Shutters are left open, doors unlatched; this will be a ripe evening for the Emperor of Thieves' children. There are so many empty homes, so many trinkets and baubles. The emperor takes most of it, but not all — enough to keep us coming back for more. I am learning from my master. One day I shall be greater than him, and I will be King of the Underworld, lord of smuggling, gambling, pickpocketry, bribery, and theft.

I move through the throng like an eel weaving through weeds at the bottom of a slow green river. A gaggle of young men in blue armbands shove their way past, and I step back into a narrow doorway to let them by. They are loud and drunk, steeped in wine already, which makes me smile. They shall be none too pleased when Demos the Great loses the race in the last lap. If they've any luck, they'll spend most of their gold on wine before they have time to place any ill-fated bets. I think of Demos, alone in the stables with his horses. How strange it must be for him, running through the race in his mind, working out when to lose instead of how to win. Poor Demos. But I'm being softheaded, a fool.

Demos is right: he chose his path the moment he laid more money on dice than he could borrow.

I slip west down near the Great Palace and turn into an alley darkened by tall houses with balconies and windows blistering out of their walls. Even here, there is a throng. A girl is selling sugared lemons from a tray hanging around her neck, and men are sitting on the steps of the houses, drinking wine and arguing about the race.

"It'll be Demosthenes again," says a fat man, gesturing wildly with his wine cup so that dark liquid splashes out and stains the dusty street. "And don't try to tell me otherwise, Mikos, because you only make yourself look like a fool. Temon can't beat Demosthenes. He doesn't have the speed."

I leave the raised voices behind. Little do they know. At the end of the alley lies a secret hole, hidden behind a tangle of warm green vines and a heap of decaying brick. My city is old beyond time, and she has many hide-away, crumbling places — I know them all, and I love each one. Drawing in my breath, I clear my mind and think of nothing, knowing that although the street is heaving with people, no one will see me as I slip into the darkness. Already my skin feels damp. It is cold down here. Someone has left a torch alight farther down the passage, and it casts a dim, oily glow on the stone walls. There is a smell of stale water that reminds me of wet metal, of rain drying on my father's sword out in the courtyard, long ago. *Don't think about him.*

Smoke hits the back of my throat. Someone has the fire going in the tin cook-pot I stole from that one-eyed stallholder up on the Mese. Who is it? Who's here? Surely most are on their way to the hippodrome, already busy liberating coin from the money bags of foolish people. Soon the cold passageway opens out, and I see a forest of vast stone pillars reflected in the long, dark pit of water spreading out before me. They are like trees turned to rock by a witch man. In places, daylight streams down through holes in the vaulted roof where the paving slabs on the streets above have cracked, worn by many thousands of human feet. Tendrils of tangled weeds hang down, twisting in the slanted light.

Some say that this flooded underground palace was once the home of a wicked empress, that she was cast beneath the earth, along with her rooms and all her riches, as a punishment from God for her sins. Some say she walks among her chambers still, her hair knotted with slime, her skin whiter than bone. You may never be sure when she will come. I know that all this is untrue — because I made it up. The Kingdom of the Ghost is nothing but a big old underground lake that keeps freshwater flowing in the Great Palace. But it pays to have my subjects leery and afraid.

When I first came here, the water was so low that I could wade from pillar to pillar, but then it rose, and last year we built rope paths. That was a lot of rope we stole from the docks. Days and days it took to get it all. I leap onto a rope path now and run — it bucks and sways beneath me, but I haven't fallen yet. Who is down here, sitting by my fire, while all the rest are out harvesting riches for our master?

This is *my* place. When I am here alone, I feel like I am lord over it all; the thought of someone else claiming my rightful kingdom makes me cold and shivery.

Don't be a fool, I tell myself. *It's probably just Iskendar or Niko waiting for you.* Yet I cannot help it: I've a sense that there's something sorely amiss down among the pillars of my dark, watery palace. I almost see the intruder now — it's gloomy here. He's big, whoever it is. Bigger than me. Who? My master's older subjects rarely visit my kingdom. I am like a spider in their soup, a thorn in the soles of their feet. I have always known it riles them, seeing that the master trusts me more, that he uses me for his more interesting and delicate tasks even though I am younger by far. Well, it is not my fault that I am better. The best thief in Constantinople.

It is Thales. Thales the Knife.

He is sitting on the ledge by my cook-pot fire, legs dangling down toward the water. His toes graze the surface. He is not frightened of the dark, glassy depths. Unlike the others.

"Why so quickly, little Ghost?" Thales says, turning to look at me in the shadows. Thales is taller than me by a head and a half — he must have fourteen summers at least — and his limbs are knotted with muscle. Everyone knows how he got his name. No one plays games with the Knife. I wish now that I had crept up on him instead of bounding in like this. A foolish mistake. My second of the day, after nearly getting caught by the guard for stealing that pomegranate. If Iskendar and Niko knew of that, they would never let me forget it.

I shrug, stepping off the rope path onto the ledge. "It is not often you delight us with your noble self down here, Thales the Knife."

Thales lifts one eyebrow. Everyone is always so fawning and slimy toward him that he cannot tell if I'm mocking or not. *Surely the brat wouldn't dare?* I see the thought flash across his mind as clearly as if it were my own. "I don't concern myself with children — that's why," he says.

I lean back against the wall and it chills my skin, but at least I can look down on him like this. "I'm all the more honored, then," I say. "How may I serve you, Thales? It better be quick. It's time I was away to the circus."

Thales smirks. "There'll be no circus for you tonight, my boy," he says.

I have to think about Tecca to stop myself from laughing at him. I'm so full of sin, using poor Tecca like this, but I'm sure she would not mind.

"You're wanted," Thales goes on. "You're to go up to the villa before the sun is down. Do you know where it is?"

We both know that I have been admitted into the chambers of our emperor more times than he has. *Fool!* I tell myself. *Don't let him see that you think he's not got the brain of an ox.* I smile, saying, "I think I know it well enough."

What does our emperor want? I wonder, feeling a tiny flicker of fear. It pays ill to get on the wrong side of our master, and he does not like us to forget this. I cannot help thinking of Black Elias. Till last summer, he was our master's golden angel-thief who could do no wrong. And then word got out that instead of tumbling his stolen prizes into the lap of the Emperor of Thieves, Elias had been selling them to traders out of Chalcedon. Elias has not been seen for many a long month. They say he was found floating in the harbor with both hands missing. The Emperor of Thieves does not make a quick end for his enemies.

But what am I thinking? I've done no wrong; I'm not like Elias. All that I steal, I hand over to my lord.

"I hope you've been behaving yourself, little Ghost," Thales says. "I wouldn't want to be in your place if you haven't. Better go directly to Master, shouldn't you?"

Thales is boring me now. And he is right. It's time I was away. The emperor does not like to be kept waiting, and besides, I'm curious. What can he want? But before I find out, I must teach the Knife a lesson.

It happens quite easily—all thought, all color drains from my mind as I step away from the leaping shadows of the cook-pot fire.

Thales shakes his head; if he a friend with him, he might try to not look scared, but he's alone—he cannot help it. "Where've you gone, you little witch? Your tricks don't scare me, brat," he hisses.

Just because he cannot see me, he thinks I cannot hear him. He is wrong: there is no ungodly magic here. I am just quiet and quick, but it fills people with fear when the next moment I am just not there anymore. Up the wall I go, digging my toes into gaps, curling my fingers over crumbling ledges, gripping at plants creeping out of cracks.

I'm climbing up to the light — there's a hole in the vaulted roof where a paving slab's fallen down into my underground lake.

I feel the breath quicken in my body; I want to laugh as I climb.

Thales is standing now, holding on to one of the rope walkways, looking around. "You think you're so cunning, don't you?" he says. "But one day soon you'll get what's coming to you, you and your barbarian witch father. He's a traitor now, or haven't you heard the news? Don't think I don't know who you really are, Ghost. You have no place in the Empire of Thieves."

My father. A cold, empty feeling washes over me. What does Thales the Knife know about him? But I don't stop climbing. That's what Thales wants. He wants to goad me into coming back, so I will try to fight him. As if I'd be that foolish. He'd love an excuse to finish me off.

Who does he think I am?

I'm nearly there, nearly out into the street. I can feel the light warm on my face. Up, up. I'm out. Out on the street, pressing my face against the sunbaked pavement. A woman nearly trips over me and looks back, cursing. She cannot see me. It is a skill I have. I can go anywhere without being seen; I can do anything.

It is why they call me the Ghost, and it is why no one can stop me.

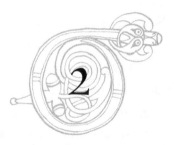

2

In the garden of the Emperor of Thieves

I GO OVER the rooftops, thirsting with the need to leap, silent and quick, through the night. It is dark now, but the shadowy city is festooned with firelit windows like so many winking, blinking jewels. To the west, the sea shimmers, a silver path laid across it by the moon. There is just a faint, fine line of purply light across the horizon, and as I watch, that too disappears. The sun has gone; it is night.

What does Thales know about him? I am thinking of my father — a sport I ought long since to have given up. He's a traitor now, is he? I will never believe that. Father is so stuffed full of barbarian notions that he has honor and loyalty coming out of his ears. He is so true to the empire that he has forgotten his own kin. I spit as I leap from one rooftop to the next, imagining my spittle landing right in his black, glittery eye. I hear word of him almost every day in the marketplace — how could I not, when everyone knows who he is? If there is not some girl cooing over his great beauty, a pack of brainless young men will be telling the latest tale of how he slayed five Arabs with one sweep of his sword. He's in the desert now, they say, bargaining with the Caliphate. Sometimes my father rides out with tribes who wander the wilderness and live all year in tents, and he listens to secrets whispered along the trade paths from a great land far to the east. God's Fire, they call him, for his skill in sending the enemies of the emperor off to the next world. Not my emperor, the Emperor of Thieves — Father has a different lord, Constans the Second, Imperial Master of the New Roman Empire.

But I'm not going to think about my father. What is the use?

I have never gone into my lord's house through the front door. The first time I tried this trick, everyone thought I had lost my senses. *He'll have your throat cut as soon as look at you,* Iskendar said. *There are rules,* Niko told me. *Ways of doing things. You have to go up to the door and knock five times, and if you're let in, you have to drop on your knees straightaway.*

I do none of those things. I go over the garden wall, like I'm doing now. There's an old peach tree growing right up it, and over I go. The Emperor of Thieves is the one person in this city who may leave his doors unlocked, his windows unshuttered for days and nights on end. Who would be so mindless as to steal from here?

The garden is heavy with the scent of jasmine and rosemary, lavender and mastic sap. It makes me feel dizzy, but the emperor likes his garden to sing to him, or so he says when he's in a confiding mood.

Grass brushes against my ankles; I catch the reek of roses, of thyme. It's not so dark that I can't see the house, and my eyes are good at night, anyhow. All the windows are lit — the Emperor of Thieves has no cause to skimp on lamp oil. The window I want is on the upper floor. Up the trellis I go; waxy vine leaves brush at my face, stickying my fingers with the juice of summer's last grapes. One hand on the ledge. The other. Nearly there. I wait, listening.

I can hear low voices — just two — and the scrapings and chewings of men eating their supper. I have caught my lord at table. So much the worse for him; if he did not want me, he ought not to have asked for me. Arms straining, I haul myself over the window ledge and drop onto the cool tiled floor, crouching immediately in the shadows. Who's here? At the far end of the room is a table; my lord sits there with Narxes, his eunuch. No one loves my emperor more than Narxes, and no one's madder or more dangerous. Apart from maybe my father. Narxes is not from the empire. He is pale-skinned, and his cheekbones are high — Black Elias told me once that Narxes was taken as a slave from Slavic lands and served in the Imperial Guard up at the palace. Narxes has got that softness about his face that all eunuchs do. Not quite a woman, but not quite a man.

He's pouring my lord more wine, leaning forward across the table. The lamplight glints off his shaven head.

"That will be enough," says the Emperor of Thieves, holding out one of his long, delicate hands. "We have a visitor."

Narxes jumps slightly and looks vexed with himself for doing it. Seeing me, he says, "It is usual, boy, to knock."

My lord laughs, and, quick, quick, I come forward to bow my head before him. I glance up and see Narxes sitting back in his chair, frowning slightly. There's a big platter on the table heaped with what looks like stuffed kid; it smells of garlic and fish sauce and has that rank, goaty stink about it, too. Narxes does not seem delighted that I've gotten in the way of their meat. He is fiddling with the stalk of a half-eaten pear by his plate. He is twitchy. Why?

"So," says my lord. "The race is now begun. How went your little chat with Demosthenes, Ghost?"

"He has not forgotten, my lord. He swears he shall not win."

My lord smiles, and the skin creases around his ruined eyes. I cannot help staring, sometimes, wondering what it would be like to lose my sight, to have my eyes scraped from my skull. No one knows what crime the Emperor of Thieves committed, long ago, but I've heard he was born to the Purple, that he is close bound to the Emperor Constans by blood, and that his eyes were taken from him so that he might not be a challenge to the throne. I've heard that Narxes was the only member of the Imperial Guard loyal to him, and that is why Narxes serves the Underworld now instead of the empire. But you never know what's true and what's made-up. For all I know, the Emperor of Thieves was nothing more than a pickpocket with a good head for trade.

I'm burning to ask him what he wants, but I know I cannot. I may come in through the window — he likes that; he admires the cheek of it — but I'm no fool. There is only so far I can go. Narxes gives him a look, one eyebrow slightly lifted, and I can tell he's not going to like what the emperor's about to say —

"You have done well," says my lord. "There are not many I could trust to deliver my messages to Demosthenes. Now there's something else I want you to do."

Narxes' eyebrow lifts even higher. He likes this very ill. It must be something good.

"Your wish is my command, O lord," I say.

"Come closer, child."

I go and sit at his feet as if I were a tiny stripling and he my dearest papa. I look up but not quite at him, my eyes lowered in respect. My lord cannot see, but he feels everything, I swear it. He can feel the way you look at him. Narxes' mouth is pursed as if he smells something bad, and now he's gazing out the window. He is probably trying to pretend I'm not here.

My lord smiles. "Do you know the house of Achaicus Dassalena?" he says to me.

Achaicus Dassalena? Achaicus *Dassalena*? I know where he lives, all right. He is the prefect of Constantinople, second in command only to the Emperor Constans himself. The Emperor of Thieves rules the Underworld, Achaicus very nearly everything else. "I know his house," I say. "It's the big villa with the blue door down near the palace." I hold my breath for a moment. "What would my lord have me do?"

The Emperor of Thieves smiles, pressing his lips together. "Now, listen, little Ghost. The Guild of Thieves has been revered as Keeper of Order in the Underworld since the days of Constantine himself, when Rome had only just been abandoned to the barbarians and the empire was still full of fire. You understand me, Ghost, do you not?"

I gaze down at the floor, wondering what I have done to besmirch this noble history. There is a chicken bone beneath the table with a shiny lump of gristle still attached; Narxes really ought to have a talk with my lord's servants. "Of course, my lord," I say.

This city runs with all the smoothness and mystery of the mechanical angels they have at the palace to confuse barbarian kings. Even the Underworld must bleed tax money into the imperial coffers. The Guild of Thieves pays its dues just as the silk weavers, the silversmiths, and all the rest of them. There is even a Guild of Sewer Workers, and they are probably taxed as well. But not so high as us.

"Well," says my lord, "Achaicus Dassalena has just made a foolish choice."

I let out a tiny, relieved breath. It is not me, then, who has offended the honor of the Guild of Thieves. He goes on: "Achaicus has deemed that our guild is no longer to be tolerated. I fear that the running of the city has softened his mind: he wants to rid Constantinople of thievery altogether. He wants to close us down."

What an idiot. Where's the use in that? It'll never work, and if there is always to be thievery, bribery, smuggling, and racketeering, why not have some coin out of it in taxes?

The Emperor of Thieves leans closer. I cannot help looking at his eye sockets. The skin is thin, purply, puckered where it healed long ago. He speaks: "Do you recall the name Callias Athenas?"

A chill slides down my spine. Callias Athenas used to be in the army, commander of the Thracians. There was a scandal — everyone heard whispers of it but never the whole tale. While Constans was away out east last year, fighting against the Caliphate over Armenia, there were whisperings that he was not fit to be emperor, that he'd abandoned the capital in her hour of direst need, leaving her like a virgin girl hemmed about by pirates. Then Constans came back, Callias disappeared, and the whispering stopped. It was fools' talk, anyway — if this city were a woman, she'd be a raddled, wise old whore, not a virgin girl.

"Your silence tells me that you know something of this," says my lord. "Am I correct?"

I nod, then recall that he cannot see me and say, "Yes, O lord."

"Callias Athenas was a fool," says the emperor. "The truth of it is that he had a lust for power himself, and when Constans was in the desert, Callias took his chance and tried to win the nobility and the army over to his side so he could take the throne. Callias had all the eastern army behind him and most of the nobility—but Constans has spies everywhere, and word of the betrayal reached him. That is why he came back in such a great hurry when Muahi'ya the Arab was still razing Armenia."

I nod, thinking, *What does this have to do with Achaicus Dassalena? Unless*—

"Constans's spies rooted out most who'd sided with Callias," says my lord, his voice dry and thin. "But Achaicus Dassalena covered his trail well."

Achaicus Dassalena, prefect of the city, upholder of the law—a traitor? Surely this cannot be true. The law in Constantinople is the will of the emperor, and he rules by the grace of God. To be sure, I am a thief, yet every coin has another face: there cannot be law without disorder. But for the prefect to betray the emperor is just unnatural. They are meant to be on the same side.

I cannot help smiling. This is going to be good. It is going to be a grand old caper, which is just what I like. Narxes takes a swig of wine, still staring studiously out the window, as if not looking at me will make me disappear.

What will my lord have me do? I wonder.

He bends toward me in his chair. I can smell the garlic and kid meat on his breath.

"Somewhere," he hisses, "Achaicus Dassalena left a trace of his betrayal. It will be in his home: he's not fool enough to leave any sign of it in the palace. You are going to find it for me, and then we'll see about him putting a stop to the Guild of Thieves. Achaicus will be as a newborn kit in the palm of my hand." My lord leans back in his chair, his thin, bluish lips twisting into a smile.

I feel hot with the thrill of it. I have broken into many a fine villa. But never into the house of Achaicus Dassalena, prefect of Constantinople.

This is turning into a fine evening.

A robbery

I T IS one of those nights when my city feels alive. The crowds surging through her streets are her blood, the jumble of buildings her ancient bones. It's quicker to go by the alleys, but I race up along the Mese, anyway. It runs like a spine across Constantinople, this street, widening out through the Forum of Theodosius, where market stalls cluster around crumbly pillars and that big old statue of Emperor Justinian on his horse. As I run, the air's rich with the stink of tanned leather, the jangle of silver. Here's a girl selling quince sweets and ginger buns, and a wineshop cluttered with stools where careless drunks sit, their purses unwatched. The race at the hippodrome has put fire in everyone. It must be over now, surely. I hope for Demosthenes' sake that he kept to our bargain.

The night air is thick with cook-fire smoke that stings my eyes, and I can smell grilling fish. Just up here's where Aikaterina the Fat has her grill-shop. I weave my way through the tangle of people, getting closer. It never pays to burgle on an empty stomach. The crowd shifts, parts, shifts again like a shoal of fish. . . . I remember, once when I was small, we were taken out on a boat and my father showed me a dark patch on the water, ruffled by white foam, and when we turned closer to the wind and drew nearer, he lifted me. We saw a great rush of mackerel, mottled and shiny in the water as if they'd been born out of a forge fire.

My father used to get such a longing in his eyes when he saw the sea. "The ocean is like a great road, little cub," he once said. "She has taken me far from home, and she whispers to me at night when I'm near her, singing me the way back."

It's one of the few times he has ever spoken of the north.

I wonder if he dreams of home now, away in the desert with Muahi'ya the Arab, and I wonder, too, what Thales the Knife meant when he said my father was a traitor. Has he gone over to Muahi'ya's camp and become an enemy of the empire? I've heard of people doing that: deciding the Prophet Mohammed had the last word after all, not Christ, and changing sides. It is not Father's way, though — he's still half in thrall to his barbarian gods, just like Ma, who hangs bread dipped in wine from the branches of the vines in our courtyard. What has my father been doing? But I'll be damned if I'll go begging news from Thales.

I push closer to Aikaterina's stall. I can see the stone tables laid out in the street now, and the crowd's even thicker the closer I get, but still I can hear her yelling, "Get it while it's hot! Three coppers for fish so fresh he's still swimming!" I smile. Aikaterina's got such a big mouth on her, I bet even the Arabs out in the desert know how much a griddled mackerel costs. Sometimes Aikaterina just gives up and hands one over to me; she knows I'll have it whether she likes it or not. But there are so many people in the way: a group of boys a few summers older than me — palace puppets all blown up with hot air, hawking, and wine. I think the one with greasy dark hair hanging around his shoulders might even be Solon Dassalena, ever-loving only son of the prefect himself. What a happy chance. I remember Solon from those parties in the palace gardens: all venom and rose-petal wine among the peach trees.

"Elflight promises to be just as fair as you, my dear," Lady Dassalena used to say to my mother, smirking. "It is so fortunate that your daughter shall grow up surrounded by the benefits of civilization."

My parents' beauty saved them from the slum quarters and cast them straight into the courtyard of the Great Palace, but it didn't stop the fine ladies from laughing at my mother because she speaks with a strange accent and could not read till she was a grown woman.

I am going to enjoy burgling the home of Lady Dassalena.

Little does Solon know where I'm bound. He and his friends have got girls with them, girls with their faces veiled and their hair covered. Not market wenches they have hooked in the street, then. These must be girls of their own kind — rich ones, smuggled out of the house. I don't blame them: if I were a female and had to spend my days cloistered like that, I would break out as well. I wonder what they've got in their little clutchy bags, ready for the taking.

Solon shoves past the gaggle of people waiting at Fat Aikaterina's stall and goes right to the front.

"There's folk waiting, you know!" says a woman with a couple of little brats hanging off her skirts.

Solon — I'm sure it's him — turns and says, "Oh, be quiet, you whore," and the fools with him laugh — all except one, who turns away as if she is ashamed. There's something about her that's so familiar: the proud way she holds her head. Solon casts a shower of silver coin at Aikaterina, saying, "Don't bother about the difference," and walks back to his table, bearing steaming parcels of fish wrapped in flatbread. My stomach growls — time to eat and be away from here.

Moments later, I'm leaning against the stone table, reaching past Solon and his heedless friends, my fingers closing around a parcel of fish, smoking hot and griddle-charred. They cannot see me. I want to laugh. It's so easy to do this in a crowd, it amazes me that anyone wonders at it, but why else do they call me the Ghost? All I do is think of nothing, allow my mind to clear, and no one can see me.

The girl who did not laugh suddenly turns. She's looking right at me with a pair of clear gray eyes. I'd know them anywhere. It's Elflight: my sister, my twin.

Oh, for the love of God. What is she doing here?

29

I run.

You're a brainless fool, Elfla, I think, clawing one-handed up a wall and dropping down into a dank, winding alley that stinks of piss and rotting food, still holding my stolen supper. If she's found outside without a chaperone, she'll end her days in the whorehouse or the nunnery. I sprint down to the little church at the far end of the alley, where it reeks less and there's a fountain dribbling greenish water over a mossy statue of a woman with no arms. Sitting in the dust outside Our Lady of the Savior, I cram the hot fish into my mouth without even tasting it. She's got muck for brains, my sister, God curse her eyes. And then I laugh, sitting there in the shadow of Our Lady.

If I were Elflight, I'd do just the same. And I am hardly at home playing the dutiful son and mopping the fevered brow of my sick mother. But I'm not a girl, and if Elflight loses her good name, what else has she got? A mother who will not move, will not speak, cannot stop bloody weeping, and a father in the middle of the desert. She is not even betrothed to anyone, because Father said she should have a husband of her own choosing. Not much use, our mother and father, to Elflight and me. I will have to do something about this — but later. The night is deepening, and before anything else, there is the house of Achaicus Dassalena to visit.

Toward the great looming bulk of the palace I run, slipping along these twisty alleys like a snake. Here's where all the high-and-mighty ones gather close around the emperor, as if nestling up to his gates might cause some of his power to seep into their own homes.

But no one is safe from the Ghost. I can go anywhere.

I've done it, I've done it. I sprint along the roof of the silk merchant's warehouse, my heart bursting with glee. I run so fast, I scarcely feel the warmth of the tiles beneath my bare feet. The alley below throngs with folk returning home from the races; the stink of hot wine, charring meat, and boiling sausages roils up from stalls jammed against the crumbling walls, overshadowed by ancient, crabbed apricot trees heavy with fruit. I have you now, Achaicus Dassalena.

I hadn't thought it would be so easy. I reach the edge of the roof and leap across the width of the alley, right above the heads of the fools below me, landing neatly on the domed roof of an old bathhouse. I can stop now. I'm safe. I edge, light and quick, around the bulk of the dome, the old brick rough beneath my feet, crumbly, sandy to the touch. I crouch in the shadows and reach into my tunic.

Inside, there's just the roll of vellum, soft and leathery. In the light of the moon, I unroll it, and here we are: a list of names. It's a letter to Callias, unsent, signed at the bottom by seven, eight, nine, ten men. I want to whistle out loud when I read the names again. Achaicus must have kept it to ensure that none of the others betrayed him. Wily old fox — but Chance has turned her face from him now.

On this day of our Lord, we the undersigned do solemnly declare our belief that Constans, son of Constantine, is no longer fit to bear the ruling of our most glorious empire, caught as he is in the grip of a cruel obsession with the Arab threat, paying no heed to the pressures brought to bear on us by the Slavs or to the sorrowful consequence of these high taxes on every man, woman, and child in the empire —

I have the devil's own luck.

It was surprisingly easy to find, hidden in a locked chest in Achaicus's own chamber. But then, he was not thinking that anyone would come looking for this wee treasure. Achaicus is an arrogant fool.

My lord is going to love me even more when I take it to him. And take it I must. I wouldn't want to be Achaicus when he sees it's missing. I put the scroll safe inside my tunic again, lying flat against my belly. I know I should go straight back to my lord with it, but there's something I must do first.

I'm afraid that if I don't do it now, I never shall.

I'm on the palace wall, stepping over trailing ivy, running east, swift as a lark. I hate coming here. Bad feelings swirl around in my guts. But if I do not tell her, who will? Sucking in my breath, I leap. This jump always thrills me and frightens me at the same time, but I make it; I've never failed, though I'd be lying if I said I had not nearly missed a handful of times. I crouch on the roof for a moment, catching my breath. The tiles are still warm after the day's heat.

This was once our stable. Elflight and I thought we might rent the space to some workman or artisan, but as far as I know, it's empty yet. Our house is not the only one pinched by this desert war. I recall the day we sold our horses. We did it down at the market, and I'll not forget the way Ares looked at us as the silk merchant's slave led the pair of them away. Zeus went more easily, but he was ever that way, trusting and easy.

A cat steps out of the shadows, sending my heart up my throat. She watches me for a moment, her eyes glassy in the darkness, then slinks off and I'm alone again.

I'm outside Maria's window, sitting in the branches of the olive tree. The twisty old bark's rough against my legs and back. Both shutters are tightly closed, which sends an odd, chilly shudder down my neck. This isn't right. Maria always leaves her window open — that's half why I chose this way in, as well as the fact that nothing shocks Maria and she won't make a fuss at the sight of me.

Slinging one arm around the tree trunk, I lean forward, peering in through the gap between the shutters. There's not a chink of light, not even one lamp lit. Where is she?

Curses — I'll have to take the hard way. I edge out along the branch till I reach the window next to Maria's. The knotted bark digs even harder into my legs. One of the shutters is ajar, and flickery lamplight shines through.

It's Ma's room. I hear voices within. I edge closer. Who can be with her? By leaning forward far enough to grip the window ledge, I get near enough to peer in through the crack between the shutters. I see a wedge of Ma's chamber: the edge of her bed, the heavy drapes drawn back, lamp shadows leaping. I can't see Ma, but I can see a woman sitting on her bed, back to the window. She's dressed in a heavy cloak, hood tossed back to reveal a mass of shining dark hair with a thin veil thrown over it. The veil's dotted with flinders of gemstone that catch the lamplight whenever she moves.

Fausta.

Oh, Mother, you may be useless and bedridden, but you do have friends in high spots, do you not? How many can claim sickbed visits from the empress herself? It's not every barbarian wench who finds herself a place at court in the Great Palace. Only the ones who are so shockingly fair of face that folk swear they've been blessed by God. But what use is your fairness now, Mother dear?

"You must have hope," Fausta is saying in a low, urgent tone. "Now more than ever, Lark. How else can you live?"

She may talk till hell freezes over and it won't change anything. I do not even know why Fausta bothers coming. Ma will not move from that bed till the day she dies.

I cannot stand to hear any more of this. Soundless, I climb higher up the tree till I reach the window above Ma's. The branches are thinner here, whippy, and I must move like a cat, light and quick. Again, the shutters are open. I reach out and draw them wider, and then I'm in, perching on the window ledge.

Here they are: two girls sitting on a bed, talking in low voices. Asha is combing my sister's hair. Elflight looks up first. She jumps, and then her face softens when she sees it's me. "Damn your eyes, what are you doing here?"

Asha drops the comb, whispering what must be a prayer in her own desert tongue. The comb clatters to the floor.

"A fine welcome for your dear and only brother," I say, swinging my legs.

Asha's covering her mouth with both hands. Her hair's grown since I saw her last; it hangs over her shoulder in a shiny black plait.

"Where's Maria?" I ask.

Asha and Elflight share a quick, hunted look. "We had to sell her," Elflight says, a hard, defiant edge to her voice.

"*What?*" How could she? Maria has always been here. "But she's an old woman—"

"What was I meant to do?" Tears start trailing down Elflight's face. Oh, God—I never know what to do with weeping girls. "We've not seen any of Tasik's pay since long before Easter. *What was I to do?* Keep Maria here for all of us to starve and shudder in the winter?"

Jesu. I untie the bag of coin from my belt and let it fall with a shuddery clink. Asha and Elflight both stare at it as though it's a burning ember that might char a hole right through the floor. The red rug's gone—has she sold that, too? She should have sent word to me.

Elflight snatches up the bag and steps toward me. "What do you want?" She stops, leaving a gap between us. "For God's sake! When did you last wash? What do you think you're doing, playing this game of thieves? Why can't you just—?"

"If you don't like it," I say, "don't take the coin. Anyhow, what fool's game were you playing, out with Solon Dassalena and his brainless friends, and no chaperone?"

Elflight laughs. "Oh, come on, now," she says. "My runaway little brother, head of the family all of a sudden? I never thought to hear this!"

Elflight is my elder by just a handful of sand through an hourglass — we shared our mother's womb, growing together inside her — but you would think there were twenty years between my sister and me, the way she goes on.

Now Asha speaks. "Ought I to tell your mother?" she whispers.

I could kill her. "Make another sound and you'll be sorry," I say.

Asha stares at the floor.

"You've no right to speak to her like that!" Elflight hisses. "Just go." She turns to Asha. "Don't. It'll only upset Ma again. It makes me ill to think of the time I've wasted trying to keep him here, and all for nothing."

"All right," I say. "It's not me who'll finish in the whorehouse, pleasing fat old men for coin."

"How dare you?" Elflight reaches out to slap me, but she's too slow. Always was, the heifer. I'm back in the olive tree before she can even get close.

"Asha," I call. "Look after her. If she must run around the streets, let it be with you."

And then I'm gone before either of them can answer.

Down in the alley, a shadow steps out of the side gate. It's

Asha, breathing hard. She must have run like a hare, but she is not fast enough to catch me. "Don't go," she says, and I stop.

I have not stopped for anyone in years.

I remember my mother bringing home a girl from the market with hair as black and glossy as the skin of a plum. I remember sitting in the fountain with Asha when we were small, shrieking and splashing each other with bright beads of water. I remember Asha talking softly to my mother till Ma took a little sup of milk, the first thing to pass her lips since we had buried Tecca. I thought my mother would die, too, till Asha had her drink the milk.

I would stop for no one else.

"Why do you not come back?" Asha says. "You only make it worse by staying away."

"I can't." There's no use in trying to make her see—the Guild of Thieves is my family now. I feel the scroll resting against my chest, safe inside my tunic. Safe for the moment. I'm sure it's getting hotter, as if it is burning a shadow of itself into my skin. "I must get back to my lord. I have my orders."

Asha shrugs. "But are you not just a kind of prisoner, then?"

"No more than you are."

"I had my freedom and my family taken from me," Asha says quietly. "You have given yours away." She turns and slips back through the side gate, and I hear the bolt drawn home behind her.

I run silently away down the alley.

After all, where is the profit in staying?

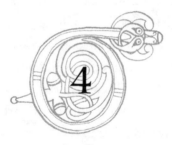

The fleet

ONE OF the striplings comes up to me as I warm my bones by the cook-pot fire with Iskendar and Niko. The brat gets down on his knees, just as he should, and bows his head before us. "If it please you," he says to me, "you're wanted by Master again."

"Well enough," I say. "And how went your morning up on the Mese, Mouser?"

Mouser ducks his ratty-brown little head again. He's fast and small, almost as good a pickpocket as me. "I slit fourteen purses with my knife, and I took all to Master, just as you said."

"Well done, then." I wonder what our lord wants of me this time. "You'd best spend the afternoon down by the docks. There's always some trader in his cups with too much coin in his purse and not enough sense."

Mouser scuttles off along one of the rope walkways where the other young ones are sitting, boasting of their day's thieving. I'm proud of them. A good morning's work by all.

"Go on, then," Iskendar says, leaning back against the wall. "Tell us. Everyone's speaking of it."

"You know I can't say." I grin at him, stirring the fire with a stick. Bright splashes of flame float up into the gloom; some land, hissing, in the water. The blind white fish stop circling and dart away.

"You want to be careful what you get tangled up in." Niko's staring at the water, his thin face pinched with worry. "There's thieving, and then there's just foolery."

Iskendar nods. He's been all morning at the silver market, and he's got a set of knives spread out before him and a heap of bracelets all bound together with a leather string. "Niko's right. Look at this — the honest end to a hard morning's work. You should stick to what you know. You ought not to get bound up in Master's plots. They're not for the likes of us. But I suppose you think you're different." He pauses then and looks away.

There's an unspoken pact among the Children of the Underworld never to ask about someone's life before they came to this. Some tell, anyway: Iskendar was cursed with fifteen siblings and a stepfather; Niko lived with his grandmother till she died. The Emperor of Thieves turns no child away. But I've not spoken a word about my past, and I never shall.

"What would you have me do?" I say. "Tell our master that he may go hang the next time he summons me?" There's a hard edge to my voice. "We all know he owns us down to the nails at our fingertips. We're his to do with as he likes, so you may as well end this half-witted talk."

I don't really believe this anymore, about our every sliver of skin, blood, and bone belonging to the Emperor of Thieves. It might be true for Iskendar, Niko, Thales, and the others, for Black Elias, who betrayed our lord and died at his order. But it isn't so for me. I delivered Achaicus Dassalena to my lord when I gave him that vellum scroll, and now he owes me, the Ghost. He cannot live forever — the Good Lord gathers every man to his fold, and the devil takes the rest. One day, I will be Emperor of Thieves myself. I will rule the dark side of Constantinople, and no one can stop me.

"You should watch yourself — that's all." Iskendar stares at the dark water.

"Is that a threat?" I say. My voice is soft and quiet. Is he envious? Surely not.

"Of course it isn't, you mutton-head," mutters Niko. "We're just feared for you. All this sneaking and secrets."

Iskendar nods. "If I were you, I'd give up this game you play — whatever it is," he says, and I wonder then how much he knows about me, how much I'm not telling. Thales knows. *You and your witch father*, he said. Some long-nosed fool's been digging around — Thales or someone else who wants to see the back of me. There must be a few among the Thief Children who do. Thales said my father had turned traitor, but I know he never would, not with all his barbarian notions of honor and fealty. Much I care about him, anyhow.

I stir the fire again, and I speak so soft you couldn't ever know how close I am to driving my fist into Iskendar's face. "Would you lead the Ghost Legion, then, instead of me?"

"That's not what he means," Niko says.

"Well enough, then." I spring to my feet, and, making myself unseen, I am gone. I hear their voices fading as I scale the wall, leaving the same way I did when Thales was here.

"Do you think he's really a ghost?" Niko says. "Sometimes I wonder, when he melts away like that."

"He's as real as you or I," Iskendar replies. "And I hope one day he doesn't find it out at the end of a dagger."

So do I, my friend, I think. *So do I.* But I'm relieved that Iskendar's not one of those who wants to see me gone, all the same.

The streets are crushed with people — it's worse than the day of the race. I wonder how Demos is now. Grateful to be free of his debt or just ashamed? Normally a crowd like this makes my spirit wild with excitement, but today I feel hemmed in by it, trapped. The air's thick with the smell of wine, and a man with three days' worth of beard stumbles toward me, his blubbery lips parting as his eyes roll up to heaven. He's in a heap at my feet, still gripping the wineskin like a brat at its mother's teat. I step over him. Everywhere I look, there's a drunk — it's like a festival.

The houses down here are tall enough that their balconies block out the sun, but it's still so hot that my back's damp with sweat. The air sizzles against my skin. A brace of fine ladies sweeps by, their hair covered with rich brocade shawls, and I realize that it's Sunday and that I'm caught up in the swarms making for Santa Sofia. Maybe the emperor is going to church today and there's one of the parades where they fill the fountains with spicy wine instead of water. That must be the reason for such a crowd, and for this tingling thrill that throbs from every paving slab and every ancient brick, and for all the drunks, of course.

I dodge a man with staring eyes and vomit in his beard. A hand snatches at my sleeve as I slip through the crowd. For the love of God, I hardly need this now. Why won't these people steal instead of begging? I dig into my belt-bag for a copper and turn, thrusting it at the girl tugging at my clothes.

It's not a beggar. It's Asha, her hair wrapped in an old blue head scarf of my mother's. Why does she bother? She's only a slave. No one cares how respectable she looks. I fight the urge to shove her or slap her or even both. I can't do that to Asha. But she's like my cursed shadow at the moment.

"What do you want?" I demand. The coin falls into the dust.

"You must come home," Asha says, her skinny chest heaving. Silly fool must've run like a chariot horse to catch up with me. She's wasting her time. I tug myself away, but her thin brown fingers are stronger than I thought and she's still gripping my tunic. "Listen to me," she hisses — but I'm away from her now, streaking through the streets, faster than thought. I can't stand looking at her: it makes me feel bad inside. She makes me think of what I should be, rather than what I am.

My heart pounds as I kneel before the Emperor of Thieves. Narxes isn't here, but I can hear him moving about on the floor below. He's talking to someone — one of the emperor's bodyguards, it must be. The guard's footsteps are heavy, Narxes' light, even though he's a big man.

So now it's just me and my lord. He is sitting in a chair facing the garden, and I wonder why.

"It is good to feel the breeze on my face, even though I cannot see," he says, his thin lips twisted into a smile.

I feel a chill chasing its way down my back. I've never liked his knack of sifting through my private thoughts. I've heard it said that when sight's lost, hearing and the other senses become sharper, more acute. "Yes, lord," I say. "What will you have me do now?"

"I hope I can trust you, child," the Emperor of Thieves whispers.

I think of Black Elias floating handless in the harbor and feel colder still. "Of course, my lord." I lean forward even more so my forehead is almost touching the rug, and I can see the soft leather of his sandals and his toenails, pinky-pale and glossy like the inside of one of those big shells. It makes me ill, the thought of Narxes paring my lord's toenails, rubbing his feet with scented oils.

"Achaicus Dassalena is in fear of his life," says the emperor.

He's met with him, then. Did Achaicus come here himself or send one of his men? Unlucky messenger, if so: he'll be dead by now, his corpse rotting where it landed in the weeds at the feet of the city walls.

"Achaicus will be gathering his forces around him," my master goes on. "Weekly, he meets with his men in the palace — the quaestor, the chief accountant, the heads of each guild. If I know Achaicus, he'll tell them we have the letter; all signed their names to it. I want you to get into the palace and listen to what they say, and then tell me what they are planning to do. If you are found, boy, I cannot help you, but if you succeed, you will be rewarded beyond all measure."

A jolt of fear and excitement rushes through my body, the way it does when you're by the sea and jump off a high rock. You don't know how deep the water is or what's waiting below, but the thrill as you fall sends your spirit up to the heavens. I say, "Yes, O —"

What's happening? Someone's banging on the door downstairs: loud, furious knocking, then talk — Narxes, sounding outraged, the low rumbling of the guards' voices. I hear a sharp crack — a broken bowl or plate? Mary, Mother of God. More shouting. My master's sitting straight upright like a marble statue, his bony, bluish hands gripping the arms of his chair, and I'm on my feet in a moment. Footsteps, pounding the stairs. Surely it cannot be the city guard? What can they prove? A blind old man sitting in a room — what can they say against him? But if my lord's made an enemy of Achaicus Dassalena, maybe it doesn't matter. The prefect of the city is the right hand of Emperor Constans, and even if Achaicus is a traitor, Constans most likely has no scent of it yet, or Achaicus would surely be dead. Is this the guard, coming for my lord?

I flatten myself against the wall next to the window as the door flies open. It is not the city guard. It is far worse than that.

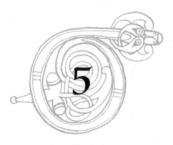

5

God's Fire

LL BREATH is sucked from my body as my
eyes rest on the intruder. He's tall: a good head
and shoulders above Narxes, who stands just
behind. His eyes are blacker than pitch, but hair the color
of fire hangs over his shoulders and down his back, woven
into plaits and strung with beads and shiny charms. At his
belt he wears a sword in a long black scabbard, and the
afternoon light slants in through the window and strikes
the silver patterns beaten into the dark leather — twisting
serpents, they are, some barbarian pattern I used to trace
over with my fingers when I was small . . . but why am I
thinking of this now?

He is a killer by trade, and some say a witch.

He is so shamefully different.

My father bows his head in a mocking salute. "Sir," he says
to the Emperor of Thieves. "I believe you have something

belonging to me." His voice is icy calm, and I know he is in a spitting rage.

Dear Christ, what is he doing here?

"What is the meaning of this intrusion?" whispers my lord; his voice is soft like rustling silk. It's scary, how quietly he speaks.

"I am so sorry, dear lord," Narxes says. There's a bruise spreading around his right eye, and his lip's bloody, swelling into a purply sausage. I wonder what happened to my lord's bodyguard. "We were unable to prevent the man from entering. Michaelis will be lucky if he sees the morning. I will call —"

My father shoves past Narxes, ignoring him. He's meant to be in the desert. Tecca: he must know by now that she is dead. How did he find me? How did he get here? His eyes travel over me and I feel burned. "Come," he says in Anglish. "Now."

What does he think I am, a complete fool? He hasn't reckoned on the window. I'm out of it in a moment, not waiting to hear what my master has to say, slipping and sliding down the vine into the garden, bumping my knees and grazing my elbows against the wall.

He doesn't call after me — but he's coming, all right. He'll be down in the street already. I run to the end of the garden and go out the back gate instead, sprinting north so fast my legs burn and my chest feels as if it wants to burst. If I can get to the hippodrome, he'll never find me in the market. When did he come back? What's he doing here? Asha must have been trying to warn me. Why in hell's name did I not listen? It's a mistake that might cost me all.

I take to the rooftops again, scrambling up the side of a market stall in the shadow of the hippodrome. I'm running, leaping, and sliding, the shrieking of a market woman echoing in my ears as her stall crashes to the ground. Glancing back, I see a wave of figs tumbling across the street, bowls of salted cheese bouncing as they hit the ground, splashing brine everywhere. Dried sausages roll in the dust. People are yelling and cursing. I can't see him, though. He's not easy to miss. I've lost him; now I must just get away.

The crowd thickens the closer I get to Santa Sofia. I shove through the throng, weaving, pushing, moving so fast that the breath scrapes in my chest and sweat soaks my head scarf. I see him again coming right for me now—damn his eyes—head and shoulders above everyone else, and I curse God that he's so tall. He plows into the mass of folk as though he does but walk through long grass.

Oh, Jesu keep me: I'm going to church, and so's half of Constantinople, it seems. I'm in, though, and the great domed roof soars above me, dwarfing the seething sea of people. The air's thick with the heady reek of sweat, wine, and stale breath all mixed with the richness of frankincense, which rises heavenward along with a thousand prayers. I come in good time: the liturgy begins. I can't see the priest above the throng, but I can hear him, just about:

"Blessed is the kingdom of the Father and of the Son and of the Holy Spirit, now and ever and unto ages of ages. . . ."

I glance over my shoulder and catch a glimpse of fiery hair. I'm a fool — I've trapped myself in here like a spider in a cup. I dash sideways and make for the gallery. The corridor that slopes up to the next floor is guarded by shaven-headed eunuchs; the Empress Fausta has come to worship with her subjects, then, rather than praising God's glory in the comfort of the palace.

Well, she does not like to grow *too* close to the common stream, for the guards let no one through.

I draw in my breath and slip by them unseen.

That's surely given me a moment's grace — he dealt with my lord's men pretty sharp, but even my father is not fool enough to start a fight in church. Or at least I do not think so.

The corridor that slopes up to the galleries is empty, so I run. The flagstones here are treacherous, worn smooth and slippy for more than a hundred years by the feet of the noble faithful. If I can get to the other side of the church, if I can just find a way out there, he'll never catch up with me. But first I must cross the ladies' gallery. A wooden screen painted with the Virgin and her child blocks the way in. Their gold haloes glow softly in the gloom. A guard stands by; he has not yet seen me. I press myself close to the wall, and the stone chills my skin, even through my tunic. I hear the low rumble of the liturgy being chanted below. The whole church thrums with it.

I run past the guard, and — oh, Lord — he swings around, staring after me, a befuddled look in his eyes that switches to alarm as he knocks into the screen. It crashes to the ground.

There's a whole gaggle of noblewomen and their insipid daughters up here, all decked out in bright silks and looped about with necklaces, bracelets, and trinkets (no common folk allowed, of course). As one, they turn, jewelry jangling, to stare at the guard as he rights the screen — some frowning, others shocked, a few ready to laugh. *Think of nothing, think of nothing.* I keep close by the wall behind them, running. Elflight's not here this day, I thank God. She'd see me; I know she would. I recall the day I laid a bet with Tecca, and smack in the middle of the Eucharist she leaned over the rail and dropped a sugared lemon. From my place down in the church, I watched it strike the head of a fat man with a beard and laughed till I nearly cried, and Maria had to march me outside till I'd gathered my wits. . . .

The women have all turned back to the gallery now, eyes fixed on the doll-size, gold-draped figure of the priest below. Their voices ring out as one, chiming with the rumble from the crowd. "We lift up our hearts to the glory of God. . . ."

The door at the far end of the gallery is ajar. There is no guard there. I'm safe; once I reach it, I'm safe. I move quietly and stretch out my hand for the worn wooden handle — and I know someone has seen me. I feel the heat of their gaze on my back. I turn.

A small, dark-eyed woman watches me; she is draped in bejeweled sea-green silk, her hair veiled with cloth-of-gold. It is the Empress Fausta. Her again. It seems like ten years ago that I saw her sitting with Ma. Can it really only have been yesterday?

Oh, dear God. I freeze, waiting. We stand there, staring at each other a moment. Her brows draw together in a small frown. She mouths a word to me, a silent message: "*Go.*"

Fausta has ever been sharp-eyed. She needs to be, in that court of finely dressed, flower-scented snake folk.

I do not need telling twice. I shut the door behind me, softly, softly, and pelt down the empty, arched gallery before me toward a row of windows in the far wall. I leap and scramble up onto the nearest ledge, and it's a good thing I've never inclined to fat: I barely squeeze through. It's a long drop down onto the roof below. I feel a tile slip, hear it clatter to the ground.

The afternoon sun strikes the bulk of the great church behind me, and the walls glow rose-pink as the rise and fall of the holy chant fades. God's eye must have been drawn to our fair city this day, for he's delivered me safe from danger. For now.

Without thinking, I reach the wall of the Great Palace. I must stop or I'm going to choke out my lungs. I lean with my back to the wall, taking great gulps of air. It tastes of rose-water — I must be somewhere near the perfume stewers'. I feel dizzy with the mangled scents of amber, lavender, and musk.

What is my father doing back here? It makes sense now, the bubbling festival thrill in the air, the streams of drunken men: one of the fleets has returned. If I were on top of this wall now, I'd be able to see them, clustering dromonds moored up in that great basin of water the Golden Horn, their masts poking up like reeds at the edge of a lake.

How is it I've not heard of this before now? I've been too tangled up in my lord's affairs, a little voice tells me, to sense the mood of the city.

And then I see it.

A long eye, graven into the sandy, pocked surface of the wall. My sign: the all-seeing Eye of the Ghost. Signs like this are all over Constantinople, carved into walls and paving slabs by Mouser and his kin to mark the city out as mine and in turn the Emperor of Thieves'.

It's just another Eye of the Ghost. But this one is not the same as the rest. A jagged line has been drawn straight through it with the tip of a knife.

My mark has been defaced, shamed. Forget my father — this is far worse. I know there must be many among the Thief Children who'd see me dead with all good cheer, but none of them has ever been fool enough to disrespect a Ghost Eye. Or at least not that I've seen. Darkness clouds my mind — maybe there are shamed marks like this all over the city and I've not chanced to see them. No, that cannot be true. It would never have escaped me so long.

Whoever did this is going to be sorry.

I squint up at the sky. It's hazy with smoke and it looks as if a sea mist's going to set in before sundown. Summer's gone for the year. It's oven-hot still, but it won't be so for long. A flock of starlings flies over, dark specks against the blue; then they scatter. There's a buzzard hovering—that's why.

A coldness washes over me, and a creeping, chilly certainty comes to rest in my mind: I won't see the winter, not this year. I won't see snow gusting around the dome of Santa Sofia, settling around the base of Justinian's statue in the forum. I won't see the chestnut sellers bound up in woolen rags, warming their red hands at little charcoal fires. I won't see the fountains of Constantinople filled with spiced wine as the Emperor Constans goes to hear mass at Christmastide.

What am I thinking? There is no time for this mawkish romancing. If that crazed barbarian finds me, I am finished. I must deal with whoever defaced my Eye another time. I've lingered here too long. I sprint along in the palace wall's shadow, hardly even noticing where I'm going till the salt smell gets stronger and I'm near the palace harbor. There's just a couple of walls and gardens between me and it—the Seaside Palace is next to the Great Palace, but much smaller: I can manage the walls easily, scrambling, climbing, running till my heart is fit to burst. I'm over the harbor wall, and I crumple to my knees on the marble quay, the bulk of both palaces rearing up behind me, the glittering sea spreading out in front. There's a great marble-framed door in the wall—that must be where Constans and his family come out when they want to get into one of their boats. I pray to God that none of them feels a yearning for life on the salty wave this evening.

I rest on my hands as sweat trickles out from under my head scarf and slides down my back, pooling at the base of my spine. I'm so thirsty, but there's nothing here to drink. I sit, breathing hard and dangling my legs over the quay as I gaze out across the silvery sweep of the Sea of Marmara. A buzzard or something is circling in the blueness above, around and around. I'm sure it's the same one I saw just now. It feels as if he's watching me. I've got that jumpy feeling in the back of my neck like someone's laid the evil eye on me. I'm like a foolish old woman. It's a good thing there's no one here to see me like this — only the buzzard. Some of the palace boats are moored down the way, the purple sails of the emperor's barque furled and gathered to the mast like the wings of a new-hatched butterfly. Maybe I should steal on board and see what he's got to drink — some choice treats, I wager.

Wind moans through the rigging. What am I to do? My head's jumbled: I think of Demos in his stable, Elflight when she saw me on the window ledge, Iskendar, Niko, my master. I can't let my father keep me away from the Underworld. Time passes quickly there. It won't be long before I'm forgotten and Thales is the Emperor of Thieves' right-hand man. Which is just what he wants —

Behind me, I hear the soft squeak of creaking hinges.

Someone comes! It must be one of the boat keepers or a slave come to sweep the quay. I jump to my feet, turning. But it's not a boat keeper or any sort of palace servant.

It is my father.

Jesu. *How did he find me?*

How did he persuade the guard to let him through? Mind, if I were a guard, I would not argue. His face is bright with anger, and his eyes are fierce and shiny like a hawk's. There's nowhere to run. It's not that much of a jump down into the sea, though, and there can't be rocks here; otherwise how would they—

He moves faster than a hunting dog and he's got me now, gripping the top of my arm. "You had much better not," he says, nodding at the water. "You've already led me a dance through the streets. You'll be sorry if I must swim after you as well."

I'd forgotten this—it freezes my blood, the way he's clear ready to rip off my head and spit down my neck but does not even raise his voice.

He lifts one eyebrow—a trick I've never been able to master. "Nothing to say?" he asks with horrible calm. "Will you tell me the aim of this game of thieves you play? I fear it defeats me."

I stare down at the ground, my heart thundering. Game of thieves? How much does he know? And how? I can't believe he's here, that he caught up with me. How in God's name did he do it?

"No?" he goes on. "Very well—it's done with now." And then, as if he knows how much it means, he tears off my head scarf and my hair comes tumbling free, hanging in my eyes. Bright white, marking out my northern blood, branding me his: the son of God's Fire.

I feel naked. My scarf lands in the harbor, and I watch the water draw it under till it's nothing but a faint dark red stain, growing smaller as it sinks. I am filled with anger; it burns my throat as though I have just vomited. That scarf's part of me, part of the Ghost, and he knows it.

My father sighs. He looks more tired than angry now. His face is burned all coppery, and the lines around his eyes are deeper, grained with dirt. "Sit down," he says. "I want to talk to you."

Maybe I should run again now, while he is distracted. But instead I sit next to him on the edge of the quay. We stare down at the water. After all this time you'd think we should have a lot to say to each other, but I don't know where to begin. There are scores and scores of tiny fish nibbling at the fronds of green weed growing out of the quayside.

I pray he does not talk of Tecca. I will not be able to hold on to myself.

"So," my father says at last, picking up a pebble and throwing it far out into the harbor, where it kicks up a small white splash, "aren't you a mite young to be making such powerful enemies?" He throws another pebble.

I just sit, staring down at my dusty feet. *What does he know?*

"A letter was stolen from the home of the prefect two nights since," he says. "The talk is that there's only one thief in Constantinople with the skill to have taken it." Another pebble. *Splash.*

I think I want to be sick.

"I was not pleased to learn after hardly a moment on dry land that this thief was my son."

It's out, then — they all know who I am, who the Ghost really is: not just another of the Emperor of Thieves' orphaned street rats after all. What's worse, Achaicus Dassalena knows who delivered him into the hands of the Emperor of Thieves. This is vexing, but I see my path now. I turn, meeting my father's dark eyes with my identical pair.

My father speaks many tongues, but he brought two with him from that cold, wet island of his childhood: Anglish from the tribe of his mother, and a strange, silvery manner of speech from his Briton father. Words of love he always speaks in British.

"Oh, *Tasik*," I say — *Papa* — and the British words fall clumsily from my lips. "Help me."

It is as if he's been bound in ice, and now all has melted. He puts his arm around my shoulder, pulling me close. He smells the same as ever: hot somehow, and salty. "You need not ask, my honey," he says. I've got him now; he's drawn in up to the hilt. I am a poor victim, tricked into a life beyond the law.

"I want to get away from them," I whisper, burying my face in the front of his tunic. My voice is muffled. "But they'll kill me if I try. They do that: a girl tried to leave the guild to marry a soldier and they found her body in the harbor." I keep on talking, the words rushing out, not daring to stop lest the spell be broken. "It started out just for fun, stealing things from the market. I know it's wrong. And then this older boy — Elias — he said I'd joined the guild just by thieving, and that I could never leave. He said . . ." I draw back, allowing my eyes to brim with tears.

He's got that dazed look that comes over people when I talk like this. I could persuade the sun to roll backward across the sky if I could get close enough to it. I'll talk him into a daze and then I'll slip away so fast, he won't ever be able to catch me.

But then something changes. Tasik shakes his head slightly, as if he's got water in one of his ears, and his face clears. His eyes are narrowed into black slits, and I feel a sudden jolt of fear.

"Cai," he says — and it's a shock to hear my given name after so long — "I may have named you after my father, but by Christ I wish you did not have his talent for deception. Come, you and I are going home."

I will never forget the look on his face: it's as if he has just seen someone he hates with all his soul.

Tasik never speaks of his life in the north, and neither does Ma; I know nothing about my grandfather, but I am cursing his memory now. He has just cost me my freedom.

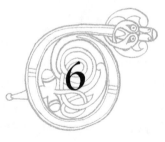

6

Home

I'M RUNNING to keep up by the time we reach the courtyard gate. Tasik has not said a word all the way back, just dragged me along as if I'm a cur on a string — an ill portent, if ever there was one.

Asha and Elflight leap up from the table and stand there beneath the vines like a pair of stuffed quail. Oho, there's a storm coming, all right.

"Tas," Elflight says, a touch shaky, "will you have some — ?"

He ignores her, slamming home the gate bolt, and rounds on me like a wolf. "Where is it?" he shouts, his calm burned away.

I know what he means. I reach into my tunic and pull out the leather thong that hangs around my neck. He snatches it and holds up the ring so the gold loop glitters before my eyes.

"What did I tell you about this?" he demands. "I ought never to have trusted you with it."

The words fly out of my mouth. "What good was that when Tecca died? It's nothing."

He lets the ring fall so it dangles against my chest once more. "It's but cold metal." His voice glitters with anger. "It was the trueness of your heart that failed. You swore to look after your mother and your sisters, and you did not."

How could I have helped it? How could I have saved her? Does he believe I can forget Tecca lying in this very courtyard saying, *Where will I go when I die? Will I be all by myself?*

I hate him.

I lower my head. "I am sorry," I whisper, and he steps away, sighing, his anger and his wits blunted by those little, shining words.

Fool of a man: I'm ashamed my father's so easily taken in.

I spring for the wall, dodging him so fast that he doesn't have a chance. I grab the vine — one of the girls is screaming, Elflight most likely — and I push up, up. I'm within grasp of the top, but then I'm hauled sharply backward. I fall to my knees and scramble up again, breathless and afraid now, and red-hot with rage.

No one stops the Ghost.

Faster than a striking snake, Tasik reaches out and fetches me such a clout that I'm knocked back against the fountain. "Never do that again," he hisses. "Not if you value your skin."

I'm filled with a curdled mess of anger and savage joy that I've managed to rile him so much. My whole body is fiery with pain and a fierce ache. I feel like Greek fire, that slop of pitch and trickery sailors shoot at the Arab warships — a shuddering flame that will not go out.

"You should have come home!" I shout, trying to catch my breath. "All she wanted was to see you! We sent word, but you didn't come!"

"Dear heart, be calm."

A thick quiet falls on the courtyard. Elflight and Asha cling to each other as though they're actors in a tragedy. I have not heard that voice in more than a year; it is cracked and faint, but I know it straightaway. A rail-thin figure stands in the open doorway, shadowed by the lamplight behind her.

"Ma —" Elflight begins, but no one is listening. Poor Elflight — it's a sad reward for being the good and dutiful child.

The Angel of Constantinople, they used to call my mother because she was so fair. But Ma's so frail now, so wasted. She moves slowly across the courtyard, letting the door swing shut behind her.

Tasik is just standing there, looking at her as if he's forgotten that I'm even here, which I for one am not sorry about. My face stings and aches where he hit me, and he'd do it again, I know.

"Lark." He speaks her name so dearly.

"Essa," Ma says to him, "be a little kinder. The fault was mine." She folds her arms around me. She is so frail, I'm afraid I might break her if I move.

Ma never used to be like this. She used to be strong, and quick, and merry. She was the first to put a bow in my hands, long ago. I can't have been more than four summers old, out among the grapevines at Hieron. We shot wooden cups off the rim of the fountain. When I hit my first cup, Tasik lifted me in his arms and threw me high into the air, so I felt as if I were flying. *You'll soon be a better shot than your mother!* he said, laughing. *Which means you'll be better than your* tasik, *as well.* Ma laughed, too, and said, *Dear heart, I know.*

The Angel of Constantinople, dotted with jewels, adorned with silk scarves, shooting cups in the courtyard at Heiron. All of a sudden I want to cry, but I cannot. I feel hollow, like a dry bone. "I am sorry, my honey," Ma says to me. "I was so bound up in my own grief that I forgot yours."

Well, fair game to her for saying so, but it comes a year too late. I do not need her anymore.

"Grief does not make a liar," Tasik says, "or a thief, and it does not make a coward, either. He's all three. Now, come." He takes my arm and hauls me inside, leaving Ma in the courtyard, standing there in the fading light.

Upstairs, he shoves me into the first chamber we come to and bangs the shutters closed, barring them. I have a bad feeling—he's not going to lock me in here, is he? He can't do that. He won't. He knows how much I hate being closed in.

I watch, alive with fear, as Tasik tears a linen coverlet from the bed and rips off a great long strip. What in hell's name is he doing? He's not watching me, though. I step softly, softly toward the door, but he whirls around, snatches me by the arm, and twists it behind my back. He pushes me hard into the corner. My elbow strikes the wall, sending a jolt of fiery pain up my arm, and I cry out. He says nothing; he doesn't even look at me, just leans over the bed, binding the bar across the shutters so I can't lift it, pulling the linen strip into hard, tight knots.

I sit there watching him in the gloom. Everything hurts: I'm going to have a bad bruise on my knee from where I fell, I've skinned the palms of my hands, my face is still burning where he struck me, and now my arm is throbbing, too. I don't cry, though. I never do. But I'm scared. "Tas!" I fight to keep my voice steady. "Don't. Don't shut me in here."

He turns on me. "Do you think I've lost my senses? I've had my fill of your coaxing and lying, so be quiet. Give me all you have — everything."

Wordless, panicked, I hand him my knife. What will I do if he locks me up? I can't stand it. I can't.

Tasik laughs harshly. "And the rest."

I crouch down and pull out the dagger that's bound to my leg, and he takes my belt-bag, which has my lock picker in it. I am the Ghost, but I cannot do magic, and without that and my knives, I'm trapped.

He raises an eyebrow at the dagger, unsheathing it. The blade glints; it's sharper than the devil's tooth. "You should take care, carrying such blades," he says. "She'll get you into trouble, but she won't get you out."

For a moment he sounds like his old self again. If he hadn't seen through my lie, we'd be sitting down to our meat in the courtyard with the girls, and maybe even Ma, too. Tasik is not like other people's fathers: he would have forgiven me if I hadn't lied. But then he goes out and closes the door behind him, leaving me in darkness. I hear the key scrape in the lock and have to clench my fists hard to fight this awful sense that the walls are closing in on me. I scramble to my knees and run my hands over the barred shutters, but the knots Tasik tied are fiendishly tight, and I know I'll never get them undone without a knife. I can't lift the bar: I'm trapped. I sit on the bed, breathing deep.

Just how in the name of Christ am I to break into the Great Palace when I cannot even get out of my own house?

Tomorrow, Achaicus Dassalena meets with his fellow traitors, and if I do not bring word of their plot to the Emperor of Thieves, I may as well slit my own throat and save him the trouble.

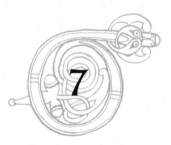

The Great Palace

I CANNOT breathe. I am in a dark place, and there is no way out. I shout to be let free, but no one comes. I will lie beneath the earth, alone in darkness forever. I am crushed by the weight of the black earth and by the knowledge that I have lost something, have done a deep, dreadful wrong that cannot be repaired.

Tecca.

I must find her —

At last I hear voices — coming from a long way off, it seems — and I have the sense of a dim light somewhere, the hot smell of an oil lamp.

"What in God's name is this riot?"

"He shouts like this every night, or at least he used to before he left."

Someone sighs. "Well enough, dear heart. Now, get to your bed."

I'm panicking now. "I can't breathe. I can't—"

"Na, be easy." He speaks in British: soft, as though stilling a scared horse. "Go back to sleep." He pushes the door open wider. A thin stream of cool night air slips in through the window from the corridor outside.

Am I awake or still sleeping? "Tas?" He has been gone so long.

"Yes, it's me." Even in the shadows, I can tell from his voice that he is smiling. I sit up and he holds me tight, rubbing my back, knotting his fingers in my hair. I clutch on to him, my heart racing.

He has come back, but there's no use in it.

Tecca is dead; she's gone.

And I remember now: Tasik thinks I'm a coward; he said so. It's my fault she's dead, and he hates me. I pull away and lie facedown. I can't stand this. I can't stand being locked up with my misery, and he's not going to let me out.

Tasik rests his hand on my shoulder.

"It will be all right," he says quietly. And now I know he's a liar, for even he can't do anything to fix this. Even God's Fire the hero cannot bring Tecca back.

It's morning now. Nothing's changed. Whenever I wake up in this cursed house, there's the light moment when I think it was just a dream. And then I remember. I will never see Tecca again; she's beneath the earth, trapped. I sit in the dark, waiting. The shutters are barred, bound tight, keeping out the sun; the door's shut, and I know without even checking that it's still locked. A dull ache throbs across my left cheekbone where Tasik hit me last night, stinging where his ring drew blood. I still cannot believe that he caught me — twice. I cannot believe I fell: me, the Ghost. I pick a speck of dirt from my hand, wincing.

What am I going to do? Achaicus could be meeting with his traitors in the palace this very moment, and I'm locked up here.

I kneel on the bed, running one hand over the shutters, trying to find a weak spot. There's a rotten old chair in the corner — it's the one that was left out in the rain too many times. It wouldn't be hard to snap off one of the legs. I could use it to lever the bar away from the shutters. It'll make a lot of noise, but what choice do I have? I'll have to be fast, though. If I don't get out of here soon, I'm finished.

Suddenly the door opens behind me and light gushes in.

"Lost something?" Tasik leans in the doorway.

I'm still half blinded by the flood of sunshine. Jesu, how did he come so close and I didn't hear? Is the Ghost losing his touch? I could get past him now, if I were quick enough —

He steps forward into the room, blocking the way out. "Any of your tricks and I'll make you sorry. Here, eat this." Tasik hands me a lump of bread smeared with lemon preserve. I can smell its sharp sweetness, and my belly lurches. I'm so hungry. "Be quick," he says. "You're going to your lessons."

I laugh at that; I can't help it. The Ghost, studying ancient verbs and counting on an abacus? Come on, dear Father. It's been more than a year since I went to my tutor; old Yannis wouldn't even know my face.

But Tasik just smiles. "I'm glad you think it funny. Hear this, Cai, for I'll only say it once: your life is about to change. The Ghost is gone, do you understand? You no longer have the freedom of the streets. You leave this room only to attend your lessons, and you will go nowhere alone."

I swallow a gush of panic. I must get to the palace. "You can't keep me locked up forever."

"Na, perhaps only till you are about twenty."

"No!" I know half of him is joking. But the other half is not, and with the fix I'm in, a day locked in this room is as good as years.

He laughs, shaking his head. "What choice do you give me, you foolish brat? I know very well that you'd be gone the moment I turned my back given half the chance. If you want my trust, you must earn it. Now come, I've enough to do this day without acting as prison guard to you."

Tasik drags me through the streets as though I am a sack of rags. People stop and stare; I see them marveling at his great height, at the bright hair hanging down his back all woven with plaits and glass beads and silver charms. He pays no heed, but I feel as though I am naked; I am used to moving through this city unseen, silently — the Ghost. They stare at me, too, at the whiteness of my wet hair. With my head scarf on, I looked just like anyone else, but now my northern blood is plain for all to see. I wish he would let go of my arm: it is so undignified being hauled along like this. I will die if Iskendar or any of the boys lays eyes on me.

When we were at the bathhouse, he made the slaves in the caldarium lock the door and shutter the window as if I were a prisoner — a murderer or worse. There was only the spice merchant in there, and a couple of tired-looking soldiers, all soaking in the warm, misty waters. The spice merchant's face went even redder when we came in, like the skin of a ripe peach. I've lifted more from his market traders than any thief in the city, but none of them has ever come close to catching the Ghost.

"*You!*" he said, half choking as he jabbed a finger at me. His pale, flabby chest looked as if it had been hewn from old cheese.

Tasik paid him no heed, tossing a gold coin to the slave who shuttered the windows and lit the oil lamps. "I'm desolate sorry to make this a jail," he said to them all, not the least sounding it. "Wilder than a tiger is this brat of mine. He's gotten clear beyond control while I've been away."

The soldiers saluted him, grinning; they must have come off the same fleet. "Is the brat crazier than you are, God's Fire?" one of them asked. "We should have him in the legion."

Tasik just said, "Don't wish that, Iarchos. He'd steal the rings from your fingers while you slept. God alone knows how I bred such a wretch. How is your head this morning? Drank a lot of wine at Aikaterina's grill-shop? I was sorry to miss that."

"Feels like my eyelids got boiled in oil," said the other soldier, and everyone laughed.

Oh, ha ha, I thought sourly.

The spice merchant was staring at me still, goggle-eyed with rage. If I hadn't been so full of misery, I'd have laughed myself. "That boy," he spluttered, pointing wildly. *"That boy—"*

Tasik turned to him. "What, raided your spice stalls, did he, Helios? Well, do not rile yourself about it, I beg you, not while these good men have such sore heads." Tasik tossed the purse of coin at him, and it fell into the waters with a splash.

The merchant glared at him but snatched it up, anyhow.

Tasik looked down at me, a smile flashing across his face so fast it was barely there. Then he said in British, "Don't do anything foolish; I'm in no mood for it, I promise you."

I sat on the edge of the pool, staring at the high, domed roof above while Tasik had rose oil rubbed into his limbs and the journey dirt scraped from his skin and his hair combed and rinsed with lemon water. A thin trail of daylight lanced down from a gap between two bricks, and I stared at it, wishing I knew when Achaicus had summoned his fellow traitors for their meeting.

"Do you not desire to bathe, young master?" I looked up to find a slave standing there with a bowl of oil and a drying wrap.

Oh, for the love of God, I thought. *I'm meant to be breaking into the Great Palace at risk of having my throat cut, and here they are, bothering me about baths.*

"No," I said.

"He'd better, or the womenfolk shall have my hide," Tasik said, and the soldiers laughed again. "Cai, get in."

Let him believe I'm ready to obey his every word. I climbed into the steamy, greenish waters and sank to the slimy tiles at the bottom. Thoughts swirled around my head like oil and vinegar shaken together in a jar: Tecca before she was sick, so thrilled whenever Asha and Elflight took her to the girls' baths; Ma carrying her there later when it hurt too much to walk; my lord's silk-thin voice, whispering that I must learn Achaicus's secrets.

I think of my dream, the stifling darkness of it. Always I ride the same nightmare when I'm in that house. It's one of the reasons I left it.

If I tried to tell Tasik about the Emperor of Thieves and the task my lord has given me, what would he do? He would not even let me out of that cursed chamber for my lessons. I would be a prisoner forever.

I do not know what I am going to do.

Tasik does not knock or call for a slave when we reach my tutor's villa; he just sweeps straight in. We burst through the house and out into the courtyard, where I blink in the morning light. Old Yannis is standing under the apricot tree, his face slack with shock when he sees us. The boys slumping at the table sit up and stare. It takes me a moment to remember their names — there's Peri, the silk merchant's son. His face is swollen now with pimples. And that's Timaeus, who was always slow and had to copy my work.

Solon Dassalena used to come, too, but he is not here now, thank God.

"Good morrow, Yannis," says my father as though they have just crossed paths in the marketplace. "I beg you will accept my apology for my son's laziness. I find he has not been attending much to his lessons these past few months."

Yannis gathers his wits pretty quickly, all considered. He grasps Tasik's hand, saying, "It's no matter, sir. I only hope you've had success bringing the Arabs into line."

"Let me have the Arabs any day." Tasik lets go of my arm at last. It feels like it's going to fall off, but I resist the need to rub it.

Yannis smiles at me — I am quite fond of him — but I can see that his eyes are full of worry. "Sit down, child," he says. "There's a spare stool at the end of the table."

Tasik turns and speaks to me in Anglish. "Do you hear this: if you're gone when I return, I will find you, and when I do, I'll take you home and I shall bind you before I lock you up." I know he means it, and the thought makes my gorge rise and chills the back of my neck. I must just hope he won't catch me.

And then he is gone, striding off across the courtyard without looking back, without another word to me. Timaeus and Peri stare as if I have grown a second head. Was it really me who used to play catch-ball with them while our mothers drank rose tea in the garden? We are the same age, but they are just children. How well fed they look: sleek, like the dolphins swimming in the Golden

Horn. I think of Niko and Iskendar, who know they'll get their next meal only if they are quick enough.

"I believe Hector had just killed Patroclus the last time you graced my home with your presence, Cai," Yannis says, "but you'll find we've moved on since then. Timaeus, where have we reached?"

Timaeus smirks. "We're not even on the *Iliad* anymore. We're doing the *Odyssey*, when Telemachus leaves to search for his father."

I could not care less, and Telemachus was a fool. I heartily wish my own father were lost on a far-distant sea where he could do nothing to bother me.

"Very good," says Yannis, and he starts burbling about ships with twelve masts and the wine-dark sea, and that fool Penelope weeping and weeping. Then we all have to repeat it back to him till we've got it by heart: a tangle of such ancient verbs that it hardly makes sense. What's the use?

If I don't get to the Great Palace soon, I'm dead, but Yannis is watching me closer than a cat watching its prey. It's Peri's turn now, and he's droning on when Yannis comes and stands at my side. His old knees crack as he crouches down to speak quietly so that Peri and Timaeus cannot hear. "I am glad to see you, my child," he says, "but I have been keeping my ears open to the market talk lately, and I'm afraid you're in a row with the sort of men you ought not to have crossed." Yannis pauses, as if he's waiting for me to say something, but I keep quiet. He sighs, and his eyes travel across my face, taking in the graze on my cheek left by Tasik's ring when he hit me. "Remember, if there is anything you feel you ought not to . . . well, not to bother your father with, I am always here, and perhaps I can help." He smiles, and I smile back.

"Yes, sir," I say, and I feel ashamed of what I'm about to do to him, because Yannis is a kind old man, and for a moment I almost want to tell him everything. But of course, I do not.

Time slides by till I'm nearly bursting. The whole morning has gone, and Yannis has hardly taken his eyes off me. The slaves have just cleared away what's left of the midday meal — dried sausage, partridge broth, bread, and peaches. It tasted like dust in my mouth. I have to get to the palace. What if Achaicus has already met with his fellow traitors? What if I am too late?

Curse Tasik. The fault's his.

I watch the shadow of the apricot tree lengthen across the courtyard. Yannis paces in the shade, spouting the *Odyssey*. Timaeus and Peri listen; Peri's lips move as he desperately tries to follow the God-forgotten tangle of age-old grammar. Timaeus gazes fixedly at the wall. How can they do this, day after day? Doesn't it make them want to shriek? Yannis is paying too much heed to me; he keeps looking over as if to make sure I haven't disappeared. Poor Yannis. Tasik's going to have his throat when he finds I'm gone. If I weren't such a wicked person, I wouldn't do this to the poor old man. But I have no choice, do I? I am starting to think that they aren't so foolish after all, Iskendar, Asha, and now Yannis. I am in deep water. I know too much.

Achaicus Dassalena has found out who I am, and that I stole his letter.

I must bring an end to this somehow before he ends me, and I must do it now, before it's too late. I breathe in, long and slow, clearing my mind. It's hard today: there is too much stirring around in my head. I think of Ma, of Tasik, of Elflight. I think of Iskendar telling me I shouldn't be entangling myself in our lord's affairs, of the thin smile on my lord's face when I handed him Achaicus's letter.

Yannis is looking at me again. *Come on*, I tell myself. *Time to go.* I let myself become swept up in the sound of my own breathing: in, out, in, out. My mind's clearing. Neither Timaeus nor Peri is paying me any heed. They are probably secretly planning the stories they'll tell when they get home: *And you won't believe this, but then God's Fire walked in with the Ghost. . . .* I slide off my stool, take a couple of paces toward the courtyard wall. It's hot away from the shade of the apricot tree. Yannis stares at where I was sitting, looking dazed. Was I there or was I not? He's confounded. Did he dream the whole thing? The Ghost was never here, old man; return to Odysseus, climbing up the rocks to the island of Circe.

My heart sings as I scale the wall. I have done it. After Tasik saw through me yesterday, I've been fearing that my skills were lost. But they are not. It will be hours till he'll return to Yannis's house for me. Maybe I can even be back there, and he'll never know I was gone.

I go across the rooftops—I don't dare to risk meeting Tasik in the street—scrambling, leaping, jumping over alleys shaded by great, sagging trellises of grapevines that send long green stems down into the cool shadows of the streets below. I realize as I land in the lee of the palace wall that I still don't know why Tasik is back. Did word of Tecca reach him at last? Are the Arabs subdued? Has he talked Muahi'ya out of Armenia? Perhaps Constans won't send Tasik away again, and he'll always be here.

What'll I do then? A year ago, that was all I wanted, but not so now.

I sit in the shade of the wall, one of the palace courtyards spreading out before me. It's easier to stay hidden when I'm in the shadows. Some folk have sharper senses than others, like Fausta, who saw me in church. I hope to God that I don't lay eyes on her today—she might let me off a visit to the ladies' gallery, but if I'm found sneaking around her palace, she'll want to know why. There's a gate on the far wall guarded by a couple of Africans. Not eunuchs, so I'm not in the empress's quarter or near Constans's inner chambers, which Tasik told me once are guarded by the fiercest, most cunning eunuchs in the known world: folk who could slide a knife between your ribs without your even feeling it.

The guards are leaning back against the wall, eyes half closed against the sunlight. I run around the edge of the courtyard, keeping to the wall. There's a fountain dribbling greenish water, a few peach trees heavy with forgotten fruit that no one but the birds will eat. The Great Palace is so ancient and so huge — there are great rambling swaths of it that no one ever goes to — but it's all guarded, just the same. I remember Constans once telling me that he got lost for a day and a night here when he was my age (I was in my eighth summer then). He told me that there are chambers lived in only by bats and spiders the size of your fist, and others filled with great heaps of gold: the dowries of long-dead empresses, princesses who came from far-away kingdoms to wed the Purple long ago.

The prefect's quarters are off to the west, I'm sure. I glance up at the sun and skirt around to the far wall of the courtyard. One of the guards yawns and scratches his nose. The other looks as though he might be asleep. Luckily for me, the wall's old and crumbling, easy to climb. As I get closer to where I think Achaicus's chambers are, everything looks cleaner. There are no pikes lying rusting against the wall, no broken chairs rotting in the sun. The guards here stand straight, watchful, sunlight glinting off the heads of their spears. It's harder to remain unseen. It's not easy to keep my mind clear and find my way west through this rambling maze of a palace.

I slip silently through a courtyard where lines of rose-bushes breathe out a heady scent. A slave boy in a white tunic rakes the dusty pathway. I pass an open window, and, peering inside, I see scribes sitting at two long wooden tables, heads bent over their work. Maybe it's my barbarian blood, but a life like that would drain the spirit from my body. How can they sit there, day after day, copying out reckonings and laws and declarations? But this must mean I'm somewhere near Achaicus's quarters.

I slip past the guard at the west gate of the rose courtyard. One of them blinks as I stir the air in passing, but that's all. Another courtyard, this one cast into green-dappled shade by a roof of trellised grapevines. There are more scribes here; I can see them inside. I haul myself in through the nearest window. The room is cool. The quiet is interrupted only by the sound of stylus tips scratching at vellum. One of the scribes speaks in a low voice to another. None of them notices me. When I slide out the door, I just brush the guard, a shaven-headed eunuch. I freeze and I glance back. He is shaking out his robe; he probably thinks there's a spider up there or a mouse. I have to bite my lip to keep from laughing.

I run off down the corridor and come to a corner. It's all the same in here: quiet, dark hallways, windows looking out over jumbled palace roofs, some with glimpses of the sea. I don't know where I'm going, and time is slipping away. I must ask someone. I wait by a window for what seems like years, and in my mind I see Achaicus and his men gathered, but I am not there and I cannot hear what they're saying. I have to fight a sick, panicky feeling. Achaicus probably has men all over the city looking for the Ghost. He is going to have me killed if I give him the chance — and now here I am, making straight for his chambers.

Sometimes I wonder if I am not clean out of my mind.

At last. A pair of slave boys in white tunics are coming down the hall, carrying great bundles of parchment.

I step forward. "You there," I say. They stop and bow their heads before me; they must, even though they are taller than me and probably three summers older. I would hate to be a slave. I would rather die. "I have been charged with a message to the quaestor's office," I say. The quaestor's chambers are right next to the prefect's quarters, where Achaicus will be. "Some fool gave me the wrong direction. Tell me how to get there, and be quick. I'm late as it is."

They tell me, in lowered, respectful voices — the way slaves must always speak lest they get beaten — and finally I'm there.

Two huge eunuchs guard the door of Achaicus's chamber. They could kill me with just a pinch of their fingers around my throat, but they shall not catch the Ghost. I am afire with the thrill of it. I wait behind a pillar, drawing deep, slow breaths, watching the door. I hope it isn't bolted from the inside. All color drains from my mind. I am here, but not here. I must just walk straight by them. It is the only way in. There can be no fear, no pause.

I smell their sweat. One oils his body with orange-flower water; the other has not been near the bathhouse for perhaps two days and has a stale stink about him. He has been eating onions; I can taste his breath. I press both hands flat against the door, feeling the old, polished wood, cool and smooth beneath my palms. Very slowly, it creaks on its hinges. For the briefest moment, I listen: there is no one within. It's a vast room, with a high vaulted ceiling criss-crossed by wooden beams worn dark with age. Then I slide past both the guards. I do not have long to find a hiding place. They heard the door creaking—they have seen that it's open. I run toward the nearest couch and duck behind it; I know I can't remain unseen for long. They are wary now, ears pricked up like dogs'. They're looking for an intruder.

"Strange," I hear one of the guards say. "Must be the damp."

Go on, I think. *Close the door.*

"Wait. Did you feel something just then?"

One of them has stepped into the room; the soles of his sandals slap softly against the flagstones. If they find me in here, I won't live to see the sun set.

I can hear him breathing. I stare at the rich red folds of damask hanging over the back of the couch. Why did I not steal a scarf on the way here to disguise my hair? If I'm caught, they'll know who I am. But then the footsteps sound quieter. The guard has left. I hear the door click as he closes it behind him.

Thank God. Now, where to hide? I look up at the ceiling and see the place straightaway. I step onto the polished oaken table. It's inlaid with gold and mother-of-pearl. I haul myself up till I'm standing on the window ledge—

Achaicus certainly has a wonderful view of the sea. I leap for the beam and catch it, then pull myself up till I'm sitting astride it. Then I crawl closer to the wall and lie facedown on the beam, with the whole chamber spread out beneath me. It would be a long way to fall — but I won't fall.

I just pray that none of Achaicus's men is in the habit of staring at the ceiling.

I hope I haven't missed their little gathering. I think of my lord, sitting in his chair by the window. Does he wonder what has happened to me? What if he has given up on me and passed this task on to Thales? Not that the fool could manage it: he is good at cutting throats but doesn't have half my cunning. He would be dead and floating in the harbor before he knew what befell him.

How long have I been lying here? The angle of the light has changed. Now the sun slants into the room rather than glaring in through the window. The afternoon is drawing on. Poor Yannis: I would not wish to be the one explaining to my father that I have gone, just as if I had melted into the air. Tasik will be looking for me now. Oh, Jesu. A cold, sick feeling grips my belly.

I am too late; I must have missed Achaicus's gathering. It is all Tasik's fault. Well, I am not going home. Niko and Iskendar will be wondering where I am. I remember my Eye, a line struck through it. When I discover who did that, they will be sorry — and I *will* find out, they may be sure of that. It is time I went back to my underground palace. Then I will have to return to my lord and tell him that I have failed. I think of Black Elias, his bloated body bobbing in the harbor. . . .

The door opens, hinges creaking. In comes Achaicus, at last. I'm sure it's him — I think he has even drunk wine with Tasik before in our courtyard at home. His hair is thinning on top; I can see a patch of pale skin at the crown of his head. I barely breathe as he goes to the oaken desk, picks up a silver-wrought jar, and pours himself a long draft of raki. I can smell the aniseed-scented kick of it from here. He drains the cup in one go. I don't blame him: with a conscience like his, he needs all the strong drink he can get. I hear him let out a tiny sigh. He stands still for a moment, gazing out the window, then crosses to the couch and sits.

Maybe I am not too late after all.

Time drips past like stiff honey on a cold day. Achaicus sits there, quiet as a corpse; it makes my skin creep. I don't like the way he is so calm and still, as if his soul is cleaner than a newborn babe's. He gets up and pours himself another dose of raki. He's drinking, at least; that's something. This second draft goes down without a pause as well, and just as he sits again, there is a knock at the door.

"Enter," says Achaicus in his bored-sounding voice.

The guard shoves the door open and someone walks in: a stocky man about my father's age but not so tall. Reddish-brown hair curls tightly along his forehead, and he wears a close-cropped beard. He moves briskly, as if he doesn't have time to spare for anything.

It is Constans. It is the emperor.

I nearly fall off my beam and have to dig my fingernails into the wood and grip hard with my legs.

The door closes behind him, quickly, quietly. Achaicus is on his feet in a moment, bowing his head. "Your Majesty," he says. "You need not have troubled yourself; I was expecting a summons to your chamber of state. Is there anything you desire?"

"No cause to fuss, Achaicus," Constans says. "It's hardly taxing, walking the length of a corridor." He sits on the couch I hid behind, one square, callused hand resting on each knee, leaning back. Constans was brought up in the palace, but he has the hands of a soldier. Tasik used to say he felt sorry for Constans. All he wants to do is lead his men in the field, but he always has to return to the palace and be fussed over by eunuchs and flatterers, and read endless parchments. "Come, Achaicus," Constans goes on, "sit down. There's no call for all this pacing. I am here to talk about all this fuss over Essa. You must know that these things always reach my ears."

Save for my mother, Constans is the only person who calls Tasik by his given name.

And what of the letter I stole? I think. *What do you know of that, my Imperial Majesty?* I am sure they can hear the beating of my heart.

Achaicus smiles sadly at Constans. "Ah, so you have had word of it. It is a great pity." Achaicus sounds as if his dog has just died, but there is such a great clanging lie in his voice, I wonder that Constans does not laugh.

But he just leans back in his seat. "Tell me all," he says. "I am greatly confused. The last I knew, Essa was my faithful right hand in Armenia, but judging by the whisperings from my agents, and all the scrolls I have been forced to read on the subject, anyone would think he is about to stab me as I sleep."

Tasik would never do that! Constans is his dearest friend. I have heard it said they are more like brothers. You will pay for this, Achaicus Dassalena. I will make sure Constans sees that letter whether my lord the Emperor of Thieves likes it or not.

"Your Majesty," Achaicus says in a low, sorrowful voice, "we must open our eyes to the truth. God's Fire has become too close to Muahi'ya. Almost every evening, they would speak long into the night. God's Fire spent more time with the Arab's retinue than he did with your generals. Even Theodosius doubts him — the commander of your own desert army."

Constans shakes his head irritably. "Theodosius is the fool who let Armenia fall into Arab hands in the first place," he says. "I do not trust his word. Essa's task was to learn the secrets of Muahi'ya's soul by befriending him, and that is what he has done."

"It is not just Theodosius," Achaicus says quietly. "It is widely known that God's Fire is a traitor not only to you, Your Majesty, but also to the True Faith."

Constans laughs then. "Gone to the way of Mohammed, has he? Well, Essa was always thorough in his work. Not many of my men would have themselves circumcised in service to me."

So is it true, then, that Tasik has turned to Islam? He would not, surely. He is barely even a good Christian — I have heard him pray often enough to the strange warrior-gods of the north.

Achaicus sighs heavily. "Your Majesty, I know not how to make you feel the severity of his betrayal, and the danger to your own soul in allowing this infidel to —"

"You speak to me as though I were a child, Achaicus," Constans says. His voice is light, playful even, but I would not wish to be sitting where Achaicus is now. "You have served me since I was fourteen summers old, and much as I value your devotion, you would do better not to forget that I am well able to look after the needs of my own immortal soul."

Achaicus bows his head. I would sell my own mother to see the look on his face. "Of course, Your Majesty. But you are always so bound up with the needs of your people, I wonder if there is one thing you have forgotten."

You liar, I think. The words of the letter ring in my head: *On this day of our Lord, we the undersigned do solemnly declare our belief that Constans, son of Constantine, is no longer fit to bear the ruling of our most glorious empire. . . .*

"If I have forgotten something, I pray you may tell me what it is," says Constans in the same low, dangerous voice. He is looking up at the ceiling. His eyes widen for the briefest moment, but then he looks away. He saw me! But he can't have. I would surely be in the hands of those guards by now if he had. I have been up here so long, my mettle is sunk; I will be seeing phantoms next, and shivering at breezes and floorboards creaking in the night. I close my eyes and cling tighter still to the beam. It is pressing into my belly now and I wish I could get down, but I cannot move.

"Your Majesty knows better than anyone the importance of his own dear people," Achaicus says, almost in a whisper. I think of the bishop again, the one they dragged through the streets and tore to death. I think of the fear in Demos the charioteer's eyes when I threatened to spread word of his cheating.

They say there is no man more powerful than the emperor, that he is second only to God. That is true, but nothing and no one wields more strength in this land than all the people of Constantinople when they are stirred up into a rage.

A strange stillness spreads over Constans. "I would be a fool, Achaicus, if I did not know the strength of my own subjects," he says.

"Well, then," Achaicus replies. "It is a true shame they have chosen to believe all this foolish talk about God's Fire. The word in the marketplace, Your Majesty, is that your dear friend is a traitor and a witch, that he converses with beasts and employs strange barbarian powers a faithful Christian ought never to think of. He is also a brigand and a thief of the first order, and thinks nothing of plundering gold wherever he can."

Well, it is true enough about the gold — before Tecca died, hooded men used to knock at the door in the thick of night, delivering up locked chests full of treasure and rich spices. We thanked God, then, because Tasik's soldier pay — even though he was Constans's most prized assassin — had been dwindling as the palace's coffers drained. But as for the rest of Achaicus's tale, I do not understand why he is serving my father so.

What in Christ's name does he mean by saying that Tasik converses with beasts?

Is it to draw attention away from Achaicus's own misdeeds, like the sleight of hand used by the traveling magicians who bite coins in half and hide hen's eggs in your ear? But then I realize there's most likely another reason for Achaicus to blacken my father's name: me. He knows I was the one who stole his letter, and he is taking his revenge.

If anything ill befalls Tasik, it will be my fault.

Constans passes one hand over his face, as though he desires to wipe away his weariness. "These past ten years, God's Fire has ever been spoken of as a hero," he says.

Achaicus shakes his head. "I am sorry, Your Majesty. But too many now say that God's Fire has sold his soul to the devil and his services to Muahi'ya. Have you not heard of the strange powers he is thought to possess? And by retaining him in your favor —"

Constans holds up one hand. "I know, Achaicus. You need not go on."

Strange powers? What strange powers?

A deep quiet falls on the room. How can they not hear me breathing? I can hear them: I can hear their hearts beating. Oh, Tasik. I must warn him. I shall show him I am no coward —

"Do I have your leave, then, Your Majesty?" Achaicus says at last.

After what seems like ten long winters have passed, Constans nods his head. "Do what you must," he replies. "And may God save both our souls."

"Very well." Achaicus is on his feet in a moment, and he sweeps out of the room, his crimson robe sailing out behind him.

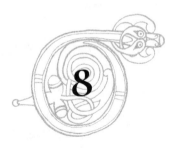

8

As the door closes, I sit up, clutching the beam. "What will they do to him?" My voice comes out in a harsh whisper. I might have known Constans my whole life, but he is still the emperor and he could have my neck wrung in the blink of an eye.

Most people would leap with fright to find a child looking down on them from up in the ceiling beams, never mind after a delicate conversation like that, but not Constans. He does not even get up from the couch; he just sits there, looking at me. He smiles, shaking his head. "I thought I had seen something. What odd talents you must have, my child, to hide and sneak in the way you do. To think, the son of my dearest friend has become the most wanted criminal in the empire. You had best come down from there."

"You're no friend of my father!" I hiss. "You have just ordered his death. Achaicus is the traitor, not him."

"Come down," Constans says. "I do not wish to call the guards. Good God, Cai, if all I hear is true, you have been leading those who love you a merry dance long enough. Do as you are asked."

I scramble down as far as the window ledge and sit there, glaring at him. "I'll come no farther," I say. "You've just betrayed my father. How do I know you won't order your guards to cut my throat?"

"Well enough," Constans says. "You have no reason to trust me, but hear this: I have already seen the letter you stole, and I know that Achaicus Dassalena tried to finish me. Nothing will ever convince me that your father is a traitor, but Achaicus is right: however the tale spread, this city is no longer safe for your family, and anything is better than meeting death at the hands of the mob."

"What will Achaicus do to him?" I say. I cannot bear it. I cannot stand to think of Tasik coming to a traitor's end, the breath choked from his body, blood pouring from his mouth and eyes.

"Nothing," Constans answers. "He will not get the chance: you will all leave the city before the sun rises. But it must be you who warns your father—I can trust no one else in this place to do it. Till I saw you, I thought I would have to hide my face and go to him myself. Go quickly."

He pauses, and our eyes meet. His are light hazel, slightly slanted and flecked with greenish lights. The lashes are pale, rusty-looking, darker at the tips. I will never forget this moment, I know. It is just me and the emperor. He is the most powerful man in all the world, but he is a coward. He should have ridden through the streets till he found my father. He should have stabbed Achaicus Dassalena through the heart where he stood. "Go quickly," he repeats, "and may God watch over you."

I am running. I do not even care if anyone sees me; I must get home. What if Tasik isn't there? I must find him. Darkness is drawing across the city sky like a deep blue curtain, and one by one, unshuttered windows begin to glow. How can folk light their lamps and think about their suppers when at any moment, Achaicus Dassalena's men might find my father and take his life? I should have gone back to my lord, to the Emperor of Thieves, many hours since, but I do not care about him anymore. If I have crossed his mind at all, he must think I am dead by now, my throat cut in an alley for stepping on the wrong foot, just like so many other Thief Children. I've been a fool to give him my service all this time.

I must go the quiet way, through the secret alleys and lonely streets that decent folk never visit. I do not go across the rooftops; I just run, shouldering people aside whenever they get in my way. I am used to moving quickly, but now I am running faster than I have ever run in my life. My legs feel as though they are burning, and I cannot draw enough air into my body; I'm gasping as if I have swum underwater for leagues and leagues.

I must make it home before Achaicus's men get there.

Tasik will not go easily with them—if Achaicus is even of a mind to allow him a trial. For all his honored bravery and beauty, for all the songs they sing of him in the market-place, Tasik is a barbarian, and most likely his trial would be nothing more than a thin wire pulled tight around his throat till he breathed no more.

But I will reach him first, and we'll get away—by sea, most likely. There's always some boatman willing to look the other way if the coin's enough. Oh, my beloved city. I cannot bear this; I cannot bear to see her, smell her, for the last time. I cannot bear to look on the lamplit windows, the shadows of the grapevines as they droop down from the rooftops to the streets, the great dome of Santa Sofia, mother of all churches. I am leaving the perfumiers' quar-ter, and the rich, rolling scent of rose oil, spikenard, cloves, ambergris, and lavender makes me want to weep because I am smelling it for the last time. Now I am running past a tavern, and the smash of broken cups, the roaring of drunken men, is my city's farewell song. I will never rule the Underworld; I will never replace my lord, the Emperor of Thieves.

Will he mourn me? Will he wonder, ever, what became of the Ghost?

But wait. Someone follows: I hear breathing, I feel their gaze burning into my back. Surely Achaicus can't have men on my trail already. Should I run or face them? I must—

"Ghost!" a voice calls. I'd know it anywhere; it's just

Niko — trust him always to find me at the wrong moment. Probably he wants to ask me some foolish thing. I turn —

My head. Something has struck the back of my head — a burst of pain so deep, I feel it run through my whole body. I am betrayed. All is going dark — and look: there is Niko. I can see his foolish, round face — his open mouth a black hole, his eyes gaping. Oh, Niko, why did it have to be you? I hear someone laughing.

"Not fast enough this time, little Ghost." It is Thales. Niko and Thales. Not Iskendar, then, who I always thought might be the one.

The darkness closes in on me; it clouds my sight.

I cannot see at all now; everything is black.

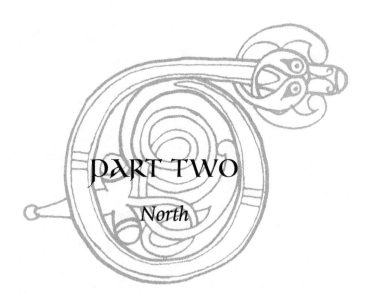

PART TWO

North

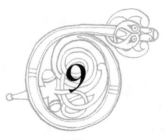

9

Slave ship

The DREAM shifts—somehow I know I am dreaming—and now I am back in the courtyard at home. The fountain bubbles softly, but I don't hear any voices. It is so quiet here. Overgrown vines hang loosely from the trellis, stroking the dusty flagstones. Fear slips through my body like ice water. Sunlight sears the flagstones and the white, crumbling walls. Everything is too bright. The windows yawn, open black mouths revealing nothing within.

I have come home, but there is no one here to meet me. They have all gone.

"Tasik!" I call. "Ma! Mama, Elflight, Asha!" Why do I call? No one can hear me. I move toward the cook-room door, but I can't go inside: I am too afraid of what I might find.

But I must find Tasik. I can't be too late. And then I see a dark pool spreading across the bright, hot flagstones. It comes from the far side of the courtyard. I can't bear this. I can't — but I must see. I am not moving fast enough; the air has thickened and clings to my limbs like warm honey, trapping me.

"Tasik!" I shout again, but there is no reply. The dark pool is spreading and it seems to shine, forming a trail beneath the eaves. A breath of wind stirs Ma's chimes as they hang in the vine, and their soft clanging is the only sound save the regular whisper of my own breathing.

I force myself to move, pushing back the long green tendrils, still heavy with grapes, now rotting where they sprouted.

Tasik lies on his back, arms and legs spread awkwardly, bright hair clotted with blood. His eyes are open, staring sightlessly up at the tangle of green leaves above. Blood still seeps from the tear in his pale, freckled throat. It is like a big grin, a mockery of a smile. Oh, my father. I am too late. I kneel by his side, closing my fingers around the cold, yielding flesh of his arm, crying, "Tasik, Tasik," even though I know he will not wake, because he is dead and I delivered him to this end.

"For the love of God, shut your mouth!" It is the boy who sits by me on the oar bench. I can just make out his narrow, bony face in the gloom of the hold. He is shaking my arm, gripping it so hard that I flinch. The stench hits me like a wall as I wake up. There is no way to get relief when you are chained to the oar and the deck is awash with piss and ordure. Every now and then, one of the overseers comes with a bucket of seawater and the filthy mass of it swills around our ankles and spills down into the bilge. On the rowing deck there are tiny oar-shaft holes, which let in thin, salty air. Down here there is nothing but the smell of our own bodies and waste, and of stale breath. I am sure misery has its own scent, too: the sweetish hint of decay, the smell of all hope dying.

"Leave the poor child be, Amin!" I hear a woman call from somewhere in the darkness.

"All we get down here is sleep," Amin says roughly. "Is that to be taken from us as well?"

"Get used to it, my friend," calls another voice. "You don't even own your dreams now."

Amin ignores them. "Just be quiet," he says to me savagely. "We need all the rest we can get in this hell pit."

"I do not choose my dreams," I answer, shivering. I can still see Tasik lying there, the awful ragged tear in his throat. He is dead; I am sure Tasik must be dead, and the fault's mine, for I didn't reach him in time. And what became of Elflight, of Ma? Asha?

I wish Thales had killed me, but it is worse than that: he sold me.

Amin raises a thin black eyebrow. "Oh, so you speak a civilized tongue after all?" I must have been calling out in Anglish or in British as I slept. "Well, little barbarian, you will be glad to know where these sons of demons are trading us. Maybe your mama will buy you back in the northlands, if they don't sell you first in Ephesus or Syracuse."

I don't have the spirit to tell him that I have never been farther north than my father's estate at Heiron. "Where do they trade to, then?" I ask. "The Gaulish lands?" My voice is cracked. I have barely spoken to anyone since I was in the Great Palace with Constans. I have become like an animal on board this hellish boat, knowing only hunger, pain, and what little relief we get. I don't know how long I have been here: it might be six days, or it might be twenty. I never see the rising sun. I never see the night, only darkness.

Amin laughs. He has square white teeth and a crooked nose that looks as though it has been broken more than once. "Farther than that, my friend. Bright-haired angel-brats like you fetch a fine price, and they are going to get some more. This boat goes all the way to the end of the earth — to Britannia."

Where did you and Tasik come from, Mama? I asked long ago.

Mama looked up from her spinning, the coil of red yarn limp in her hands. *Britain, my honey,* she said. *The island of Britain.*

Why did you come here, then?

Frowning, Mama became very busy with her spindle, retying the weight. *Cai, the past is best left where it is — behind.* She smiled. *Now, find Maria and ask her when the broth shall be ready. I wager you're as hungry as me.*

And now God or the devil or whoever rules my fate has chosen to send me to Britain, island of my forefathers, island of secrets.

For the first time since I lost my life, I smile.

On the oar deck there's scarcely room to stand. Even the overseers are forced to walk hunched like olive trees twisted by the wind. Little wonder they are so free and easy with the lash. This boat must be one of those old-style dromonds with two decks of slaves at the oars and a couple of masts. Many's the time I've seen them sliding up along the Golden Horn and then hauling sail where the wind picks up on the strait down toward Chalcedon. I never thought I would be on one of them, rowing. I can see one of the masts — it passes up through the wooden-planked roof to the deck above, climbing up toward the open sky. How I long to see the sky.

I am racked with pain: I have been hit so many times by the oars before and behind that my flesh roils with bruises. The overseer always has a whip, and the skin on my back and shoulders is raw and stuck to my tunic with dried blood. My hands are burning, blistered, but I cannot let go of the oar. I am so tired, afire with the heat of rowing. I feel my eyes closing; my head droops forward.

"Row, you fool," hisses Amin over his shoulder. "Row, or else we'll all suffer." He looks a few years younger than Tasik — more of a boy, really, and although he's skinny, his arms and shoulders are thick with coils of muscle.

I clench my fingers around the oar handle and try to heave in time with everyone else. I cannot make myself do it; the shaft flies from my hands, and shouts of rage boil up from the oar benches. My hands scrabble uselessly, there's a choking blow to my belly as the shaft flies back, and I can't breathe. I am knocked backward off the bench, the shackles rending the skin from my ankles as I fall. Rough hands grab my tunic, and I'm hauled upright. Someone is shouting at me; fiery lines of pain wriggle across my back and shoulders. The lash comes down again, and I feel thick, warm liquid seep beneath my clothes.

"Ya Allah," Amin says. "Follow the way I do it: watch."

And now, even though every fiber in my body is swollen with pain, at least I heave in time with everyone else and do not get smashed in my belly by the oar shaft.

We have got out of rhythm only one other time this shift, and then it was not my fault: an old man died a few moments ago — just three rows ahead of me. I watched him slump over his oar, and then a great shout went up. The overseer, the one with the gingery beard and the belly that looks like a deflated pig's bladder, came and tore about the old man with his whip, and the shouting grew louder till I thought the air would burst with it.

"Stop!" Amin yelled. "Can't you see he's finished? Or must we be scourged all the way to hell as well as every day of our lives?"

The fat overseer didn't trouble to reply, just laid about Amin's back with his whip. Amin made no sound, though, just set his teeth hard together and carried on heaving the oar as though the lash were nothing more than a fly. I wish I had the courage to bear it so.

And I wish Thales the Knife had cut my throat that night. Hell can be no worse than this, and I know I don't have a hope of the other place.

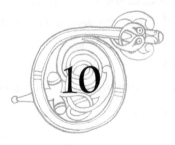

10

Tecca

I DO NOT know if I'm awake or asleep. Cold fingers
brush my forehead.

Then I hear it: laughter. My little sister always had a
spluttering, snorty, unladylike laugh. *You will have to change
your ways when you are old enough to go into society, you ragged
kit,* Ma used to say, *or they will throw you out of court.*

I don't care for court, anyhow, Tecca would tell her. *It's
nothing but a bunch of cheese-faced old women, and I would
rather die than paint my face and sit on my behind waiting to
be married.*

It is a long time since I heard Tecca laugh, but I'd know
the sound of it anywhere. I am at home again.

"Where are you?" I say to the silent courtyard. "Come
out, Tecca. This isn't a game."

The laugh again. Is it coming from behind the fountain?
But there is no one there, and I see now why all seems so

wrong. The fountain casts no shadow, and neither do I. The courtyard is filled with nothing but blank light. More laughter.

"Tecca! Where are you hiding?"

And then she is standing before me, her fire-colored curls tangled with mud, her dark eyes alive with mischief. She is wearing her favorite blue tunic, the one with crimson stripes around the cuffs. It is earth-damp, though, and clinging wetly to her pale limbs.

I step toward her. "You little fool," I say. "You're all dirty. Ma will be in a rage with you."

She smiles, slipping just out of my reach, and her round white teeth are blackened with earth as well. "Silly," she says in a strange, whispering voice. "It's dirty in the ground. How can I help it?"

"You're not going back there," I say, reaching for her.

But Tecca just looks at my outstretched hands and laughs. "Even you can't bring me home, Cai," she whispers, and as she smiles, a clod of earth falls from her lips.

The dream shifts.

"Cai, wake up." It is her again. If I open my eyes, I will be in my bed at home, Tecca sitting at my feet. Oftentimes she comes to me in the early morning, before anyone else is awake. She likes to tell stories about what she will do when she is grown: *I shall be like Tasik*, she always says. *I shall ride around the desert with the Arabs and have battles. I shall live with the wild tribes in my own tent and sleep outside at night, and ride along the trade paths all the way east till I see the sun rising at the end of the world*. She will push her chilly feet beneath my sheets, pressing them against my legs till I get out of bed and go down to the cook-room with her, where we'll dip our fingers in the ginger preserve and tear strips of chicken off the carcass one of the slaves has left out. . . .

I know this is nothing but a dream, a memory, yet still I hear Tecca whispering my name. I must see. It is hard to know what is a dream and what is not. Perhaps this ship is but a nightmare, and if I open my eyes, I will be at home, and Tecca will not be dead, and I will not be a killer.

But it is not so; of course it is not. I'm awake now. The darkness of the hold closes around me, and I feel the familiar squeeze of panic. How will I bear this for the rest of my life? My belly aches with hunger. It is strange, I did not think it would be possible to feel hungry this long, but the cramping, sick longing for food never goes away. It just gets worse. For a moment, I think I see the gleam of Tecca's bright hair in the gloom of a far corner, but I know she is not here, not really. Only now I am sure I feel her chilly fingers in my hair, against my face.

Her voice is like the whispering of wind in the trees — a sound I don't think I shall live to hear again.

Never forget that you are bound by gold, Tecca says softly, and then I can't feel her touch anymore. *You are a child of the Serpent, and you must go home.*

Is she here or not? Is my sister living somehow or dead? "Tecca!" I whisper. "Where are you?"

But in reply, I hear just a silvery trace of her voice, an echo. *You are a child of the Serpent.*

My heart is thundering. I am dreaming again — that's all. The Serpent? What does that mean? But I am bound by gold; this is true enough. I reach beneath the rags of my tunic, and my fingers close around the leather thong and then the ring itself. Its smooth coldness brings a strange calm. How can they not have taken it from me? They must have searched me for booty when I was first captured, but they missed this. And how could I have not cared to notice before whether it was there or not?

I still have my father's gold: I have Tasik's ring.

One day I shall take my revenge for his life, and for Ma's, and Elflight's, and Asha's, too. But before that, I am going north, for what can I do now? I'm just a child. For the first time since I left Constans in the Great Palace, I am making a choice: I will not be getting off this godforsaken ship at Ephesus or any other port till we have crossed the northern seas and landed upriver on the island of Britannia, the home Mama and Tasik left behind so long ago. I shall learn there how to kill, and I pray that the devil does not take Achaicus Dassalena before I return to my city.

We laid off rowing just now, and one of the overseers I'd not seen before is walking up and down the oar benches, pointing with the end of his whip at anyone hale. Everyone looks half dead to me, but some, like Amin, are wreathed with muscle from the rowing while others are weak and thin, their knobbly spines and delicate, winglike shoulder blades pushing through their ragged clothes.

There's a lot of shouting, and I can hear a great rattling of chain, so they must be dropping anchor. Some of us will be going ashore, and some shall not.

The overseer points his whip at Amin but pauses when he looks at me.

"Will we not take that one?" Ginger-Beard jerks his head in my direction, as though I were a sack of beans or a bolt of cloth, something anyone might find in the market.

The chief overseer stands back a pace and looks at me from beneath lowered eyelids. He is a thin-faced man with dark hair that falls down over his forehead, even though most of it's scraped into a tail at the back of his head. "No good. Nothing but bones." He turns away.

He is doubtless right. I have no way of seeing what my face looks like, but my arms are scrawny and my legs look like sticks.

Then the overseer pauses and turns back, snatching a handful of my hair. "Fair, though," he says to Ginger-Beard. "Could get more coin for that, though his hide's dark."

No, I plead silently.

Amin is going. Although we have barely spoken, it feels as if I am losing a dear friend. He stares straight down at the oar, looking at his hands, flexing his long fingers. But I cannot go with him to be sold at the slave market in Ephesus. I am staying on this boat all the way north.

The overseer snatches at my arm. My whole body aches these days, and it hurts so much when he touches me that I have to squeeze my eyes shut and grit my teeth. "No meat on there," he says sharply. "Useless." He turns to Ginger-Beard. "They're no good to us if they're too weak to work, and we're losing too many. We'll have to keep this one and feed it up till Carthage at least if we're to get decent coin. I want it off this boat by the time we trade at Athens. You know as well as I that the fair ones fetch less the farther north you go."

Thanks be to God — we are to get more food. I feel my eyes grow hot, and for a moment I think I am going to cry with gratitude. I watch the overseer walk away, jabbing the butt of his whip at a few more people, and then I know I shall not shed one tear. He is not kind. He is a trader, a merchant, and all he wants to do is make sure he sells human flesh for the highest price he can get.

But he will not sell me.

Someone barks out an order, and we are all unchained from the oar benches. It seems to take a lifetime as the overseers fumble with the keys. Some of the locks stick, and pig grease is sent for to loosen them. The chosen ones get to their feet and shamble off toward the companionway; the rest of us are to go down into the hold till the shore crew returns to the boat. Amin rests his hand on my shoulder as he passes, saying, "May Allah protect you, little one," and he is the only one who walks with pride, his head held high, his back straight.

I watch them go, blinking as my sight blurs once more. I am so tired that I can barely see. I think I hear her again. . . . I must be losing my senses, for Tecca has been dead over a year, and I shall never talk with her again. Yet I am sure this faint whispering voice is hers.

Are you the Ghost or no? No one binds the Ghost.

It makes no sense: when Tecca was still alive, I was not even the Ghost — I was but Cai, son of God's Fire. I hear the ringing music of her laugh — just behind me, it seems — but when I turn my head, I see only the miserable, hollow faces of those left on board: Africans, Slavs, people far, far from their own lands.

Ginger-Beard is bellowing again, and everyone slowly starts unfolding their ruined bodies from the oar benches, stepping out of the unlocked shackles. "Get down below!" roars Ginger-Beard, and his whip flickers about, stinging my flesh like a fly over a midden-pit in high summer. I would like to take that whip and ram the butt of it right into his gullet till he chokes.

I am not going back down into the hold. This is my chance: they are not expecting anyone to run. After all, where is there to go but the wide open sea? You can be sure we are anchored too far out from Ephesus Harbor to make swimming a chance. I hear the creaking of ropes, splashing, and shouting. They must have a skiff somewhere, tethered to the upper deck, or maybe they tow it behind, even though it must slow us. Amin and the rest will be put in that — all chained, if the slavers have any sense — and rowed for once, instead of taking the oars themselves. I wonder if it would almost be worth being sold just to see one of these overseers strain at the oar instead of us.

No, there is nowhere on this ship that any mortal might escape to — but they have not reckoned on the Ghost. The African man who sat next to Amin is passing me now; he speaks in a tongue I cannot understand and rests his hand on my head. He looks at me as if I am running crazy. He speaks again, gesturing at Ginger-Beard, who is elbowing his way through the throng toward me, his face sweaty and red with anger because I have not moved from the bench.

I am not here. None of you can see me, for I am the Ghost. I do not know where I get the strength, but I dart to my feet and run to the bow, where the benches get shorter and shorter as the dromond narrows toward her prow. I want to laugh — the African's face twisted with surprise as I left, his eyes widening. I duck below the nearest bench and flatten myself against the filth-mired floor. When they sluice down our deck, the water must not reach this far forward, because I swear I am lying in all manner of human mess. It surprises me that I do not even care. Had this happened at home, I would have been reeling with disgust. I hear the African laughing — Ginger-Beard must be stamping around like a small child who has lost a saffron cake, but I am nowhere to be found, or at least I hope to God that I am not. It's the first time I remember anyone laughing in a long while.

Ginger-Beard shall either find me or decide that the chief has changed his mind and taken me ashore. I curl up into as small a space as I can manage, bunching my knees up to my chest and wrapping my arms around them. I was always rangy — like a yearling colt, Tasik used to say, but now my legs feel weightless, the flesh melted away.

I close my eyes. I must think of nothing but my breathing, and the beating of my heart. I must try not to be in the world. If I am caught, they will most likely kill me. Or if not that, I shall be chained in the hold for the rest of the voyage till they haul me off this barque and sell me in some dusty marketplace.

I have never been so far from home. Oh, my city. I dream of her high walls and her rooftops, my secret pathways; I long for the blue smoke of cook-fires rising in the air by the Forum of Theodosius, for the sight of white-winged gulls wheeling about the statue of the Emperor Justinian. Who holds court now in my underground palace? My heart burns to think of Thales down there with Niko. He will lead poor stupid Niko to his death; Niko has not the spine for ruling the Underworld. And what of Iskendar? What did he say when he heard that Thales had bested me? Did he clap and cheer as the others surely must have done? Thieves are ever loyal to the winner in any battle, and Thales won out over me. I hope that Iskendar was sorry and looked away while the rest raised the victory shout. I was the one who conquered that palace — it was nothing but a grand, ruined old storm drain before I made it mine. And now here I am, curling up in a foul swill of human waste on the deck of a slave ship. But at least I am free.

I think I must have slept. For the first time in the Lord God knows how many days, I have not woken up in the dark. Grayish, pearly light slants in through the nearest oar-hole. Moving silently, I stretch out my arms and legs, biting my lip so hard I draw blood. I cannot let out even the faintest gasp of pain. The deck is empty. Crawling, I reach the oar-hole and peer out, and my eyes burn with the golden glory of it — the sun setting over the sea. Tears scald my face. I can see just a sliver of sky — a fire-tinged swirl of cloud and clear white light. The sea is like cloth-of-gold, and I remember waiting on the roof after I had stolen that pomegranate, and the sea looked so then, a spreading swath of light.

Move — you have no time.

Tecca again. I must have lost my senses. I cannot bear hearing her voice, and I wonder if it is a punishment from God for the sinful path I followed this past year and more. But whatever she may be, Tecca is right. I must go. Once the slavers have done their trade in Ephesus, we'll be away again. I wonder, do the crewmen who take the slaves ashore to sell spend the night drinking in the taverna? Maybe we do not pull up our anchors again till tomorrow morning. I think of those still imprisoned down in the hold — the African man who laughed, all those hollow-faced folk I see at the oars day after day. Is it worse for the women, who must spend all their time below, for they never row? It surely is. I could not bear to stay down there in the dark all the time; I should lose my senses. I think I have already gone mad, hearing the voice of my dead sister. It is unholy of me.

I know what I am going to do first, now that I have the run of this hell ship. I am going to do something good in thanks for my escape. This is a strange notion, doing something good, one I have not thought of for longer than I can recall. Being wicked is usual for me, but there is enough of it already on this boat.

I crouch by the oar-hole a moment, steadying my breathing, trying to clear my mind. It will not be easy, remaining out of sight on a boat this size, and it will be worse when they find out I was not taken ashore after all; it is hard to stay hidden when someone has sworn to find you.

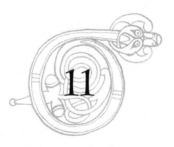

Two months later

CᏥᎯᏞᏟᎬᎠᎾᏁ, Nicaea, Nicomedia, Smyrna, Ephesus, Athens, Syracuse, Carthage—I have passed by them all. Always we drop anchor far enough from shore that no one might chance a swim, and all I see are the domed roofs of churches and the pale bulk of warehouses where silks and spices and slaves are held. I climb the masts and cling to the furled rigging; I hide belowdecks in the shadowy hold, among great bales of silk and barrels of wine meant for kings of the frozen north. I sleep curled in piles of looped-up hawsers or right in the bow on the upper deck, and no one has seen me.

I am sitting on the bowsprit, right out over the rushing sea, when Tecca comes again and perches behind me, putting her cold little hands over my eyes.

I never know when she is going to arrive. Sometimes I do not see her for days on end, and I wonder if I am bound up in a waking dream.

"I know it's you," I say, laughing. I do not know if Tecca's spirit is walking the earth or if my mind has rotted on this boat, but I am glad she is here. I am glad of the company.

"Look," she whispers into my ear. Her breath is icy cold. "Dolphins." She takes her hands off my eyes and wraps her arms around my waist, the way she did when we rode one of the ponies in the countryside up by Hieron. We stare down at the dolphins, at their glistening backs and pointed fins. There are four, five of them and they swim alongside the ship as those still chained to the oar benches groan and heave. At least they do not starve now.

"Tecca," I say. "Are you a ghost?" I half want to laugh because once I was the Ghost and now my sister is one. Tecca and I were always of a kind, more so than Elfla and me, even though we quickened together in our mother's womb.

"No." Tecca's voice has grown softer, and I can no longer feel her arms about my waist. "I am no ghost, but you are a traveler."

A traveler? Not by choice. I know not what she means, but I understand so little now — I am never even sure whether I am awake or asleep — and then she is gone, and I am alone again.

I wonder what happened to Amin, and if the folk who bought him treat him kindly, as we did Asha, or if his life is worse now than it was when he was on this ship. That would not be easy, but folk treat slaves ill. The thought of Asha being taken on a boat like this when she was but a child makes me feel bad inside. I should have been kinder

to her. I wish I were with her now, at home in the courtyard. But I cannot think of Asha, or any of them.

I have work to do, and I must be gone from here. I crawl
back along the bowsprit and drop silently onto the deck,
slipping past the rows of heaving oarsmen. There are one or
two who see more than the others. When I go by, they raise
their eyes from the rowing, and they look afraid, as if they
have just seen a spirit walking.

I want to laugh, but I know I cannot.

Am I dead? Maybe that's what happened, and Tecca is
trying to lead me to the next world — she coming back to
take *my* hand for once, and not the other way around. But
whether I am dead or not, I still have a duty, and I run toward
the looming shadow of the tower. It squats just behind the
mainmast, and back in the days when this dromond was a
warship, they must have fired arrows from the top of it at
the Arab fleet. Now there's just an African woman up there
who cooks. I think she must be a slave rather than part of
the crew, for they're leery of having women on board as it is
and would no more pay one than they would release all the
cargo. I've heard more than one of them blame a squall on
the women prisoners belowdecks.

I squat in the shadow of the tower; it is early evening,
and the gray light is slanting. I have noticed these past few
days that the sea looks more slate-colored than deep blue,
and there is a bite in the air. We are heading north, and
winter is coming. There are not many slaves left, only a few
who looked too sickly to sell at Carthage. They are bound

for the port of Londinium now, I know, where the slavers will buy many fair-haired brats like me to sell. An overseer ambles by, walking down the lines of oarsmen, idly flicking his whip, and stops to talk to his chief down by the stern. He is not looking at me.

I fix my mind on reaching the top of the tower, and spring. My body is getting stronger again, my muscles warmer and looser, and I scramble to the top, hauling myself onto the roof, where the cook-woman sits by her pot, chopping onions into it. Steam drifts. None of this food is meant to reach the mouths of those below, but I shall make sure it does. The cook-woman is scrawny like everyone else—she looks as though she can barely lift her arm—but she works fast and smooth, her heavy knife slamming down and down again. I wonder that she has not gotten fatter and more hale in charge of the cook-pot. She pauses and scrapes white scraps of onion into her pot. I am so hungry, I could eat it raw in handfuls. My mouth fills with spit at the thought. A shiny pile of fish lies next to her. She sighs, reaches for one, cuts off its head and tail, slits it down the middle, and pulls out its guts. All this goes into another pot behind her, the one destined for the cargo.

I curse myself—I have come too soon. What was I thinking? I ought to have waited till I smelled the food cooking before stealing what I could. I have to do this at each change of crew so that I can get it down to the hold, to the resting rowers and the women, without any of the slavers seeing. But the cook has barely begun her work, so I must either wait or come back when the sun's even lower and she has finished. What is wrong with me these days? Every time I move about in daylight, I risk being caught. There will be someone on this boat who is quicker than others, someone who will see me even though I do my best to remain hidden. The Ghost is losing his touch.

I stifle a sigh.

The cook-woman looks up. Right at me. Her eyes are locked on mine. She smiles and laughs softly. "Careful, child," she says in a low voice. "You grow reckless."

I feel cold to the bone. She can see me. And I did not know she could speak Greek.

"It's well enough," she goes on, stirring the onions. "They can't spy you from the deck, even if any of them were sharp enough to spot you, child, with your cunning. I've been watching you. Sit down."

I obey. There is something about her voice that commands submission. I glance around quickly. There's a pile of rotten-looking blankets folded neatly in the corner and a row of sacks lined up next to a few barrels. They must shelter the woman and her fire from the wind. Oftentimes I have seen the crew sitting with the cook-woman, looking out to sea or up at the night sky as they warm their bones around her flames.

"I know what you have been doing." Her voice has a musical lift. She gazes down at the simmering onions as she speaks; if anyone on deck were to glance up, they would not guess she was talking to anyone.

"I don't steal it for myself," I say quickly. "Only a bit. I take all the food below and leave it in the hold. It's — it's for the prisoners."

She laughs softly, her thin shoulders rising and falling. "What a good little thief you are." Then her face changes: she looks afraid. "And so the prisoners all think you died that day we anchored by Ephesus and that your spirit haunts this ship and brings them mortal food. I hear of everything, sooner or later, up here. But I am not talking about you stealing scraps from me, child. It's your wandering I speak of."

I hear Tecca's voice in my mind again: *You are a traveler.*

"I have to move about the ship." My voice sounds dry and cracked; it has been so long since I spoke to anyone. "If I stayed in one place, I would get caught, and I would not be able to steal any food."

The cook-woman shakes her head. Her hair is woven into hundreds of thin plaits, and they swing about her face. "Come, do you not see what you are doing? You walk too close to the other place."

A strange, fluttery feeling bursts in my chest. "What other place?" Of all the talk to be having after such a long silence, this must be the strangest.

I fear I already know what she means.

The woman leans forward, and her skinny fingers grip my arm. "Hear this," she says, and I feel her warm breath on my face. "You stray too close to the land of your ancestors. You are a powerful one indeed to do so, but you must take care or you will not come back and your body shall be as an empty shell."

I grow cold as I recall Thales the Knife calling Tasik my witch father and Achaicus Dassalena sowing his poisonous words in Constans's ears. *That ungodly craft,* he said.

What manner of man was he, my father?

I will break open if I think of Tasik; I stare at the woman's cook-pot instead — a blackened iron thing, shaped like a bowl with a rough handle on either side.

"There, now," the cook-woman says, rubbing my arm. "The ancestors have such sweet voices when they call, and this life has no light for you at the moment. But you must resist and live in the world of men." She cuts open another fish and spears it with a wooden skewer, holding the flesh to the flames. The skin begins to spit and crackle.

"I see my sister," I whisper. Why am I telling this to a stranger, to the cook-woman on this damned boat? But the words come pouring out of my mouth like grains of wheat rushing out of an upturned sack. "I hear her voice, but she's dead. She's been dead a year and more."

The cook-woman nods slowly, turning the skewered fish so its other side begins to blacken in the flames. "She is trying to help you, child. The ancestors know they cannot linger here too long. But if you call her, she has no choice but to come."

I call Tecca? She seems to come and go like a leaf floating on the wind. I cannot call her any more than I might whistle for a wind. The smell of the cooking fish is making my guts rumble. I am hollow and dry inside like an empty nut.

The cook-woman smiles. "Are you a Christian?"

I nod, though I know not what kind of Christian I have been. I have not prayed to God in as long as I can remember. It seems He doesn't listen to me.

"All you People of the Book forget," says the woman. "You forget how close the ancestors are to us. You call your sister with your longing for her, but you cannot bring her back. She is gone from this world, boy. She has moved on." She draws her skewer from the flames and holds it out to me. "There, my dear, eat that. Put some food in your body, and it will bring your spirit closer to your flesh and bones."

The fish burns my fingers and then my mouth, but I do not care — I strip it from the soft, translucent bones and tear lumps of it from the charred and blackened skin.

The woman smiles. "Easy, or you'll sicken."

She is right. It hurts my belly, but I don't care. I swallow the last mouthful. "Thank you," I whisper.

"It's no matter. I grow lonesome, with no one to talk with but my captors," she says. "You rest now, boy. Get in behind those sacks, and sleep, and I shall let you know when it's safe for you to steal from my cook-pot."

I am tired of taking orders, but all of a sudden I want nothing more than to sleep, so I crawl across the floor — which is the roof of the tower: what lies below, within? — and slide behind the barrel, covering myself with a half-empty sack. My fingers come away pale with the dust of crushed oats. I feel the waters of sleep rising up to claim me as I watch the woman get to her feet. She comes to kneel beside me, scooping oats from the sack in a cracked earthenware cup with whorls graven into the side.

"Tell me your name, little barbarian, since you are hiding in my domain. I am Sia." She smiles, showing crooked white teeth.

"I am Cai." It has been so long since I heard my own name spoken that I say it again. "Cai, son of Essa."

I dream less now. I do not know why; maybe it is because I eat more and talk to Sia when I can. She tells me of the hot, yellow land of her childhood, of the white sand where the sea meets the sky. She tells me of the war between her village and the next one and of being sold in a marketplace to the wife of a spice trader. She tells me how she spent long days grinding cardamom seeds and weighing out turmeric on a pair of bronze scales till her hands were stained yellow. She shows me her fingertips, still tinged a faint gold-green, as if each one has been bruised. That was more years ago than Sia cares to count.

Most often I sit astride the bowsprit, watching the sea rush by beneath me. Sometimes I hear Tecca laughing, but when I turn, all I see is a flash of her red hair, a glimpse of her blue tunic.

We are sailing fast now; what few slaves remain are chained in the hold. Till but a few days since, they were using some of the men as crew. I was clinging to the rigging, and I saw the African who used to be chained behind Amin hauling in the big sail they've rigged on the mainmast, and I'm sure he looked straight at me. He said nothing, though. He just finished hauling in the line — and then he jumped overboard. They cannot keep the slaves chained if they wish to use them as crew. I watched it happen, so full of horror that I felt bile fill my mouth. I could not see him fall from where I sat, but I heard the cries from the crew and the slaves, and I wondered why more of them do not end it so.

Folk will cling to their lives no matter what. Perhaps everyone has something to finish, just as I do. Maybe that drowned man had nothing left at all — no family to treasure hopes of finding, no enemy whose dying face he ached to see. Unlike me: I will watch Achaicus Dassalena's eyes darken as he faces the next world, and I will send him there with my own hands.

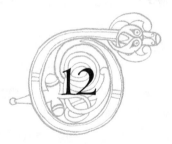

Off the Gaulish coast, mid-October

A FTER NIGHT upon night of being lashed by
a storm, our world has returned to a cold, quiet
gray. We lost five men all told, each one washed
overboard by waves that overtopped the mainmast. Now
that they use the slaves again as crew, they can only pray
that more of them do not end it all by leaping for the cold
embrace of the sea. The air gets ever colder, the water darker
with each day that passes. Some days I catch glimpses of
gray humps of land on the horizon: the coast of a land
called Armorica, Sia tells me. At night she covers me with a
ragged blanket that I am sure she cannot spare.

"You keep it," I whisper as I curl up by the oat barrels.
"I'm well enough." I am not, of course. It is bone-chilling
freezing up here in her tower, but now that I am set on
being good instead of following my own willful path, I
ought to keep to it, come what may.

"Take it: Sia's bones are older and stronger than yours," she says.

I have not seen Tecca in such a long time that I wonder if I was dreaming, if I never really laid eyes on her, never heard her call to me, speaking those strange words: *You are a child of the Serpent*. I cannot tear my mind away from all that strange talk about Tasik and his un-Christian powers. He was my father, but what did I really know about him? I wish more than anything that he were here now; I feel sure that he would understand about Tecca and this Serpent she speaks of.

Sia tucks the blanket around my shoulder and I half want to laugh — I am no longer a child. Who does she think I am? But it's kindly meant, and it is good to be warm. I would be lying here easy were it not for what Sia said before she left me: "They tell me we are nearing the port of Londinium, child, and so soon your journey will start anew."

If Sia thinks I shall be meekly sold to some barbarian trader she is sorely mistaken. I have not spoken to her of my plan to get ashore without any of these fools seeing. How hard can that be, after sailing for weeks with none of them even glancing at me? Sia is kind, I cannot deny that, but I know I should not entirely trust her. Oftentimes the dark-haired overseer comes up here, the one who seems to be chief of the whole boat, and they lie together beneath the night. This is how Sia has survived so long unsold, I am sure. If she would give up her body, what else would she sell at such a cheap price? Loyalty and honor are always the first to go: she'd give me away at once were it to save her life or lessen the burdens she bears. Yes, Sia is kind, but she is not a fool.

I have already plotted the way I shall do it: I've stayed hidden long enough, and I know what a rambling mess it is, moving the slaves anywhere. Even though there are not many of them left, only the ones who did not sell in the southern markets, there will still be a muddle as the traders get them onto dry land. We are bound to sail into harbor as well this time, instead of anchoring offshore and sending in a skiff. When they are all tangled up with getting the slaves, silk, and wine ashore, and hieing off to whichever market they mean to sell them in, I will sneak off this hell boat once and for all. I'm sure none of the traders truly believes that I am still on board, so they are no longer looking for me. It has been many weeks since we passed by Ephesus, and three whole new moons have risen, waxed, and died in the night sky since that time. Never once have I been seen, apart from by Sia, and I am sure she is possessed of some kind of witchery.

With each moment, we grow closer to Britain. Lying on my bowsprit, I watch the shifting gray waters, and as we surge forward, I wonder why Mama and Tasik spoke so little about their homeland. If I've kin left alive on the island, where are they? How shall I find them? I'm named for Tasik's father, but all I know of him is that he's dead: no use to me.

Inside my tunic, Tasik's ring presses against my chest, and suddenly I am on the quayside in Constantinople again and Tasik is leaving with the fleet for the desert. He holds me close, saying, *Wear this ring for me, little cub. No matter how far the distance between us, it binds you to me, and while I am gone, you must look after the girls and your mother. It was given to me by a dear friend, and we each spared the life of the other, so it holds power. Wear it for me, my honey.*

And Mama says, *Oh, Essa, you and that wolf and your rings!* She is trying not to cry, and she sounds very young. I look up, catching the secret glance that flashes between them. Sometimes it's as if they talk without speaking.

When Tasik had gone, we stood on the quay waving at the ships as they grew smaller and smaller, and I held the ring in the palm of my hand, looking down at it: all I had left of my father. *Mama,* I said. *What did you mean by "that wolf"?*

But Tecca had started to weep, and Mama just shook her head, saying, *Come, it's time we were gone.*

I cling to the bowsprit, gazing out at the heaving sea, and I curse myself for not asking more questions, for not forcing my mother and father to unravel the secrets of their lives.

What were they hiding?

We have left the open water and are rowing against the wind up a slow brown river that grows narrower with each day that passes. But even so, it is still a huge vein of water, so wide it must be next to impossible to see from bank to bank on a cloudy day. I had never known there were so many shades of gray till I sailed beneath northern skies. Sometimes I think I would sell my own right hand to feel the sun on my back once more, to lean in the shade of a white-domed church and watch the sun shimmering off the paving stones, and feel the day's heat beating from a crumbling wall.

But now at last the time has come. The sails have been taken down, for the wind goes against us, and apart from Sia and me, all on board have taken an oar — even the slavers themselves, even the women who have been kept chained below these many months. A couple of them have been brought up to row on the upper deck; they are pale, unearthly creatures with sunken eyes and bone-white skin. They remind me of the fish who used to swim in the waters of my underground palace. They keep time badly, but the slavers need them up here come what may. They need all the help they can get, for the wind pushes us away from the dockside and they shall be lucky to get in.

They shout to keep the rhythm, and it sounds like the beating of a drum: *heave, heave*.

"You grow careless again," Sia says to me.

I shrug, gazing upon the slate-gray, glittering water. I think of nothing and slip away from her. She mutters beneath her breath as I slide from sight, away behind the now-empty oat barrels. I have been living beyond the reach of men's eyes so long that I sometimes wonder if I have truly earned the name I bore when I was the greatest thief in the known world: the Ghost of Constantinople, Lord over the City of the Rising Moon.

I have not seen Tecca in so long, though. I miss her, although I should not, for Sia is right: she is gone, and there is no having her back. She will never take me by the hand again — not in this world, anyhow. I believe Sia is a witch. I wonder if the tale she told of being stolen from her sandy homeland is true, or if she ran, hunted like a wild creature by Christian folk afraid of the way she sees what others do not.

I think on this as I lie belly-down on the bowsprit. We are nearly alongside now, and I can see men on land, shrunken by distance. I feel a strange thirst to drink in their faces with my eyes; apart from Sia, the slavers, and their captives, they will be the first folk I have seen in months. I am so close, so close to the homeland of my father and mother, so near to freedom. For what kind of life is this, to be always hiding, sneaking? It holds all the demands of thievery and none of the rewards.

We are much nearer the shore now. There is shouting both on board and ashore, and the youngest slaver, the one with the pimples, runs forward till he is but an arm's length away from me. I could reach out and touch him. Kneeling, he rapidly uncoils a rope and clambers onto the rail, holding it. Looking over my shoulder, I see Ginger-Beard doing the same down in the stern.

There is not very much water between us and the shore now. Brownish waves lap at the slimy quayside, which has been shored up by a fence woven out of whip-thin branches. The young one has the rope in a coil; leaning landward, he is ready to throw it. I am amazed he does not slip overboard, balancing the way he is, and for a moment I am forced to forget my hatred for his trade and admire the way he moves so adeptly and swiftly with the dromond, as if he is part of her.

And then — oh, Lord — I feel a hand close around the top of my arm, and a voice says roughly, "You have evaded me too long, little shadow."

I whirl around, afire with fear, and there he is — it's the dark-haired slaver, the chief, the one who decided so long ago that I was too skinny to sell in the slave market at Ephesus. His face is alive with laughter, and he is deaf to the shouting between those aboard and the men on shore. I watch, half dazed, as the young sailor throws the rope ashore. It makes a graceful arc through the air before one of the shoremen catches the loop and wraps it fast through an iron ring set in the ground. The rest of the crew all rush to fend off from the quayside, and the great dromond is brought quietly to rest after all these long weeks at sea.

I hardly feel it as the chief hauls me backward off the bowsprit.

"Quick!" he hisses. "I want no one to see you. They all think you are dead and that your spirit wanders this boat, and I need no fuss as I get the cargo ashore." He pulls me along with him so fast that I stumble. Where are we going? He is trying to hide me somewhere, but I am damned if I'll allow him to lock me up or bind me.

How can I have escaped his eye for so long, only to let myself be caught just as I'm so close to freedom?

There is a doorway in the tower, and the chief shoves me within, into a dim chamber. A shuttered window looks out across the great river, away from the shore, away from freedom. He follows the line of my gaze and says, "I hope you do not think of swimming, boy; there are tides here that will pull you under before you've time to scream your last prayer."

My mind's darkening: I cannot breathe as I should. Tides? What are tides? Some kind of sea creature that stalks the river bottom? How can he have caught me? Why did I allow him to see me? He pulls the door shut, bolts it, snatches a tinderbox from a table wedged into a shadowy corner, and lights a lamp, looking at me all the while. My nostrils fill with the stink of burning oil, pulling me back into myself. My eyes prickle, and for a moment I think I am going to weep, but I do not.

"I wonder what kind of un-Christian powers you must toy with, to have escaped me so long," the chief says. "What price does a little witch boy fetch?"

"You're the one whose soul's in the devil's hands," I hiss. "I do not deal in human flesh."

The chief turns away, and for a moment I feel a flash of victory. I have riled him now, I know. "Their souls are lost, anyhow," he says, and his voice drops lower. "They are none of them People of the Book."

I throw him a scornful look; Amin was a follower of Mohammed, and I have heard others mutter prayers I recognize. Why doesn't he just tell me bold-faced that he cares not whether he deals in Christians, Jews, Mohammedans, or the damned? It's worse that he tries to excuse himself. Any moment now, I shall be out of this prison and away onto the quayside. Just as soon as he looks away. . . . Here's my chance —

Shaking his head, the chief goes to the door, draws back the bolt, puts out his head, and shouts, "Gregorios, I need you!"

Ginger-Beard comes in — he must have been near — and there's no chance I can slip out now: he's closing the door behind him, blinking in the gloom like some kind of foolish beast.

I am scared, now that there are two of them. How am I going to get away? Calm, I must be calm. If they take me to a market, more than likely there'll be a chance to escape on the way or when we get there. But where will I go in this strange land? Time enough to think of that later.

Gregorios looks at me, his eyes widening. "But — but, sir, that boy went overboard weeks ago!" He can hardly spit out the words. I can see the whites of his eyes now, and a quick flame of satisfaction flares in me. I'm glad I've scared him. Does he think I'm a ghost returned to pay him out for those long weals on my back that I shall bear for the rest of my life?

The chief smiles thinly. "Well, Gregorios," he says, ever so softly, "you can see that the boy is very much alive. Feel his arm if you do not believe me. He's as solid as you or I."

"But — but how's he not been seen all this while?" Gregorios cannot keep his eyes on me. Every time they turn my way, he looks away with the next breath, as if he is afraid the sight of me will burn him. He certainly does not want to touch me.

The chief shrugs in one long, loose movement that reminds me of the cats I used to slink with on the rooftops of Constantinople. "The boy's a thief," he says lazily. "Or that's what my man told me. Said he'd got on the wrong side of the emperor and that's why we had him. No doubt he's used to sneaking and hiding."

I wonder if he means that coward Constans or my long-ago master. I had nearly forgotten about the Emperor of Thieves.

Gregorios is shaking his head, blinking. He thinks that next time he looks, I will be gone, that this is all some unpleasant dream.

"The question is, my man," says the chief to Gregorios, "what do we do with the brat now?"

"Bind him," Gregorios answers without pause, and I feel the sickness rushing up my throat. I thought that after being chained so long, I would have bettered this old fear of confinement, but if it has not gone now, it will never go. I draw in deep, quiet breaths, trying to steady myself. There is a way out of this. I have not hidden so long only to be sold, bound hand and foot, to some fat old barbarian merchant's wife.

"Bind him," Gregorios says again, "and sell him quick. By the time his master knows what a sorry handful he's got for his coin, you and I shall be long gone."

He is already looking about for rope, and the chief has tightened his grip on the top of my arm as though he is afraid I will melt away. But that kind of magic is found only in fireside stories. Oh no, the chief has me surer than a frog in a barrel, and that's the truth.

But if I cannot get out of this by force, I must let them have the full strength of all the silvery talk I can muster. "Wait," I say, and they both stare at me. They were not expecting me to bargain with them. I suspect that not many of their slaves think it worthwhile, but I am past caring if they slice my skin with a whip. "Wait. How much will you get if you sell me as a slave? A few coppery coins? Maybe some silver if you're lucky. I'm but a scrawny brat after living as your guest these many moons."

The chief smiles, but his eyes are colder than stones at the bottom of a drain. "Is that so?" he says. "You must accept my apologies that our table was not quite up to its usual standard. And what else do you suggest we sell you as, if not a slave?"

This is it: if this does not work, I'm finished. I suck in a long breath and reach inside the ragged remains of my tunic, pulling out the ring, clutching the leather cord so hard the veins in the back of my hand stand out. The gold shines in the dim light.

The chief reaches out and snatches the ring from around my neck. I want to shout at him to give it back, but I cannot, for I must keep my head. He holds it up by the leather string and lets it swing before his eyes. I have to clench my fists to stop myself from snatching it. "How was this bauble not found when the boy was taken?" he demands, glaring at Gregorios. "You know the rules."

"You may ask Leonides that, for I never laid eyes on the brat till he was in irons," says Gregorios.

The chief spits on the floor and shoves the ring into a leather bag hanging from his belt. I have betrayed my father again — I swore I would keep that ring, and I have just let it go into the hands of a stranger. But it is my only chance. I turn and look at the chief. Strange that he's quite a pretty man — I have always been taught that beauty means the bearer is blessed by God, as my mother is, and the chief has got to be one of the devil's own.

"Sir," I say — I may as well lay it on thick — "my lord, you may sell me as a slave, but think how much you will get for a hostage."

"What is he talking of?" Gregorios says. "We should get him ashore, sir, with the others, afore he slips away again."

The chief ignores him. "What say you, brat?" He is smiling now, but there is no merriment in his eyes. "Spare me the thief's tale. I have no desire to hear some legend you've woven about a ring stolen from a market stall."

He has met my eyes now: a mistake on his part. I gaze full into them, whispering, "Only, if you please, sir, it is no thief's tale. I was stolen from this island when I was too young to recall it, stolen from the arms of my mother — a princess of the royal house."

I hear Gregorios laughing, scornful, but the chief does not laugh. "Which royal house?" he says briskly, and for a moment he has me. Not for the first time, I wonder why Ma and Tasik would never speak of their life in the north.

But then I recall the time I dreamed of Tecca and the words she whispered in my ear. "The House of the Serpent," I say softly, not letting the chief avert his eyes. *You will not sell me, slave-man. I will be the one who got away.*

The chief stares at me a long while, our eyes fixed on each other's. I know I have him now. Even if I were lying, I would have him now. No one can ever see past my words once I look them in the eye. My gaze befuddles and freezes people, as if I were some offspring of Medusa who could turn men to stone with just a glance.

I wonder how much the chief knows about the kings of Britain — he's all tangled up in thoughts and memories now, I can tell — and then he says, "Northumbrian, then, are you, child?"

"Yes," I say in Anglish.

The chief's eyes narrow even farther. "Well enough," he says. "Well enough. We shall see if you are telling the truth or not. A pity it is for you that my ship has docked in the port of Londinium. You'd have been best off a slave, boy."

A cold thrill of fear passes through me. What does he mean? I do not think it shall be too long before I find out.

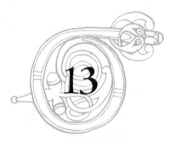

The Devil's Cub

My Legs are useless on dry land, buckling beneath me as if the bones have melted. There is a throng of people, but this place is nothing like Constantinople. I can feel gravel somewhere beneath my bare feet, but I am up to my ankles in such claggy, thick mud that it is nearly impossible to walk, and the chief drags me so fast that I keep stumbling. The streets are much wider than at home, but clustered with buildings all of wood and what seems to be dried mud plastered over woven twigs; I have seen a few crumbling, overgrown walls, but the people seem not overly fond of stone here. Their preference seems to be for mud.

My hands are bound together, and the chief walks on ahead so fast with the rope that I am sure my arms are about to be torn from their sockets. The folk look unnatural, too, some of them tall and pale with long hair — even the men! — while others are slighter and darker. No one is wearing decent clothes, and hardly any of the women cover their hair. Some of them even have bare arms as the poor do at home, even though the air is so damp that it feels like walking through a sea fog. A woman shoves past me — she is pudding-faced, but her hair is the color of fire, and my eyes burn for a moment as I think of Tasik and Tecca.

This place, this Londinium, even smells different from my city. There are no lingering scents of rose water and ginger buns mingling with the stink of dung, and thick, woody smoke hangs everywhere. A little girl no older than Tecca walks by, balancing a basket on her head. I can just see inside: it writhes with long, wormlike fish. It's been a long time since Sia spared her last bowl of food for me — how strange and sad that I shall never lay eyes on Sia again. I wonder what will befall her. I am hungry, but I'd rather starve than eat those wormy fish.

The smell of stale human bodies is everywhere, too: I have not seen a single bathhouse yet. I long to rest in a pool of warm, steaming water and have the oil and muck scraped from my skin, but I'd bet anyone a handful of coin that won't happen in this barbarian straggle of hovels.

The streets are getting wider, the crowd fuller; it is like fighting my way through a rushing river of folk. It's not like at home, where I could slide and sneak, knowing the streets and alleys like the veins on the back of my hand. I have not seen anything that looks like a church since I set foot in this mud-ridden city of wood and crumbling stone.

At home, the Great Palace can be seen from almost any-where in the city, and its shadow falls far, but I have seen no such thing here. Is there a king of Londinium? Where does he live? Maybe the chief is not taking me for a hostage after all, and I am going to be sold as a slave, anyhow. But I haven't seen a market yet, either. Now the people seem to be getting fewer, and the gray sky shifts and spits down rain that lands in my eyes when I look up. I've not seen rain like this before; it's falling thick and solid. What's left of my rags is soaked, and my hair is sticking to my face. It's easier to walk now that the rain softens the mud, though, and the sickness of being on land instead of the sea is fading.

And then, without a word to me, the chief suddenly wheels off to one side into a straw-blasted, mud-splattered courtyard, yanking me after him toward a gate in a high wooden fence. A couple of tall, bored-looking men stand on either side; both have long, straggling beards and are leaning on their spears. Hardly seeming to move, they slowly straighten when they see us approach, fingers closing around the hilts of narrow daggers sheathed at their belts, and I know that I could very easily lose my life here in this barbarian midden-heap. I wonder what trade the chief has had before in this place where they'd kill you without even thinking on it.

Giving the rope a sharp tug that wrenches my shoulders and makes me want to shriek, the chief turns and says, "Stow your gab if you value your life, little thief-boy."

He doesn't need to warn me: I know when it's best to keep words the right side of my teeth. The chief strides up to the gate, and the rich red of his brocade cloak is bright against the mud and grayness.

The chief says something to the guards that I can't unravel. It sounds like garbled Anglish. Do the folk here speak differently from my father and mother? Maybe the chief has northern blood in him, too, or does he just make it his trade to talk in as many tongues as he can? Most likely they'll just laugh at him — a jumped-up little slave trader striding up to their gate; in Constantinople the chief would be sent on his way before he had even time to blink.

But one of the guards is nodding, slow and steady, and I wonder if he has seen the chief before and what other trade this seller of human flesh might ply. The selling of news, perhaps?

The guards draw back, and we are through into another courtyard, a smaller one this time. A pair of tethered horses pull pale scraps of hay from a muddy pile in the corner. I remember our own stable at home, before Zeus and Ares were sold, and I have to look away and stare at the chief's flapping red cloak as he strides toward a high-walled wooden building slumped at the far end of the yard. This door is manned as well, but the guard just stands back to let us through, swapping a few muttered words with the chief that don't carry any meaning to me. Who is behind these walls? Who will I be sold to?

"Sanctus here?" says the chief. Again, it sounds not quite like Anglish, but I can still see his meaning, I think. But who is Sanctus? The name sounds Roman. Doesn't it mean "the Holy One"?

The guard, who gazes straight ahead, his eyes only once flicking toward us, replies in that mangled-up Anglish, "Himself and the Devil's Cub." Can I have heard that right? The Holy One and the Devil's Cub? I must be half crazed to have started this. I ought to have let them sell me as a slave. I am the Ghost — I need not have been a captive long. Oh, for the love of God, why did I begin this game of hostages? This time tomorrow, I might have been free, but now it looks as though I bargained with my life when I showed the chief my gold ring.

"The Devil's Cub, so?" says the chief quietly, and he nods to the guard, who steps back to let us through. I wish the chief were not smiling. I do not like it at all. I follow the chief into a high wooden hall, a forest of pillars writhing with carvings — beasts and birds and trees and men, all twisted and toiling together, carved deep into the wood. The shapes remind me of the pattern on the scabbard of my father's sword, and I feel another twist of longing that sucks the breath from my body. It is so smoky in here that I can scarcely see the shadowy figures of the chief and the guard — more of a boy, if truth be told — who met us on the way in. Flaming torches mounted on the walls send leaping shadows across the floor. I feel wooden boards beneath my mud-clagged feet, and the filth drying on my bare legs makes me want to scratch. I shall never suffer myself to be bound again, not by any man. I would rather die.

We have stopped. Again, there is talk I cannot quite hear nor make sense of, and the boy who led us in walks off, looking me up and down as he goes. I am but a slave in rags. Who am I to be in his hall? I see the thoughts as clearly as if he had just spoken, and I have to swallow my shame and the thirsting need to hammer him in the face. As if I could, trussed like this.

"Come forward, brat," the chief says in Greek, and I am shoved into the firelight. A handful of men and one woman sit on benches by the blaze. A thick silence has fallen.

The woman lifts her head and gazes at me, dark-eyed. Her hair hangs in heavy braids over her shoulders; it looks like plaited black glass. "What means this, Sanctus?" she says. Her Anglish is clearer, easier to follow than the others'.

One of the men shrugs. He is old, much older than my father, maybe nearer the same age as Achaicus Dassalena. He wears a crucifix around his neck — a rough thing, hewn from wood. "I know nothing of it," he says, "but it looks as though the good Lord has brought us a child."

Now they are all staring at me — except one of the men, who gazes into the fire, fiddling impatiently with a dagger. He keeps pulling it from its sheath and trying the edge against his thumb. Dark hair spills forward, hiding most of his face, but in the firelight I can just make out the freckles spattering his cheeks.

"Well, trader?" says the woman. "What have you to do here with this child? He is not one of mine."

"I bring you a hostage, my lady." The chief seems very sure of himself.

The woman raises an eyebrow, and holds up her hand as one of the other men laughs. "Be quiet for once in your life, Helm," she says, and levels her gaze upon the chief. "A hostage? But the child is no more than a ragged little slave, God preserve his soul. Why do you not stick to your trade and not bother us with these games?"

My heart is thumping, and despite the damp chill, which the fire seems barely to cut through, I feel a trickle of sweat slide down my face.

The chief tugs the rope binding my wrists and pulls me close, gripping my aching shoulder with one hand. With the other he digs into the goatskin bag at his belt and brings forth the ring, letting it dangle in the firelight at the end of its leather thong.

At the sight of it, the air in the hall thickens still more. The gold draws them all up in their seats, straight as arrow shafts. It is as if this tiny, shining loop of metal has tugged each one of them sharply out of sleep. Even the dark-haired man lets go his dagger and allows it to sit in his lap as he stares first at the ring, then at me. His eyes rest on me a moment, and he shakes his head slightly as if he is befuddled with wine.

The one called Helm speaks in a dry, rasping voice. "Where did you steal that gold from, trader?" he demands.

"How dare you come in here and try to fox us with thieved treasure and some brat from your slave boat—?"

"Peace, brother," says Sanctus.

Helm looks away sharply. He hates the old man, I can tell. He thinks him weak, soft like a woman. For that matter, he does not think the lady should be here stirring things up, either. It is written all over his face and in the way he turns his body away from her when he speaks.

"What is the tale behind this?" Sanctus says to the chief.

The woman's eyes linger on my face. I do not like this; I feel as though she looks at me but sees another.

"The child was sold to me in Constantinople," the chief says. "But I did not learn who he claims to be till we reached your shores and this ring was found in his keeping." He shrugs lightly. "How can I tell whether to believe him or not when he says he's a Serpent child? But I thought you, my lords, would rather know that he was here. If the child lies, take my sorrow for having broken in on your talk."

My ring dangles in the firelight, swinging gently from the leather string.

"A Northumbrian royal brat in Constantinople?" says the man seated by Helm. They are very like, fair with high-colored cheeks; I wonder if they are brothers. "Come, are we to believe this?"

"Step over here, child." The dark-haired, freckled man speaks for the first time. He picks up the dagger again, running the blade against his forefinger.

The chief shoves me forward, and I stumble.

The man reaches out and steadies me, then turns my face to the firelight. His touch is light. "Let me see that ring," he says, and takes it from the chief.

The woman lets out a sharp breath. "But look at him, Wulf," she whispers. "Look at his eyes."

Wulf. What did Mama say the day Tasik left for the desert? *Oh, Essa, you and that wolf and your rings!* What if she didn't speak of a beast but a man?

"I see it." He lets me go, sliding the ring onto the middle finger of his right hand. It sits on top of another, which shines there, glittering in the leaping firelight. The leather string hangs down between his fingers. "They call me Wulfhere the Devil's Cub, atheling of Mercia," he says, "but what name do you go by, child?"

Once I was the Ghost, but no longer. My throat is tight and I can barely breathe. "Cai." It comes out in a whisper.

The Devil's Cub glances sharply at the woman, who is now resting her hand on his knee as she leans forward to look at me. I wonder if she is his wife or if she is paid good coin for her beauty and her opinions. "Well, Cai, what is your father's name"— his voice cracks a little —"and where is he now? Constantinople? How did you come to be here?"

It's him, Tasik's friend. It must be.

I stare at the ring and hear Tasik's words echoing in my mind: *It was given to me by a dear friend, and we each spared the life of the other, so it holds power.* Everyone around this fire is staring at me; I feel the heat of their gaze.

"Do you not talk when I have commanded it?" The Devil's Cub speaks softly, but there is something in his voice that sends cold fear right through me.

"My father's name was Essa," I say, much louder than I meant to. "And he's in the next world because I killed him."

14

I HAD NOT expected the Devil's Cub to laugh.

The rest of them stared at me as though I were something that had crawled up from beneath the floorboards, but this atheling of Mercia or whoever he is let out a great crack of laughter and sat there shaking with it; more than a few moments passed before he could speak again, and I thought he had given up his wits.

"My dear child," he said. "Your father could not be killed by the whole of the Mercian army, nor all of the Northumbrian court, nor even by falling headlong off a horse, as I recall, so I should like to know how a skinny wretch like you might be the end of him." He turned to the chief. "What price do you ask for this child?"

Twenty gold Francian coins the Devil's Cub paid for me, tumbled out of a leather bag.

That was the cost of my life, and now the chief is gone. I know not why, but I am sorry: he is one more person I will never see again, just like my family; Demos the charioteer; Amin; Yannis, my kind old tutor; Sia; the Emperor of Thieves; Iskendar; Niko; and even Thales the Knife.

"You are lucky, little witch boy," said the chief, looking down on me before he left with his coin. For a moment he almost smiled. "May chance stay on your side." And then he went, leaving me here in this dark, smoky hall; my last link to the empire, to the Queen of Cities, broken and gone.

Wulf turned to the woman, grinning. "What says your Christian God to this, Anwen, my love? If this is not the wyrd, the working of fate, I know not what is — Essa's child, here in my hall."

I did not miss the look Helm shot to his brother: I am sure they mean no good toward me, those two.

"Who does the child belong to, then?" Helm said sharply. "One of Godsway's brats? Surely not. We all know Northumbria's twain down the middle like a split log since Godsway came to the throne. Which of the two parts does this brat belong to, Bernicia or Deira?"

"Both. His grandmother was the niece of Edwin, who held all the north as one and was High King of this land when you were still puking in your cradle. Elfgift has had two brothers on the throne of Northumbria as well as her uncle. Her brother Godsway sits there now, High King over us all." Wulf looked at me and smiled, showing sharp white teeth. "Half Godsway's own kingdom has turned its back on him, but who knows, Helm, maybe such a child as this would be prized high enough by Bernicia and Deira alike. Who are we to judge northern tastes?"

How is it that this stranger knows more of my kin than I do? Can he truly have known Tasik? Does he mean *I'm* of royal blood? I thought the devil had forgotten me, but it seems I still have all his luck on my side.

"Who knows, indeed," Helm said, sour-faced, "but like as not, you'll find a way to work it to your profit. You already have Godsway's son as your hostage."

Wulf paid him no heed but smiled at me. "Did your father never tell you how your kinsmen rule as the greatest in Britain, high kings over all her realms?"

I shook my head. Why did they never speak of this, Ma and Tasik? I should not have even cared when I was lord over the City of the Rising Moon whether I was bound by blood to some barbarian king, but now it seems strange, how close-mouthed they were about the past. How might this news serve me?

"What do you mean to do with the child, my lord?" said Sanctus, the old man. "Elfgift still lives, does she not, with the holy men at Bedricsworth? Ought you not to turn him over to his grandmother and the monks and let him be cared for by God, or do you mean him to be used as a gaming piece against Godsway and the Northumbrians?"

He has courage, that old man, but I have never liked being spoken of as if I am not there. "I'm no man's gaming piece," I said before I had the sense to stop myself.

Anwen arched a black eyebrow, and Wulf laughed again. "His father's son, and no mistake," he said. "But better my gaming piece than yours, Sanctus. You might turn the child over to the monks, but I'd wager your brothers would sooner have him an arrow to a Saxon bow. What say you, Frith?"

The fair young man next to Helm bowed his head in a mocking salute. "My dear lord," he said. "You know we are ever loyal to Mercia and would never treat against you with anyone, Northumbrian or otherwise."

Sanctus turned to Wulf. "I am King of the East Saxons," he said, "and you know full well that my folk are loyal to yours, Wulfhere. Your father is my overlord as the High King is his. The child is yours to do with as you will. I speak only of what is best for him."

Wulf laughed once more — he seems to think everything funny. "I thank you, Sanctus," he said. "Right deep I'll sleep at night, knowing the truth of your loyalty." Then he turned back to me. "Now, tell me what really happened to your father, boy. He and I were friends long ago, and I still miss his company, for it is hard to escape flatterers and liars when you are the child of the most hated king in Britain."

And I just stood there, the words dried-up husks stuck in my throat. I could not bring myself to speak of my shame, of how I did not reach Tasik after Constans's warning, of how I dreamed of his lifeless body bleeding in the court-yard, his throat cut.

"Surely I have not paid twenty Frankish coins for a boy who will not talk?" said Wulf, but he was not laughing anymore.

"Leave him be, Wulf," said Anwen quietly. "Think on how the child came here; nothing good can have led to that."

"Very well." Wulf ran his finger along the dagger's blade again. "But I will have the tale out of him one day. If Essa's met his end, I would know how."

The lady Anwen smiled at me. "Come, since we have parted with gold for you. Let me find something for you to wear. You can't go about in rags, and you're not much smaller than Cenry."

I have lost the power of speech. I, the Ghost, who once could persuade the sun to march backward across the sky, can no longer spit out a single word. I know not why, but I feel that if I open my mouth again, I shall spill the tale of how I betrayed my father, and I cannot bring myself to do it.

At least I am clean now. Anwen had a woman heat water for me, and when it was steaming, Anwen led me out into the courtyard and told me to strip off the rags while she poured bowl after bowl over my head till my hair dripped into my eyes and my whole body was running wet like a dolphin streaming along the Bosphorus and the front of her gown was splashed. She seemed not to care about that: strange creatures, they are, these barbarian princes and princesses. Anwen gave me a scratchy woolen blanket to dry myself with, and I was glad she kept her tongue between her teeth and said nothing of the scars on my back where I was scourged on the oar benches, and nothing of my flesh-less, bony body. Instead, she spoke of her son, Cenry, who she told me was shooting arrows down at the blinds, and of her two little daughters, who she was missing dearly, for they'd been too young for the journey and were at home on the farmstead.

So this Londinium is not the home of Wulf and Anwen? I thought. *Where am I to be taken?*

Anwen led me back into the gloom of the hall, took me to a row of wooden trunks lined up against the wall, and dug around inside one, saying, "Cenry grows so fast, I'm sure these are too small for him even since we left Repedune."

She gave me a tunic of rough wool, nothing like the soft stuff we have at home — bright red, with woven strips around the collar and the cuffs.

"Here, take these as well; Cenry shan't miss them." Anwen handed me another tunic, this one of pale linen, with longer sleeves, and a pair of leggings. She even found a pair of boots worked out of sheep's hide. They bind tight around my legs up to the knee.

Sitting here in the darkness, I wonder what this Cenry is like and how pleased he will be that I wear his clothes. Anwen took my rags to burn, and watching her walk away with them, I felt my final link to home was about to be blown up to the high thatch with the rest of the smoke in this hall, for those rags were once the blue tunic of soft wool my mother wove for me out in the courtyard when Tecca was sickening, lying there in her little bed, watching the fountain, listening to the loom-weights clink together as Ma made cloth for me.

Anwen laid a blanket and a sheep's hide on the floor for me; they do not have chambers here, or even beds, which seems a cruel trick of fate after my months at sea. But at least there is no way of being locked up. They all sleep here in this one hall, from the highest to the most low. I do not know yet where I fall in the order of things. Anwen bade me rest, but I cannot sleep, lying here in this shadowy place, listening to the low murmuring of voices from by the fire, and the floorboards creaking as unknown folk move about.

I am alone.

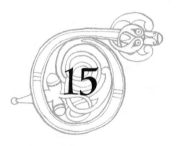

Thorn

SOMEONE is coming — maybe it's this Cenry whose clothes I wear. But it's a girl: a girl in a long, woolen robe held up at the shoulders by a pair of coppery brooches, with a linen dress underneath. Her hair hangs in twisty curls over her shoulders, and there's a slanted, wicked look to her eyes that makes me sit up.

Oho, my dear, and who are you?

"So, another hostage," she says — in proper Anglish that I can understand. "I've heard a lot of pretty tales about you, and I shouldn't wonder they're all lies. A Northumbrian child from across the sea in Constantinople? Could you not have thought of a better tale than that, my friend?"

I raise my eyes and look at the girl. Her face is alive with merriment. I'm glad she finds the tale amusing, because I do not.

"Still nothing to say?" she goes on. "I wonder what you're hiding and who you really are. Well, it's no matter. Our tasks don't go away. Come with me, whoever you may be." She pauses. "I am called Thorn."

It suits her: she is sharp and lovely, though I wonder why she was given such a sorrowful name. I do not offer her mine, though. I cannot.

I sit there long enough to let this Thorn know that I come of my own mind and not because she ordered it, and then I follow her. She is taller than me by a finger's width. She must be a summer or so older; I'm long-legged for my age. The hum of voices in the hall has grown much louder, and torches have been lit, flaming in iron stands screwed into the walls.

We walk past long tables where men and women sit, talking and laughing, and the smell of charring meat hangs in the air. How long has it been since I ate meat? Who are all these folk?

Tasik once told me that when Constans gave feasts at the Great Palace, it was only for the men, with all the women in another chamber, curtained off and hidden. It's not like that here, where they all mix together, and the women talk just as loud as the men and do not sit around looking meek and fair as they are meant to do at home. Although I do recall Ma telling me that when the Empress Fausta held court in her own quarters of the Great Palace, the women were drunker and more riotous than the men, or at least her headache the next morning was worse than Tasik's.

156

Thorn takes me to the far end of the hall, which is alive with flickering shadows cast by a great fire and bustling with women carrying pots and platters. Three long spits rammed with the carcasses of birds are licked by flames, and I watch, dumb, as a pair of girls a few years older than Thorn lift the spits from the fire and slide the fowl off onto wooden platters with strange, twisting patterns carved about their edges.

"Here, Aidith," Thorn says, dragging me to a woman with thin gray plaits wound around her head, "this is Cai. He's to help like me and Cenry do."

So she does know my name. Word spreads fast in this wooden shack.

The woman turns and looks at me steadily. She has a roundish, high-colored face, and her eyes are quick. I feel as though she can see all my secrets. "And where did you come from, child?" Aidith hands Thorn a steaming bowl of greens. "Take these, my girl — set them down at the far end first. Come back for more when you're done, and tell that foster brother of yours to hurry."

"He doesn't speak," Thorn tells her. "And Cenry's gone down to the blinds to shoot his daft arrows, so you may whistle for him."

Aidith laughs. "Imp of a wretch. Here, take this." She hands me a bowl of greens. It warms my hands, but I think I shall always feel cold while I'm on this island. "Well," she says to me, "you don't talk, then? Why?"

I shrug.

Thorn is staring. "It's no use," she says. "He's not said a word."

But Aidith just pats her on the shoulder, shoving her lightly toward the table. "Go on with your work, child, and don't be bothering me."

Thorn sighs, rolling her eyes, and marches off with her bowl.

Aidith watches her go, then turns to me. "She's trouble, that young girl. If you'll hear my counsel, be wary of her. Folk need not be sick in their bodies to be ailing sore, Cai. It's your soul that's wounded, child, and so I shall tell my lady Anwen."

Is my soul wounded? How should this Aidith know if it were? Is she some kind of witch woman, like Sia? I want to ask her, but my throat is still dry, twisted with sorrow.

She need not have warned me away from Thorn, though, for it takes one to know one, and I can spy another bad apple from more than thirty paces.

I think I will enjoy her company.

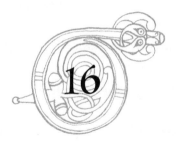

16

We have been riding for two days now. It's a long time since I was in the saddle, and my legs ache like fury. This nag I ride hates my guts. As if to mock my hunger, she dips her head and starts dragging tufts of long grass from the wayside. I jerk the reins, but she just stops dead where she is. I jerk them once more; my face grows hot with shame. I wish Tasik were here, or even Elfla. They would know what to do. We used to laugh at him and Elflight, Tecca and I, because they both said beasts spoke to them, but Tasik and Elfla had a better way with horses than anyone I know.

I would rather die than sit with the lady Anwen in that cart that bumps and jolts along the high, ridged track. She is with child, Thorn says, and that's why she does not ride, yet I'm sure that tearing along these roads is like to shake a brat from the womb in a hair's breadth. In places where the drifts of hard mud thin out, I can make out flat paving slabs, and I wonder who built these roads and why they have been left to swim in muck like this.

Cenry rides up alongside me. He's the one who led me in when I came with the chief. It's his clothes I'm wearing. Dark, floppy hair hangs in his eyes, and his face is all over freckles. He looks just like the Devil's Cub, only smaller. "By the time this moon dies, passage north'll be finished for winter," he says. "I'm glad to be going home. There's nothing to do in Londonwick. At home there's shooting, and hunting, and the river. It's good. Do you know how to catch a trout?"

I nod, shrugging. I wish he'd just leave me alone. I have not forgotten the way Cenry looked at me when the chief and I came to Wulf's hall. He talks to me now only because Thorn will not. I wonder what he has done to offend her; for the last few days she has looked through him each time their paths have crossed as though he's wrought of nothing but air.

"Why don't you ever eat or speak?" Cenry says, twitching the reins lightly as he draws closer. "You've got my mother all riled; she thinks you'll starve to death."

What would he say, this Anglish boy who thinks of nothing but catching fish and hunting, if I told him? I no longer eat because I wish my body and my spirit to drift apart. I wish to slip between the worlds, to bring back my sister, to find my own family. There must be a way. I am the Ghost;

I can run and leap without being seen. I travel across the worlds. If anyone can do it, I shall.

He grins. Like his father's, Cenry's face is ever alight with laughter. "You won't tell me anything, will you? Here, not like that, she knows you're vexed. *You* wouldn't move, would you, if someone dragged at you like that? And besides, she's hungry."

Cenry is right about that. Do the horse-kind feel the indignity of their slavery, as I did on that boat?

"Look, speak to her," Cenry says. "Talk to a horse with respect and she'll not fail you."

He sounds like Tasik: that's just what he used to say. The words rise up in my mouth like vomit — *It is my fault he is dead* — but I cannot choke them out. They are just a little handful of words, but they block the rest like old leaves in a storm gutter. I lean forward in the saddle — God's wounds, my legs burn with the strain of sitting here! — and I pat the nag on the neck, feeling the silky bristliness of her coat rough against my palm. She is gray like the sky glowering above us, gray like the inside of a mussel shell. I think of Demosthenes in his stable with Helen and Paris, and the way he spoke to Helen as though she were a woman he loved out of all reason.

Come on, darling, I think. *Enough of this grass for now. I swear you'll be fed later, so what's the worry?*

I wonder what happened to Demos. I hope that no one found him out for fixing those races and that the mob of

Constantinople didn't tear him to pieces for spoiling their fun.

Cenry rides on, grinning. I'll show him. I stroke the nag's neck again, running my fingers through her wiry mane, tweaking the reins just a little touch. And, shaking the last strand of grass from her lips, she snorts and walks on. I have done it!

Cenry laughs when I catch up to him. "Her name's Maelan," he says, "and she's my mother's. She must have taken to you, silent little slave boy, though for the life of me, I don't know why."

He seems not to mind that I don't reply.

So the nag's called Maelan, like a queen out of one of those old stories. It suits the beast: she is proud and willful as I suppose queens must be. It was kind of Anwen to give me her horse; I did not know she'd done it. It was also foolish of her, for this night or the next I am going to steal her darling horse and ride away from these Mercian folk.

I'll be bound to no man. Slave or hostage, it's all the same.

We stop in the gloaming when the light fades and the sky deepens into a haze of dark blue, as though someone has drawn a great sweeping cloth above the earth. The Devil's Cub is cheerful as ever, shouting at folk to be quick that we might get the fire lit and the ale poured. The ground is treacherous here: thin, pale grass stands high, but everywhere there are boggy pools filled with rust-colored water.

I sit by her, and gladly, too, first patting Maelan's neck one last time as she dips her head into the nose bag. Thorn is silent still, her mouth set in a hard line, but she sits down with Anwen, anyway, fiddling with the neck of a leather water sack. Cenry and one of the men take dry sticks from a saddlebag and hammer away at an iron strike-a-light till there's a blaze — though I know not how a fire's to last in the midst of all this damp. The Devil's Cub strode off with the one they call Garric, the smith, and his brother Hlafy, who Cenry says is a ranger. I knew not what a ranger is; Cenry said it means Hlafy is Wulf's spare pair of eyes and goes where Wulf cannot to make sure all's well in the kingdom of Mercia. Maybe Hlafy is a spy like Tasik was, out in the desert with the Arabs. Anyhow, they're back now with an old log and armfuls of greenish branches that look as though they'll smoke the eyes out of our skulls. The Devil's Cub is cursing merrily about his soaking feet.

I do not feel like a prisoner as I sit here, the westering sun gone now and a cow shank left over from the feast bubbling away in the lady Anwen's stew pot. The fire burns low and throws out great swaths of heat, so the skin on my face grows tight and hot even though my back's cold. Wulf's man Garric is telling the tale of some errant god who drank the ground-up bones of a goat-lord, and everyone's laughing and leaning in, waiting for him to round the next corner of the tale. A flask of honey wine goes around, and when I get it, it burns a fiery path down my throat.

Drink your fill, my fine friends, I think. *Drink your fill and sleep nice and sound.*

Cenry sits by his father, leaning against him as if he hardly sees him, as if he is but a tree trunk or a wall. The Devil's Cub rests his arm around Cenry's shoulders, and it hurts in my gut to watch them.

I have no place here. These folk are not my kin. I am but a gaming piece the Devil's Cub thinks he now owns. He is mistaken.

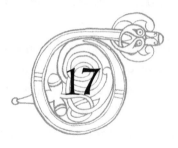

I THINK they are all sleeping now. The fire is banked
down with damp sod cut from the earth, just a dark
lump now, crosshatched with glowing cracks. It's a
clear night and there's a good moon, nearly full. I shall have
a few nights' grace before she dies and the skies are dark.
It's strange how the stars here are the same as at home. I
can see the Pleiades and, off near the horizon, the spare
scribble of Cassiopeia in her lonely corner of the night.
Webs of cloud drift quietly and peacefully, painted silver by the moon. I hear slow, steady breathing as they all
sleep. Someone mutters and I freeze, sitting up with my
blanket wrapped about my shoulders. But the words make
no sense; he is just talking in his dreams, whoever it is. My
guts clench and cramp again, and I have to close my teeth
tight together. It will be worth it, not eating, when I can talk
with Tecca once more.

If I do not do this now, I never will. I cannot let myself think on the marsh wights and the shadows, drifting across this endless bog. Moving swiftly and silently, I stand, gathering my blankets about me. Quick, quick, I step around the campfire and the humped, sleeping figures. There's Cenry, curled up with his back to the fire. And there's Garric, snoring softly. Farewell, farewell.

This is going to be the worst part, but I am not going anywhere without my ring.

I have seen that Wulf wears it still on the middle finger of his right hand, above another ring. That must be the one Tasik had first, the one he swapped with the Devil's Cub so long ago.

Wulf and my lady Anwen are lying facing the fire: two dark shapes. Softly, softly, I creep toward them — if I am caught, he will cut my throat without even thinking. He lies curled around her, his arm across her chest. I thank God that he is sleeping on his left-hand side, or I would not be able to reach. His hand rests on the blanket, just a finger's width from Anwen's face. She sleeps with her mouth slightly open, giving her a childlike look. A strand of dark hair has fallen across her cheek; it rises and falls with the soft movement of her breath. I see my ring on Wulf's middle finger, slotted above the one that used to be Tasik's. This is not really thieving, for I am only taking what is already mine.

I am not sure the Devil's Cub will share my view.

I crouch down before them and wait a moment, but neither of them moves and nor does anyone else. All is quiet. Oho, I had forgotten the thrill of this, the way it makes my whole body thrum.

I cannot believe I am about to do this. What is wrong with me? Why do I love thieving so much?

Gently, as though comforting a sick person racked with fever, I take Wulf's hand. His fingers curl gently around mine and squeeze softly. In his sleep, he must think my hand is Anwen's.

I am going straight to hell the moment I die; I know I am.

In the moonlight, the two rings glitter softly against his pale skin. I cannot breathe. I close my thumb and fore-finger around the topmost ring — mine. *Oh, dear holy Mother of God, make it come off.* The ring catches slightly around his knuckle, and I can hardly bear to look, but now it's off, and in my hand. *Thank you, thank you, thank you.* I let go of Wulf's hand and place it gently on the blanket. He sighs, and Anwen stirs — oh, Jesu! But they just shift closer together and I do not think either of them woke.

I have no time.

I clutch the ring as I creep away, then tear off one of the long ties at the neck of my tunic and knot the ring to it so I can hang it around my neck once more. It was not stealing, because Tasik gave it to me. It was not stealing.

I come to Maelan from the front so as not to frighten her, whispering into her ear to stay hushed, my pretty. I pray that none of the other horse-kind wake. But that infernal luck that used to guide me through the streets of my city beyond reach of the guard stays with me, and I get the blanket and saddle onto Maelan's back with barely a sound.

I surprise myself by feeling fairly guilty about stealing some water skins and dry sticks. Well, at least I do not take any food. They shall not starve because of me. Glancing over my shoulder at the sleepers, I lead Maelan to the road. By the time I reach it, my feet are wet and the insides of my boots squelch with water. Cursed bog. The glowing cracks in the banked-down fire have seared bright lines across the inside of my eyelids so that even with my eyes closed, I still see them.

"Wait!"

I slide my foot into the stirrup and mount in an ungainly rush. For the love of Christ, what is she doing? I see the shadowy outline of a girl running toward me. Thorn slips and rights herself with a boggy splash. I'll be caught, and all because of this sulky wench. I lean forward, squeezing Maelan's sides with my knees. I have not galloped in years and I am likely to break my neck trying it on this road with its great mountains of mud, and in the dark, but she has given me no choice.

"*Wait!*" Thorn moves faster than I expect. She's on the road now, too, and I know I should be off back toward Londonwick as if the devil himself were on my tail, but there is something in her voice that makes me stay. It is something desperate and sad, and for my sins, I stop, tugging soft on the reins. I mutter an apology to Maelan, who merely ducks her head again and starts greedily tugging up mouthfuls of grass.

Thorn takes my hand where I'm holding the bridle and grips it so hard that I am sure she is about to crush my fingers. "Cai!" At least she has the sense not to speak in a whisper, which is the most carrying talk in the world, but just in a low, quiet voice. "Cai, please don't—"

I shake her hand away. If I were talking, and not trying to escape, I'd be treating her now to such a stream of curses as she'd never heard in all her life. *Stupid, stupid*—

"Take me with you," Thorn says. There is such a sorrow in her—I can see it written in every line and curve of her face.

She is like me. We are of a kind.

Thorn gets up behind me, and I feel her arms around my waist. She whispers in my ear, "Go!"

She does not need to tell me that.

We creep down the road so slowly, it feels as if each of Maelan's steps is only a hand's span long, but I cannot risk a gallop yet lest the others be woken by the noise. I must wait till, when I look back, I can barely see the stand of hawthorn trees on the horizon. And then we shall ride, by God, till there are enough miles between the Devil's Cub and me that I can breathe easy. How far that will be? He will be pleased in his heart to see me go: fate took me to his hall and fate has now taken me away again, and he must trouble himself about it no longer. Should he wake and find me gone, once I'm out of his sight, he will but shrug his shoulders, I'm sure.

But what of Thorn? If I am chased down like a rat because of her . . . Ah, why did I wait and take her up? I'm a fool. My shoulders are all over prickles. I glance back again, nudging Thorn so she leans out of the way. I can still see the hawthorns — crabbed, black shadows clutching at the silvery night — but that is all. There is no sign of movement. No sign of another man in this marsh as far as I look.

Maelan is riding fresh, picking up her feet and putting her nose forward as though she's yearning to go quickly. The strangeness of this silvery night ride has stirred her up like a man who has drunk too much wine. The wind races faster and faster across the night; I feel it tugging the hair back from my face, and I hear it hissing through the trees, tearing over this infernal bog like a flock of devils. I look back, and the hawthorns are now so small that they look like saplings. To hell with it — I give with the reins and dig my heels against Maelan's flanks, and in my mind I hear Tasik's voice: *Let the horse think it's her choice to gallop. You must just put the thought of it into her head, and there you'll be.*

Maybe soon I will talk with him again, now that I am letting my spirit free of my body. Why have I not seen Tecca in such ages, even though I barely eat? Tecca must lead me to the rest of them. She has to.

Maelan lays her head to one side at first, ears lying flat, as if she's saying, *Ah, but why? It's nice enough walking along, quiet and peaceful.* But then I grip harder with my knees and

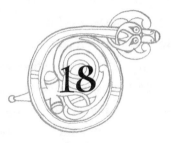

Traveling

They Lied to me; that's why I hate them so much," Thorn says.

The grayness of the sky makes my head spin — it is so many drifting shades of ash. I long for the skies at home, high and blue above my city.

"They promised I could go home for a spell, but it's been more than two years! And now something's happened with the Northumbrians, and I can't be let go." A sort of sobbing gasp creeps into her voice. "They make a great show of saying I'm one of their kin, that I'm like another daughter, but really I'm a hostage, and I can't go home because they need the Wolf Folk in their thrall against the north." She laughs harshly. "Not that the Wolf Folk care much about me. Wulfhere should have got himself a worthier captive. What good am I, with my mother and father both dead before I was even old enough to remember their faces?"

So she is an orphan. I pass the water skin back to her and hear her taking great, splashy gulps.

She swallows, then says, "If you really have just come off some slave ship, you don't know where we're going. I've a plan, though. We're but two or three days' ride from my real home, and I say we go there. Once I come back, they can't send me away again straightaway. And listen, Cai!" Thorn's voice brims with the thrill of what she's about to say. "I'll wager no one's told you this, for all they seem so kind, but my guardian at home is . . . Well, she means a lot to you, too, if you are who you say you are. Cenry and I thought you'd just heard the songs about Essa and Wulf and that you lied about the Halfling Witch being your father. But now I wonder. Wulf and Anwen are so sure, and so now I don't think you lied."

The Halfling Witch? If Tasik were here now, I would kick him. What manner of secrets did he take with him to the next world?

I turn around and stare at Thorn. Her eyes are bright, and the gold-dusty freckles are standing out against her pale skin. She reaches for the reins, grabs both my hands, and squeezes them in hers. She is so warm. Her hands feel hot, like she's been roasting them by the fire, and the shock of it makes me gasp.

"Oh! You're cold," she says. "I've a misgiving you're not well. Which is all the more reason we must hurry. But Cai, my guardian is your grandmother! Your father's mother! Don't you know the tale?"

I shake my head.

"They really told you nothing? When I . . . When I was left an orphan, your father and mother found me and took me all the way to Bedricsworth monastery and left me there with your grandmother. They rescued me. I was just a baby, so I don't recall, but it's true. And now you're here. Isn't that strange? It's the wyrd, the working of fate." Thorn falls silent. She thinks she's said too much. Why? And as it turns out, this talk of a grandmother is nothing I've not heard before. I recall the Devil's Cub saying I had one somewhere out east. I just didn't know that she was also Thorn's guardian. I did not know that Mama and Tasik had rescued a child and taken it to her. Why did they tell us so little about the past?

How can I go to this grandmother of mine, anyhow? She'll not want me when she hears how I served her son. I twist with the need to see her, though, for she's all the blood I have left. But I cannot. I know what I'll do: I will take Thorn to this place and then go away. I can't leave a girl out here in the wild marshes to shift for herself.

Thorn falls quiet, and even though my head spins with hunger and I am hardly able to keep my hands on the reins, I still can't escape the sense that she is hiding something from me, that there's some part of her tale she's chosen not to tell. Which is odd — I make no reply to anything she says, so she may as well be talking to herself. But it's clear enough that there's something Thorn's seen fit not to speak of.

I'm so weary, I don't even care.

How many hours have passed since we stole away from the camp of the Devil's Cub? I squint up to look at the sun, but since all I see is ever-shifting shades of gray, there's no use in it. We've left the road now and are aiming toward what Thorn says is the east, though how she can tell that when the sun's hiding I do not know. Maelan is slowing now, with her burden of two. She is tired, poor nag. I should not be treating her so.

What would happen if I just fell asleep? I draw the cloak tighter about my shoulders and breathe in the warmth of Thorn's body against mine. I do not feel the cold as much now. It would be so easy to close my eyes, but I cannot.

Tecca is here.

At last, she has come. I sense her. I feel the heat of her smile before she laughs, her pulsing spirit: her life. She is so close. And then I hear her laughing again, so faint that the sound's almost lost out here in the wild wide marshes.

Here she is, leaning against a crabbed-up tree, the like of which I've not seen before. Even the trees are strangers on this cold island. Tecca's hair is bright like the flames of the banked-down campfire we left behind.

Cai! Her voice comes to me as a whisper. She must be chilled to the bone, standing there in that thin blue tunic with no shoes, but she does not even shiver. Tecca always loved the feel of the earth beneath her feet and managed to lose her slippers whenever Ma took her out to the palace or to church or to one of the shrines.

Now she is closer, so close I could almost reach out and touch her, but I do not know if she has moved or if we have but ridden closer. Thorn makes no sign of having seen her. I feel the warm weight of her against my back. Her breathing has grown heavy, more regular, and I think she has fallen asleep, the silly wench.

Tecca, don't go. I want to go with you —

My sister laughs again, and her dark eyes glint with mischief. *Don't be a fool — how can you? Cai, you must not call me any longer. I can't keep coming to you.*

Something slips through my hands, burning my palms, but I don't care. Everything seems so dark. I thought it was day, but there is never any sun here, and I wonder that these barbarians can live in such a way, with this endless grayness and damp. Why does my body hurt so? I feel wet. I want to sleep. This is the trouble: I did not sleep enough, waiting through the dark hours till the time came for me to leave the campfire. I just need to sleep. We should rest: the Devil's Cub will not find us now —

Someone's calling my name — but it's not Tecca, so what do I care?

Come back, come back! I call to her. *Let me go with you!*

Life has taken a strange turn. It was always Tecca who wanted to follow me in the old days, and I who ran on ahead.

She is holding my hand; I can feel her holding my hand. Her touch is cold, but I do not care. I am not bound any longer to the earth.

A coldness rushes past me, and I'm soaring through a thick mist that dampens my face. I look down and see droplets the size of ants clustering at the ends of the hairs on my arms. Tecca is laughing as we soar along, gripping my hand tightly with her chilly little fingers. If this is what it is like to be dead, I will not mind it too much.

It's warm again now, and I catch a breath of rose water on the air, of ginger, stale wine, with that tang of rot and dung simmering beneath. I feel a hot, dusty street beneath my bare feet and the sun on my back, and we are running up along one of those alleys near the Mese, back in the City of the Rising Moon.

Tecca is not meant to be out of the house with me, but she has begged me to take her for such a long age. She is just young enough that there shouldn't be too much talk if she's seen running wild through the streets like this. If I were a girl, I would go crazy, for all they do is sit indoors or in some shady spot in a garden embroidering silks and eating sugared quinces. Elflight would never come out with me. *I ought not to*, she would say. *Only think what would happen if I were seen!* Our father has refused to betroth her even though most of the other girls her age have been betrothed for years, and Elflight thinks she will never find a husband. We are ten summers old, so why should she care? It'll be two years most likely before she's packed off. I recall my mother saying how foolish it was that the silk merchant's daughter had been wed at just eight.

Tecca's hair is damp and sticking to her forehead in sweaty little curls. *I'm tired now!* She sits down suddenly in the shade of Saint Sebastian's church, and I sink down beside her, thinking it must be time I took her home, that I don't want to be seen out with her because, after all, she is just a girl. . . .

And now I'm cold again, soaring through this endless gray mist, and I can no longer feel the heat of my sister's hand in mine. Where is she? I have lost her. She does not know these streets; she could wander for years and not find her way home. But I cannot see my way, either. I do not think I am in Constantinople at all. I am somewhere else, but I do not know where.

I want to call her name, but when I open my mouth, no sound comes out.

I am alone.

No, there is someone else here. I cannot see anyone, but I know there is someone. A man, I think. I hear mocking laughter.

A strange gift you have, cub. All is silent, but the words are clear, as if a bell tolls in my head and nowhere else. I cannot really see anything beyond this swirling grayness — hell's teeth, I am so cold! — but I have a sense of a pair of black eyes that glimmer, dark as well water, and again that laughter. The eyes are the prints of my own and of my father's.

Tasik —

Na. You will not find him here. The voice is not my *tasik*'s. I am so tired, and I cannot . . . I cannot hear so well now. The voice speaks again: *This place is not for you. It is time and time again that you went back.*

He is gone. Now there is just a great echoing emptiness. I am alone again in this cold, and there is such a wrenching pain in my belly, and I want him — I want Tasik, but even though I call and call, he does not come.

Everything is so dark. I have a sense of jolting, and I swallow a burst of sick fear: I have woken again in the dream that was the boat. I am but drifting between different dreams all the while. I have dislodged myself from the world. What I thought was real is just a cloth woven of many colors, a jumble of shadows, and behind it are other, stranger places.

We are but prisoners in a cave. I hear Yannis as though he were next to me. *All that we see is puppetry and the mere shadows of a long dream, lit by the flickering light of a fire. It is only when we break loose of our bindings and climb free of the cave that we see the world as it truly is. . . . Ah, but you boys are too young for philosophy, so back to the* Iliad *we must go.*

This place is not quite like the boat. There is no wall of stench, for one thing. It is only the way everything is moving that makes it seem as if I'm at sea. I am rocking from side to side. I'm so tired. I hear voices, but I cannot make out the words; someone is shouting, another cries. I hear the rise and fall of sobbing, cut off quick. More shouting.

Are they speaking Greek or Anglish? I want it to stop. Why will they not be quiet?

Tecca is gone. She will never come to me again. How do I know this? It's more that I feel it. Somewhere at the back of my mind, I see her walking away, hand in hand with a dark-haired man I do not know. They are getting farther and farther from me and my heart twists. Who is he? Even the brightness of her hair is fading. She is waving, her arm white against the darkness.

She is gone.

I AM WRAPPED in a blanket. It's scratching my nose, and it's got the sunny warmth of dried herbs. Lavender, and something else I don't know. It's gloomy here, but I can see the flickering light of a torch and smell burning pine-honey. I'm in a hall like the one in Londonium but much bigger, with a great soaring roof. Birds fly from rafter to rafter. Did I come here in Anwen's cart, sleeping as if dead all the while? There is someone sitting close by — I think it's a woman, for there's a warm muskiness about her. I feel a hand shifting the damp hair from my forehead. The touch is gentle. It's hard to open my eyes — everything aches — but now I can see her, a blurry, shadowy shape, a curtain of loose dark hair hanging down. It is Anwen.

So Wulf came for us, after all. The Ghost has been caught a second time.

"You're safe now." She rests a cool hand on my forehead.

Why does she say that? Did I cry out as I slept? I think she speaks the truth that I'm safe. I close my eyes and get none of the burning urge for a sprint that saved my skin so many times in Constantinople. Anyhow, I do not think I could sprint even if I were of a mind to try, which I'm not.

Her hand rests again on my forehead. "The fever's breaking."

A great wave of loss rolls over me, as if I'd just woken to find one of my legs missing. Tecca will never come back. I'll never see her again.

"She's gone." The words come out cracked and dry. "My sister."

It was Elflight who said it back then, in the early dawn light, with the rattle and creaking of the market traders' wagons rising up through the unshuttered window. We were all in Ma's room: Ma, Tecca, Elflight, Asha, and me. Toward midnight, Tecca's breathing had gotten shallower, more sparse, and in the flickery lamplight, we could see her lips turning blue.

Ma sat awake all night, I think, propped against pillows, with Tecca curled up in her lap. Elflight, Asha, and I dragged the blankets from our beds and sat up through the long darkness, piled together to stay warm because we did not have enough firewood. Although I meant not to, I think I slept a while. I don't know about Elflight, whether she slept or not, but it was she who said it in the morning light, leaning over the bed in her shift, resting her fingers lightly against Tecca's pale neck. *Mama, she's gone.*

But Ma said nothing; she just stared down at Tecca, stroking the fiery hair away from her forehead. And it was Elflight who sent me to get Father Tomas, and Elflight who sent Asha for the physician, to see if he might give something to Ma, even though we had no coin, because she could not stop weeping. Elflight cried, and so did Asha, but I did not shed one tear. I was no longer wrought of flesh and blood, but of cold iron, or stone, and so I did not weep. Nothing mattered; there was no sense in anything.

"I can't get her back." Now my face is burning wet, and my whole body shudders with it. My sister is dead, and I will never see her again. The truth of it uncurls within me like a poison I've swallowed.

"It will be all right," Anwen says, holding me. "It will be all right." She smooths back the hair from my face, and I think of Ma. I think of how I left her, to riot through the streets of Constantinople when she was sick with grief and could not even stir from her bed. Yet when I went home with Tasik the day he came back and dragged me out of the Underworld, Ma told him that the fault was hers. She was wrong, but I will never get the chance to tell her so now. I will never be able to tell her how sorry I am.

I thought the Devil's Cub would be angry. I thought he'd cast me out. Half a day's travel we must have cost them, Thorn and I, tracking us across the marsh. But he just sits down at my side, leaning against the wall, and says, "What made you do something so worm-brained, you foolish brat?"

I make no reply. Sitting wrapped in the blanket, I stare down at my hands.

"Well?" says Wulf, and I see he really means me to answer.

So I tell him the whole: of my life as the Ghost, of Tecca dying, of Tasik being away such a long time, and finally of that afternoon in the Emperor Constans's chamber, and how I ran so fast but did not deliver the message that would have saved my father's life, the lives of my whole family. "It's about honor," I finish. "I as good as held the knife that killed Tasik. I can't stay here; I've got to learn how to fight, and one day I'll go back and I'll make an end to Achaicus Dassalena, and he'll be sorry then."

All around us, folk are sitting down to eat at the long table running down one side of the hall, but the Devil's Cub stays by me, poking the guttering fire with a stick. For a while after I've fallen quiet, he toys with the embers, staring at them. Then he looks up at me, snaps the twig in half, and throws it to the flames. "You tell your tale too high," he says. "A sad and wicked thing it is indeed to kill one's own father, but for one thing, it wasn't your hand that did it, and for another, how do you know he died?"

A wild, leaping flame of hope bursts within me. "They were going to our house," I whisper. "Achaicus Dassalena's men were going there that night to kill him —"

"But who's to say they managed it?" says Wulf. "You never saw; you only dreamed of your father dead. I'm not saying dreams don't speak truth to us at times, and it's not my wish to raise false hopes, but you must rid yourself of the notion that Essa's blood is on your hands. It isn't. If he died, it was not your fault."

"Send me back!" The words tumble from my lips like milk boiling furiously out of a pan. "Put me on a trading ship and send me back to Constantinople. I'll repay you the coin one day, I swear—"

"I can hardly put you on a ship—you must see that."

"But how can you keep me here when you've told me that he might still be alive?" I reply, my voice cracking.

The Devil's Cub sighs. "You're just a boy, Cai. And if I sent you back to Constantinople, the odds are your father wouldn't be there any longer. The place had gotten far too hot for him as it was, by what you've said, and he no doubt was asking after you in all the ports. He'll not be there, not anymore. Don't think on it again."

"But if I go back, I can ask all the boatmen and find out who might've taken them and where they went, and then I can follow. You must help me! I'll never see them again if you don't."

The Devil's Cub is looking angry now. He would be an easy man to swindle: he wears his every thought and feeling like a new cloak. I hope he never gambles, because he would lose more coin than Demosthenes the charioteer. "I've given my answer," he says. "Let that be the end of it. You shall stay here."

And now I recall what Thorn said about being a hostage, how we are all just gaming pieces in a tournament of kings. "You think I'm useful because of these North-umbrians. If I want to go, I will."

"But you're wrong." The Devil's Cub smiles grimly. "I paid twenty pieces of gold for you, and you're mine to do with as I please. You'll stay here, and if you make one move to leave this place, you'll pay dearly for it — but not so high a price as I'll take if you steal from me again. Is this clear? My rangers have work enough without tracking a hare-brained brat through every bog and marsh he can find."

I shrug, staring at the fire, keeping the hot coils of my rage close and tight. I don't care what he says. I was never once caught by the city guard in Constantinople, and I'm not afraid of these rangers. If I have to take back my ring again, I will. It's mine, after all.

"It is common, Cai, son of Essa, to answer your lord when he has spoken to you."

So I look up and say, "Oh, yes, my lord, I hear you very clearly."

How dare he keep me here? After all the misery I have endured, how dare he? But I am not like my father, whose anger would fly up to the rafters like a great fiery blaze, and die just as quickly.

Wulfhere of Mercia does not know it, but I burn slow, like old, seasoned oak, with a flame that will never go out once it is lit.

PART THREE
Repedune Hall, Mercia

20

More than a year later:
A few days after harvest, AD 655

T**he greenwood** stills around me; the
world is quiet. With my heels, I urge Maelan on,
on. I reach back and draw an arrow from my
quiver, hearing nothing but the thrum of my heart.

The deer stands alone among silvery beech trees, fear-
frozen, her dappled coat a rusty blur against the greens and
grays of the forest. The rest of her kind have all fled, chased
off by the hot din of the hunt.

My dear one, I am sorry.

I let loose my arrow. In a heartbeat, I watch it fly, then
fade from my sight. One, two, three—

The young doe falls to the ground. In a rush, the forest
roars into life around me once more: birds chatter, soaring
away through the woven mesh of branches and leaves; a
tree rat scrambles up the trunk of an oak.

"Come." I urge Maelan closer, then dismount, pulling the knife from my belt, but as soon as I kneel at the doe's side, it's clear that I do not need it. Her eyes are dim, dusty with the leaf mold kicked up as she fell. My arrow juts from her neck, and dark blood oozes from the wound, stiffening the soft, pale hairs of her hide into spikes. I hear hoofbeats, but soft, and the cracking of a dry twig. Who comes? Not Hlafy, for he's ranging in the south, hunting after rumors of treachery among the marcher lords who rule the borderlands. Anyhow, he's trained Shadow so well that she moves more silently than her namesake. I gently ease my arrow from the doe's neck, taking care not to hurt her, even though she's dead. Wulf might have my every step watched, but I'm cursed if I'll let anyone see that it riles me. I wipe the blood-dark arrowhead on my clouts.

"That was neatly done."

I turn slowly.

King Penda sits astride his mare, watching me. "Aye," he says. "Neatly done, indeed. Though why do you shoot arrows like a hedge-grubbing commoner instead of throwing a spear, as an atheling ought to?"

I shrug. What do I care for being the spawn of some Northumbrian royal house when I've never gone anywhere near it? "My mother showed me, long ago. Wulf makes me shoot each morning—he says I'd as well not lose the skill."

Ma's arrows could smack the head off a nail from a hundred paces, and if I hadn't spent my youth half a world away, laying terror to the streets of Constantinople, maybe I'd be less clumsy with a spear, too, but I choose not to share this with Penda.

He smiles thinly, and I feel a chill slide down my spine. Penda may be Wulf's father, but I do not like him. "Well, boy," he says, "ride with me to rejoin your lord, and we shall tell him of your bow-snatched prize."

I mount Maelen and follow him; it is not, after all, as if I have much choice.

When we catch up to the rest, they are in full chase; the forest bursts with the pounding of horses' hoofs, the howling of dogs, the mournful cry of the horn. Penda rides hard for an old man, but Maelan's fresh today and I know we could pass him in a breath if I were fool enough to outstep my king. Instead, I hold back, and we go alongside each other, Penda and I, so close at times that I can even see the liver-colored blotches on the backs of his hands, the twisted, knobbled veins. His dried-out gray hair is whipped back from his face by the ride's rush, the heavy plaid cloak flying out behind him like the wing of some great bird. He is lost in the chase, but I could ride rings around the old snake if I chose.

I let the forest take me; the hunt's thrill burns through my every fiber. Edge and Cenry do streak ahead, killing a buck between them. Their spears fly with fierce speed, like sparrow hawks streaking out of the sky. The buck tumbles, wheeling sideways, scattering the rest of the herd around the fallen body of a hart, the greatest prize of all, and I wonder who took that. I'm among them all now. There's Thorn alongside Anwen; both are flushed with the heat of the ride, and tangled hair whips about their faces, streams of copper and black. The boys from the village howl with the joy of it: we will have meat tonight and for winter, too. Wulf leans back in the saddle, yelling and laughing.

Only he does not look so full of cheer now that the hunt's done and all are gathered about the deer corpses, making ready to heave them across the ponies' backs. He dismounts, loping over to take my bridle. "Where have you been? I told you to stay near us. If I cannot trust you, Cai, you'll spend the next hunt back in the village."

Not for the first time, I wish I had never ridden off into the marsh with Thorn. It was more than a year ago, but will I ever be allowed to forget it? It's not just that, though. Wulf has been edgy ever since Penda came here with the last full moon, and I wish to the devil he would go away again.

Before I can speak, Penda rides up. "No, Wulfhere," he says. "The boy has been with me, and a fine doe he took down, no more than sixty paces back. Very well I think it, the way he moves so quiet and quick, more so even than my finest ranger, I'd say."

So he has his uses, after all.

"I'm sorry," Wulf says, smiling at me. "I'm all of a twitter today, just like an old woman. Well done, Cai. Come, take a stirrup cup. If you've a thirst like mine, you need it." But there is still a strange shadow at the back of his eyes, plain as my hand, and I don't like it at all. I have never seen him so uneasy, like Ren when she has a thorn stuck in her paw.

I can't shake loose the feeling that something is going to happen. A year has slipped by so easily — a whirl of muddy hounds, swimming, grubbing about in the fields, horse racing, and spear throwing. But now I've got this prickling sense that it's all going to swing wild out of kilter.

"Come, Father," Wulf says, "have some ale." And they go, Wulf loping along, Penda hunched in the saddle. Penda does not even glance back at me, for which I'm glad. I do not love the way he looks at me sometimes, like a merchant in the market wondering what price he can get for a bolt of rare silk or a basket of gems. Or a high-priced slave. Suddenly, I heartily wish that Penda had not seen me track that doe. I can't escape the fear that this old snake has plans for me, and I've had my fill of other folk steering the course of my life.

"Cai! Are you too scared to race, or just too lazy?" Cenry is standing in his stirrups, calling over his shoulder, bright with the rush of the hunt.

"Ist tha tired, cousin?" Edge yells, laughing, which is not like him: mostly he holds himself high and aloof, catlike almost. And I do not blame him, because I don't much like being a hostage, either — all my body and soul bought for twenty gold coins. Edge is a child of the High King, and his price was the devil of a lot higher.

"Ah, come on!" Thorn shouts. "Let Cai dawdle if he chooses — I'm gone!" Thorn, Cenry, and Edge wheel their mounts around, stirring up a spray of leaves and mud.

I grin and lean down, whispering to Maelan, "Come on, dear heart, let's give them a gallop." I let them peel away and take the head. On foot, I can outrun any one of them, and I can ride faster, too, even through such a thatch of trees as this. I dig in my heels, and Maelan surges forward, her ash-gray mane flying in my face as I lean into the gallop.

I am still the Ghost, after all.

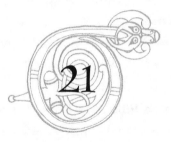

Essa and Wulf

SWEAT-DAMP, streaked with thick, dark deer blood, we chase Thorn through the village and down to the river, scattering folk out of our way like skittles, but she's already in the water up to her waist, hurling her sodden tunic onto the bank, laughing. Her skin is pearl-white, streaming wet.

"Too slow, my dears!" she calls, and lies on her back, floating.

"Off the bridge," Edge says, and we run across flat gray riverbank stones warmed by the day's heat. Shrieking like demons, we leap into the river, throwing up a great splattering spray. The water's cold, sending a shock right through me. Thorn rights herself, choking and laughing, and as we swim, the sun begins to sink, our summer-brown bodies twisting, tangling, shining wet. When I put down my feet, warm mud squelches between my toes and fronds of weed twine about my legs as I rub away the smears of blood and gore. It makes me laugh, the way these folk think themselves dirty only when they're waist-deep in mud or covered in guts and blood. There's not a bathhouse on this island.

Thorn swims a little apart from us, her hair spreading about her in the water, her pale arms glittering with beads of water. When I look at her, I feel drunk, breathless.

I turn and swim away from her.

Wulf comes down with the rest of the hunt; Cenry goads his little sisters into the water, and we duck the pair of them, too. Aranrhod shrieks, but Rhiannfel kicks Cenry so hard in the shins that he swears, and the girls splash away, sending up curls of greenish-white water. Thorn gathers them close to her, their skinny, freckle-spattered shoulders hunched as they huddle together, whispering.

"Quick," Cenry says. "They plot revenge."

"Na," Edge tells him. "Let them splash us or Thorn shall come up with aught that's worse. Tha knows what a devil's daughter she is."

So we let them do it. Bright beads of water shine in the dying light, and our yelling and shouting tears up the peace of the old, slow river. Holding the baby, Anwen sits on the bank with Edie, Wynn, and the other village women, watching over the brats too small to have their run of the water. Even Penda comes down, leaning on his stick, and sits in a chair gotten for him, and watches us all as he drinks his hot wine. The sun sinks lower still, touching the river with gold, and at last Wynn shrieks because the deer meat's been forgotten and runs to the hall with Anwen.

"Come on, Da, give us a tale," Cenry says. The meat's done with, and the village folk have gone back to their homes. Wulf sits on the bench, leaning against the wall, and I'm piled in a heap about his feet with Cenry, Edge, and Ren, his dearest of the hounds. "Give us a tale of when you were young, and rode about with the Halfling Witch — I mean, with Cai's father." Cenry grins at me. "Sorry — I forget sometimes where you came from."

I feel Wulf rest his hand lightly on the top of my head, and I stroke the soft, silky hair behind Ren's ears.

"We've had those tales more times than I can count," Wulf says. "Does no one want to hear aught that's new?"

He's asking if I mind him speaking of Tasik. Across the fire, Anwen lifts her eyes a moment from combing Thorn's tangled hair. Thorn glances at me, too; she's holding the baby in her lap, letting him cling to her finger with his fat little hand. At my side, Edge looks away from the shard of deer shin he's carving shapes into with his knife. His lap is dusted with flecks of yellow-white bone. "Dost tha mind hearing it again, cousin?" he says. "There are other tales."

What do they think I shall do, burst out weeping? "Tell it," I say. "It gets better each time."

Wulf laughs. "And you, Father?"

The old snake looks away from the fire, glaring at Wulf over the rim of his wine cup. "Ay, tell whatever you wish, although you're a fool to repeat tales of such wild disregard for your elders. What manner of tricks do you want those boys to learn?"

"Don't fear—I shan't forget to tell them how sorry you made me afterward. Now, are you ready? Aranrhod? Rhiannfel?"

"Yes, Da."

"Well enough. Cenry, pour me a drink. This time I'll give you a part of the tale you've not had before — how it started, right in the beginning. It began when the Wolf King turned to Christian ways. He gave up the care of East Anglia, going to spend his days in prayer at Bedricsworth god house, where our girl Thorn lived before she came here. The Wolf Folk fell into sadness at the loss of their king, and my father chose to help them —"

Thorn glances up sharply. "That's not how they tell it at home."

Penda laughs. "I shouldn't wonder," he says. "Be quiet, girl, and turn your ears to the tale."

Thorn glares down at her hands, but even she's not fool enough to speak when Penda has bidden her to silence.

"So," Wulf goes on, "the Wolf King had a kinsman, brave and sharp, who was not so willing to let East Anglia come under the wise rule of Mercia. That's your da, Thorn — Egric the Atheling, they called him, and a great warrior he was, famed from one end of this island to the other for his bravery. Now, Egric the Atheling had many ring-bearing men, bound to him by gold, and the youngest of them was called Essa."

"That's *your* da, Cai," Aranrhod calls.

"He knows that, dafthead! Stow your gab." Rhiannfel pokes her in the side.

"Essa," Wulf goes on, "was a sharp lad, able to move right quiet and swift—"

"Just like Cai!" Aranrhod says, in such a carrying whisper that she may as well have shouted.

"Yes, like Cai, my honey. Now stow it. So, one day Egric the Atheling gathers his men and says that one of them must sneak through the night into Mercia, right into the camp my father held at the East Anglian border, and find out when we planned to ride out and attack them. Ah, it was a crazed plot, so brimful of cheek that Egric's men could scarcely believe it. White-hearted, they were, and they begged him to think of some less risky plan, but they had not counted on Essa, who at once said that even if they were cowards, he was not and would go that very night.

"So, Essa comes to the camp, with none of us any the wiser, and honey-talks his way into my father's tent. He has his hound with him, of course. Fenrir. A fine beast, she was, and I swear to God Essa used to talk with her and understand her just as well as he did the speech of men.

"But, although Essa was a wild and canny one, my father was—and still is—wilier than the oldest fox in the greenwood. He saw at once that Essa had come to us as a spy, did you not, Da?"

Penda raises his eyes from the fire and glares at me. I feel that cold shiver slide down my spine again. It is as if he looks at me and sees another. "It was not hard to guess, for anyone with a pinch of sense," he says. "Did you never hear this foolish yarn from your father, boy?"

I shake my head. "No. We asked him and Ma lots of times how it was, living here in the north, but they never would tell us."

Penda watches me a moment longer. "Is that so? It's as well you have such a stamp of your father all over your face, or perhaps I should find it hard to believe that here before me sits the son of the Halfling Witch or whatever it is they call him. A mannerless, unruly brat is what he was."

"Anyhow," Wulf says, "my father took it in his head to get Essa out of the way. It chanced that the time had come for his youngest son to marry, and so he agreed with Eiludd, King of Powys, a kingdom far to the west of here, that I should take his daughter."

"That's you, Mama!" Aranrhod whispers again.

Anwen laughs in the midst of plaiting Thorn's hair and says, "Don't I know it."

"So, my father bids me to ride west to Powys with Essa and to cut his throat one night, when we are far from anywhere."

The air in the hall seems to thicken. The fire crackles and spits out a stream of crimson sparks, which rise up with the smoke and fade into ash. I have a sudden sense of falling away, of fading into nothing, which is what I should be if Wulf had followed Penda's word long ago. For a moment, I feel as if I'm looking down on the hall, at Wulf on his bench by the fire, with only Cenry and Edge sprawled at his feet.

I am not there.

Elf-led fool, I tell myself, and sharp, too. What's the use in that manner of idle dreaming?

"And I might have obeyed him," Wulf goes on, speaking softly, "had Essa and I not been set upon by outlaws deep in the western forest. Right hobbled we were, and knocked cold, dragged along the forest floor like a pair of dead hares, but Essa woke before I did, and I came out of a daze to see him fighting like something from the spirit world. Never had I seen aught like it — Essa and his hound, bringing down men as if they were nothing more than flinders of wood."

It hurts in my belly to hear this. No wonder Tasik hated me: they will sing of him for all time as a hero, but what did he get for a son? A liar and a thief.

"We bested them, between us," Wulf says, "but to this day I owe Essa my life. So you see, don't you, that I could not take his, even though my father had ordered it. For the first time in my life, I disobeyed my father and my king."

"And, sadly, not for the last time," Penda says. "Cursed near two months you made me wait to ride on those sheep-faced Christians."

"Essa and I did what we thought was right, which is all any man can do." Wulf speaks to the whole hall, but still I feel that really he talks to Penda, and Penda alone. "When we reached Caer Elfan, hall of the King of Powys, I was wed to the fairest maid in all Britain, who sits before us now, her brightness not a pinch dimmed—"

"Oh, move on, Wulfhere!" Anwen says. "Quick, before your son casts up his supper." She is right, too, for Cenry looks sicker than if he had eaten a week-old herring. To cheer myself up, I make kissing faces at him till he jabs me in the ribs.

Wulf laughs, then takes a long draft of cider. "Well enough. Give me the chance to speak, and I will. Essa was cunning, as I've said, and we both of us were sore afeard at Caer Elfan. We could not trust King Eiludd, nor his sons, either, and so we took it in our heads to ride out from there before they could do us any harm. We needed to take Anwen, though, so I told her the plot, not knowing if she'd go screaming to her father of the betrayal. We'd have been dead in a heartbeat if she did."

"But I did not!" Anwen says merrily. "I went with the harebrained fools."

"We took a hawk with us," Wulf goes on, "to fool the gate guard into thinking we were riding out only to hunt. But it wasn't long before we were followed."

"How did you know they were coming?" Rhiannfel asks, forgetting her place as the wise older sister.

"I'll let your mother give you that end of the tale," Wulf replies, "for I never knew, till she told me."

Anwen ties off the end of Thorn's plait and begins weaving the second one. Thorn is staring at me, a strange, frozen look on her face.

What? I mouth at her. What's the matter with her?

Nothing. She shakes her head, looking away.

"Whenever I tell this," Anwen says, "there's folk that say I've lost my wits, but that's their own outlook. We pelted off down the hill, chased by my brothers, and I've ever had the feeling Essa heard of their coming from the hawk: flying high above the hillside, it saw the riders and told him."

"The Halfling Witch," Aranrhod says, breathless. "He spoke to birds, and horses, too, and turned your brothers, Mama, into great teeth of ice with his elvish spells!"

I can't breathe right. I hurt. It's too hot by the fire, too airless, and I can't stay in here anymore, listening to talk of Tasik when all I want is for him to walk in the door this moment. But he will not, because he is dead, and the fault is mine.

I get up and stumble over Cenry to reach the door. I hear my name called, but they might shout all they like. Footsteps pound — someone is coming after me — but they shall not be fast enough. No one is. I stream across the yard and past the village houses, with their unshuttered windows all firelit and warm. Down at the riverside, I sit beneath the bridge and look at the moon rippling on the water's dark skin, listen to the river slip along, and try to steady my breathing.

How is it that I've come so far across the world to live with strangers who know more of my father than I do?

Why did Tasik never speak of this to me? Why did he never tell me he saw into the hearts of horses and birds?

I think of the poor heretic bishop torn apart in the streets when I was just a child, before Tecca was even born, and I remember Ma dragging Elflight and me home so that we would not see such an awful thing, saying furiously, *What manner of place is this, where they treat men like nothing more than lumps of meat?*

Not only have I lost my father and mother; I never really knew them at all.

Someone is down on the riverbank. I hear them breathing; I hear the clink and rattle as they walk across the pebbles, moving quietly — but not quietly enough.

"Cai! Where are you, tha feckless brat?" It's Edge; Wulf must have sent him.

I lift a stone and pitch it into the river as my answer.

He's here in a moment, kneeling beside me. Edge can be very swift and surprisingly deft given that he's so big. His pale red hair is drained of color in the moonlight. "Why didst tha let Wulf tell it, you great fool?"

I shrug. "I don't know. I didn't think it would bother me."

"Chaff-for-brains. But tha must learn not to run off whenever you're overset. You're an atheling of the House of the Serpent, and you'd do better to face what the wyrd throws your way rather than skelping off. You're not short on courage."

"Oh, I'm so sorry to smirch the honor of our kin."

I can tell that Edge knows he's scored a hit, because normally he clobbers me when I give him cheek. This time he just cheerfully damns me to hell and stares out at the river. "I feel it, too, you know," he says after a while. "I miss my home, and wonder if I'll ever see my folk again. The sun shall be high over the fells this time of year, the harvest in, and my father and his men will be hunting roe deer across the moors — and I'm here, a hostage. Tha must just bear it, Cai." He smiles. Edge hardly ever speaks of this, of why we are here — he, Thorn, and I. He can't quite keep the bitterness from his voice. "Come, let's go back, before Anwen works herself into a fit."

I lie down to sleep with just Ren stretched out beside me, leaving the others on the far side of the fireplace. Anwen has gone off with the baby to her pallet behind the long red blanket that hangs from one of the roof beams. Penda sits in his chair still, a blanket draped around his withered shoulders, staring at the fire as if we were not even here. He doesn't flinch when Thorn whispers to Aranrhod and Rhiannfel — some girlish foolery, most likely, but it makes me feel lonely when I hear Cenry saying, "Ah, stow it, I'm tired. *Ow*, Edge, there's no call to kick me."

"There is if you don't keep quiet." Edge lies on his back, so easy in his own skin, one arm flung across his face to keep the firelight out.

I wish I were next to Thorn.

I lie watching the shadows ripple, soft blackness against

gold, firelit wood. The old shields hanging on the wall seem to move up and down, as if they are fastened still to the boat that brought Wulf's ancestors here from the east long ago. I watch as, one by one, the torches sputter in their iron sconces and go out. I can just see Wulf, all shadowy, as he walks from one to the next, snuffing them. The darker it gets, the keener my ears seem to grow; I hear the crackle and hiss of the fire, old floorboards creaking beneath Wulf's feet, the others breathing, Ren's heartbeat — a slow, comforting thud — wind sifting through the dark trees outside, the river.

Wulf comes and crouches at my side, holding a tallow lamp. The hot, greasy smell of it catches in the back of my throat. He draws up the blanket, covering my shoulders. "Not tired?" he says, speaking quietly. How did he know I wasn't asleep? Nothing gets by him.

I nod. "Wulf, I'm sorry I skelped off."

"It's all right. I should have told another tale."

"It's just that I wish he were here." I couldn't say this to anyone but Wulf. I wonder if Penda is listening. He just sits there, still as a hawk.

"I know." Wulf looks at me, searching. "Cai, is there aught else that's riled you?"

I swallow. Sometimes I wish my noble lord were not so cursed knife-witted. "No," I say. "Just that."

"You've not enough to do with yourself." He smiles, shaking his head. "Let me see if I can't think of aught to take your mind off it." I feel his hand rest on my hair a moment. Then he says, "Sleep well," and I hear him walk away.

Oh, this is grand. Now he will have me chopping wood for the next month, or laying fish traps, or some other such brain-numbing task. How I wish I could fly and leap among the rooftops of Constantinople, running from the guard. How that used to set my blood afire. I never had time to think on my sorrows then.

I should not have lied, but how can I tell him? How can I tell Wulf that I wish Penda had not seen me track that deer and that I did not like the way he said, *Did you never hear this foolish yarn from your father, boy?*

Why do I feel so sure that some part of the tale has been kept from me?

I remember sitting in the courtyard with Ma, Asha, and my sisters, watching them thread necklaces of bright glass beads as I carved faces into a curl of vine-wood with my knife.

"Mama," Tecca said suddenly, "don't you miss your mama? Why did you and Tasik leave behind all your kin in the north?"

Elflight and I swapped a glance. We'd long given up asking such things.

But this time Ma just smiled, looking down at the pile of glossy beads in her lap. "It's all such a while ago, dear heart, and there are some things it does one no good to brood on. Look—here's a nice green one for you. Have it, and I shall keep the blues."

All told, what do I really know about my mother and father? That Tasik is called a witch, and his father a liar.

What were you covering up? I think.

It is as if part of myself is hidden, veiled behind a smoky mess of unspoken stories.

If the truth be told, I don't really know who I am.

Two days later

OHO, I HAVE changed my mind about Penda now.

I can't believe it. I don't dare to believe it. This'll be the best sport I've had since Thales the Knife sold me out to the chief, and Anwen's going to stop it if she can.

"I cannot like this." She shakes her head. "Wulf, it's the same all over again, don't you see? And Cai is too young to go riding off into Elmet, spying on some rebel chief. They are *both* too young."

Wulf says nothing. He slouches in his chair, shoulders hunched, wolflike, long legs stretched out before him. He gazes into the fire, toying with the dagger at his belt, which I know means he is thinking deeply. I don't dare to want it. I don't dare to think about it. Wulf doesn't fully trust me; he'll never let me go. I sense the heat of Cenry's joy from here, and his dread that Anwen will put an end to this before it has even begun. He stands oddly still, as if turned to stone.

"My dear girl," Penda says, taking a long draft of wine, "you are too careful. For every woman, there comes a day when she must watch her son ride out into the wide world. Take comfort in your daughters and the young bairn, and speak not of what you know not." He nods at Aranrhod and Rhiannfel, who up till this moment have been playing cat's cradle at their mother's feet. Both now freeze, the web of yarn hanging limp between their outstretched hands. No one ever spoke so to Anwen in my hearing, nor in theirs, either, I'd wager. Aranrhod flushes bright red and covers her mouth with her hands. She's trying not to laugh. White-faced, Rhiannfel reaches out and pinches her, hard by the look of it, holding a skinny finger to her lips.

Anwen only lowers her head in a slight bow. She is smiling but her eyes glitter with a sharp look, and I like it not. I pray to God she has the sense to keep her tongue behind her teeth. "Of course, my lord, I know nothing. I beg you, excuse me. I hear the baby crying. Come, girls, such manly, noble talk is not for our ears." She rises from her seat and walks away, graceful as a swan.

Aranrhod and Rhiannfel huddle after her, whispering. Aranrhod steals a look back over her shoulder, but Rhiannfel grabs her arm, hauling her along so fast that they nearly tumble over each other.

Beside me, I hear Cenry let out a long, low breath.

"I see the need for someone to go," Wulf says at last, looking up from the fire. "I trust the Elmet-set no more than you do, Father. We must make sure that they remain loyal to us: the last we need is Orhan pledging himself to Northumbria now. But this is the work of a ranger, and my man Hlaf shall return from the south before the moon is full."

He is not going to allow it; he is going to defy Penda and not let us go. I will stay here in this wretched village till I rot. I can't look at Cenry.

Wulf smiles suddenly. "So let them go to Elmet, if they are willing to take the task. They grow restless of late, and I shall only have all manner of riot and strife on my hands if they're kept here. They must learn a man's work sooner or later."

Yes, oh yes! I don't dare to speak lest Wulf change his mind. I know that I am the restless one, though. He is not speaking of Cenry.

"You won't be sorry, Da," Cenry says, grinning as much as I am. "Will he, Cai?"

"I had better not be." Wulf gives me a long look and pulls the dagger from its sheath, watching the firelight gleam off the blade. "The Elmet-set move faster than thought; they're not easy to track. Strangers in their land are meant to sound a horn as they ride. You'll not be doing that, so they'll suspect you from the start if you're seen from afar. And once you find them, you'll not be able to let down your guard for even a breath, and do not forget it. They'll tell you one thing and do another, so you must judge for yourselves if Orhan's loyalty is true or not."

"Why so edgy, Wulfhere?" Penda says mildly. "Do you fear this little chief shall take a brace of hostages for himself? He's not such a fool; it would do him no good."

"It would if he sold them to Northumbria," Wulf replies, just as calm, as if he is talking of nothing more than a clutch of eggs or a few barrels of ale. "And I am not such a careless father nor heedless guardian that it doesn't cross my mind."

"We can do it, Da," Cenry says, and I can tell it costs him dear to sound so cool. "We'll take care. You must send someone to make sure of Orhan, and both Cai and I speak British, which you don't. It'll seem a sign of respect that you send me; it'll make Orhan think that you trust him."

"Of course you can do it," Penda says. "Orhan shall swear you as many false oaths as he pleases, Cenred, and Cai will learn how the land truly lies." His gaze falls on me. "I'd wager my right hand that you could wheedle the truth from Orhan or one of his men without putting yourself to the sweat."

I feel cold, and slightly afraid, if the truth be told. How does Penda know I have that knack? How does he know I can befuddle men and draw words from their lips they don't mean to spill? I haven't used this trick since I was on the slave ship and talked the chief into selling me as a hostage.

It has never seemed right to do it here.

"Cai?" Wulf says, a touch sharply. "What's amiss?"

Cenry is staring at me, narrow-eyed. Penda does nothing but smile.

I shake myself. "Nothing. It's only that, well"— I grin at Wulf—"a few days back, you near had a fit when I lied about weeding the kale. Remember?"

Wulf laughs. "There's a world of difference between lying *to* your lord and lying *for* him, so don't fret on that score. Lie to Orhan's men all you wish. I order it."

"Well then, Cai, son of Essa," Penda asks. "Do you take this task?"

"Of course, my lord." He knows I have no choice. "And what should we do if we find Orhan to be a traitor?"

Wulf only glances at his father a moment before replying, "Kill him. What else would you do?"

Jesu. Every now and then, Wulf reminds me why he is called the Devil's Cub.

23

From Mercia, north into the rebel marches

IT'S A PEARL-GRAY dawn, brightening in the east. Mist hangs in the air, dampening our faces; small silvery beads of water glisten in everyone's hair. It's chilly now—Anwen wears a heavy blanket around her shoulders—but we shall get warm later, for we're still in the time of the long days, though they're getting shorter. I don't know that I'll ever be used to the stretched-out, drowsy light of midsummer on this island, and the darkness of winter.

In the courtyard, Anwen frees me at last from a hug, planting another kiss on my forehead. "Be safe, my *cariad*," she says, trying to smile even though she is crying fit to flood us. Why are all women and girls such water-pots? Anwen turns to Cenry, weeping all the more. I am only glad they did not wake Aranrhod and Rhiannfel, or we should probably have drowned. Elflight and Asha were the same.

But I cannot think about them.

Thorn would not have cried, though.

Wulf gives me one of his quick, bright smiles, squeezing me so tight that I'm crushed against his chest. "You'll do well enough," he says. "I said the same to Cenry, but if you get the flicker of a hunch that something's not right, then be off, even if you must leave Orhan alive. Your da and I would have had our throats cut scores of times if we'd not listened to that feeling in our bellies. You know what I mean, don't you?"

"I wasn't the greatest thief in Constantinople for nothing." I grin at him. "I've only been caught the once, you know."

"Twice, wretch. I'll not soon forget tracking you and that hussy across the marsh. I beg you will not do anything so tiresome this time." Wulf's smile fades, and he looks grave again, drawing me a few steps away from the others. "Do take heed, Cai: I wouldn't be sending you to spy on Orhan if I thought it beyond your skill. But I do not want Cenry to come back from Elmet alone. Do you understand what I'm saying? I hope you're not cooking up some stew-brained plot to go off seeking your father once you're out of my sight."

Why must he be so wretchedly knowing? Suddenly, it's hard to speak. "I wish I were so sure that he's still alive."

I can't begin that back-and-forth talk with myself again. If Tasik were dead, would I not know? And what of Elflight, who grew beside me in our mother's womb? Surely I would know if my twin were dead. Sia was right: my longing to see Tecca took me too close to the other place. But never a shadow did I see of Tas, Ma, or the girls. Never once did they come to me when I was on the slave ship. It was only Tecca. And I can't forget that voice saying, *Na. You will not find him here.*

Which means they live, does it not?

But then there was my dream. If I close my eyes, I see it again: Tasik lying dead in the courtyard, his throat cut. I can never be sure. I will never know. I wish Sia were here. I wish someone could tell me.

Wulf smiles. "Your father's gotten out of tighter spots. I know him: if he lives, he'll seek you till his last hour on earth. And if he ever comes here and finds you gone, he'll knock me senseless. You don't wish that on me, do you?"

I draw in a deep breath. "No. But, Wulf — can I have my ring back, at least?"

The sunny cheer drains from his face. "We've spoken of this before. You'll have that ring when I judge that the time is right for you to keep it."

Anger twists deep in my belly. "It's not fair."

Wulf gives me a dangerous smile. "Na, perhaps not. But you sold yourself to me, remember? I paid good coin for you, too. Twenty gold ones, so don't make me sorry. Cai, give me your word you won't go off on some foolish search for your father."

God take his eyes. "All right," I say. "I swear I won't go looking for him."

Not this time, anyhow.

We pick our way through the village, past Garric's smithy, past the weaving hall and the god house, the cluster of lop-sided wooden houses topped with thatch, golden in the dawn light.

Voices drift on the still, early-morning air. Strange, since I hear no clattering of cook-pots or yawned greetings. Even the hounds are sleeping yet. And though Wulf and Anwen may have woken to see us off, I'd have thought the village folk would be enjoying their last moments of rest.

Cenry glances at me, grinning. "Seems we've a farewell party."

But he's wrong. I can see them now: it's just Wynn, Garric's woman, and one of her brood of daughters. What's her name? Mildreth, that's it. She's bidding fair to be as fat as her mother one day, too. What are they doing huddled in the doorway of the weaving shed like that? The sound of sobbing drifts toward us. Jesu, how many weeping females must I see in one morning? Wynn stands with one hand on her hip, jabbing her finger at Mildreth, who cringes like a whipped pup. She's such a milksop, that wench.

I can hear what Wynn's saying now. "You foolish, foolish girl! Well, you've made your bed, and you must lie in it." If they weren't so wrapped up in each other, they'd have spotted us.

What are they talking of?

"Come," Cenry whispers awkwardly. "This isn't for our ears. I've no urge to hear Mildy have strips torn off her for breaking another bowl, the clumsy wench." He glances behind us to the bright line of yellow light where the sky meets the earth. "This way—northwest. We've a long ride ahead."

But I do not think that Mildreth has broken a bowl or spoiled the milk or dropped a cheese. Wynn loves nothing more than making a great fuss over naught, but not at this hour of the day, when all are still abed and she's no one to watch her. Cenry is right, though: it's not for us to know what they're squabbling about.

Anyhow, we should be elsewhere by now.

Be swift, dear one. I dig my heels into Maelan's flanks and stir her up to a gallop, following Cenry as he thunders across the bridge, over the river to the reaches of the wood shore.

"That's Cassiopeia." I point up at the night. "And that's Deneb, the bright one."

Cenry laughs, rolling over to poke at the fire with a stick. "Whatever you say. Da always told me they're jewels, dropped all across the night by Lady Frigya. Jesu, I ache. I've not ridden so far in months."

"He still believes in those old gods, doesn't he?" I ask, pulling my cloak tighter around my shoulders. "And your grandfather, too."

Cenry shrugs. "If Granfer had any sense, he'd let the god man baptize him. We're the strongest kingdom in Britain, truth be told, and if Granfer were Christian, or at least seemed it, Kent, Wessex—all the rest—they'd take him for their high king, well enough. But they're too afeard for their mortal souls."

"And meanwhile, Penda and your da harry Northumbria as much as they please and no one has the courage to stop them."

Cenry pokes the fire again, roiling up a shower of amber-bright sparks. "It can't go on much longer. We'll fight it out with the north before the year's done, if they can stop brawling among each other long enough."

What will happen to Edge if Wulf fights his father? What will happen to me?

"Do you think the Elmet-set have truly gone over to the high king, then?" I ask quickly.

"They're fools if they have." Cenry falls quiet. What's gotten to him? It's not his way. Is he asleep? "Cai," he says at last, leaning on his elbow and looking right at me, "what did Granfer mean when he said you'd have no bother drawing the truth out of Orhan? Do you *know* something about him?"

Cenry's too cursed sharp-eared at times. Just like Wulf.

I roll onto my back, drawing up my blanket. It smells of the lavender Anwen scatters to keep out moths, and I'm reminded with piercing strength of Ma. She used to rinse her hair in lavender water, and always the smell of it hung about her, warm and peaceful.

What if I just tell Cenry the truth? He'll never believe me, anyhow.

"No," I say slowly, "I don't know anything about Orhan. I've nothing to bribe him with."

Cenry spits into the fire. "I knew you couldn't. You came straight off the slave boat to Londonwick, and you said yourself that your parents told you nothing about living here. So —"

"Do you want me to tell you or not?" I sit up, wrapping the blanket around me.

Cenry sits up, too, grinning. "You know I do. There's something going on. Come, you can't fool me."

"All right. I don't know how Penda got wind of it, but you know how I can run so quick, and hide, and no one can ever find me if I don't wish it?"

"They don't call you the witch boy in the village for nothing. And most handy it was, when you stole Garric's home brew from under his nose in the spring." Cenry lets out a crack of laughter. "They never did find us out, did they? But what's it to do with Orhan, some rebel chief you've never laid eyes on?"

I draw in a long breath, and let it out. "All right. I can make you tell me anything I want. You can't keep a secret from me. I could make you walk over to that stream and lie down in it if I chose. I could make you do anything."

Cenry stares at me, his freckled face still. I thought he'd laugh. I wish I hadn't told him. It's like when I cheated at Fox and Geese — I reckon there's no use in playing games unless it's to win, and the devil may care how. But Cenry and Edge looked at me as though I'd thrown a baby in the river when they found that I was sitting on half my goose pieces.

"Well enough." Cenry lets each word drop from his lips as if it's made of glass. "Show me."

Iskendar or Niko would have laughed, but this island is not the same as Constantinople: here, the woods and streams are haunted still by old gods, and the elf-kind wait behind every shadow, fair and immortal, ready to tweak the affairs of men just as Cenry's sisters play with wooden dolls.

I swallow. My throat's drier than sand. I get to my feet, blanket wrapped around my shoulders still, and I walk around the fire till I'm near enough to crouch right by him. *All right, my friend, no one could say you didn't ask for it.* I gaze right at him; his eyes glitter in the firelight.

Cenry looks puzzled now, afraid almost. "Cai?"

I smile. "You don't truly think I can make you do anything, do you? No, don't look away. I do but talk of Thorn. We all know what's to become of her, don't we? Do you feel aught for her at all, Cenry? Or will you just be hand-fasted to her because you've been told to?"

He stares at me, his mouth slightly open. "Both. I'd choose no other girl, and I know my duty."

My heart's yammering. I'm burning. "Well." I sound breathless. "That's lucky, is it not?"

Cenry shakes his head slightly, then looks at me, stricken, and scrambles to his feet. "You sneaking *cheat.* How could you do that? You — you made me speak my private thoughts. You *stole* them from me."

I jump up, afire with a mess of shame and rage. "You asked me to do it!" I yell. Before I even know what I'm about, I'm running headlong away from the firelight, into the shadows of the greenwood night.

It scares me. I'm afraid of myself. Oh, God, I would give anything for Tasik to be here.

I'm fast but tired, and it's as if the trick has drained my strength somehow. I hear Cenry crashing after me, cursing and shouting my name. I only want to get away from him, away from his disgust.

"You little fool, I'll wring your neck one of these days." He grabs my arm, sounding just like Wulf. "Stop!"

"Don't talk to me like that — I'm not that much younger than you!" My face is wet with tears. That's all I need — to start crying like a girl. I can't help it, though. I can't stop.

"Cai, be calm, will you? I'm sorry." Cenry talks softly, as if to an uneasy horse, which makes me think of Tasik again, because that is how he used to speak to me when I was riled up. Tears burn down my face, and I wipe them away with the back of my hand, trying to catch my breath. Cenry shakes my arm gently. "I'm sorry, all right? I didn't mean to shout at you. But I wasn't thinking you'd do that; it was — it was *strange*." He laughs uneasily. "And you might have asked about something other than Thorn, like what I most like to eat or who in the village I can't stand. Christ, Cai."

I draw a long breath, steadying myself. "I'm sorry. I

shouldn't have. But I know you like roasted ducks most, and you hate the cursed god man just as much as I do."

But part of me is glad I asked about Thorn, and I don't even know why. It is like pressing a bruise, a strangely gratifying ache.

It is because, inside, she and I are wrought of the same stuff. And she is going to marry my dearest friend, and I can't stand it.

Without thinking on it, I know the truth of this. It'll hurt me, too, one of these days, if I'm not careful, just as Achilles was brought down by the heel of his foot.

Cenry stares at me a moment, shaking his head. "Come on, you crazed witch boy, we've a long ride on the morrow." He slings his arm around my shoulder, and we walk back toward the fire. I'm glad, for I'm shuddering with the cold. We lie down in the warmth, and after a while Cenry says sleepily, "Well, if you can do that to Orhan's men, we'll have no trouble."

"We've to find them first," I reply, but what I'm really thinking is how in God's name did Penda know I could twist the thoughts and words of men, when I have done my best to forget it?

Elmet, three days later

I T'S A WILD land: rolling, rock-strewn, green, and tangled with great swaths of stinging nettles and a wiry brownish plant Cenry calls heather. Streams crisscross the hills in lines of white and tumble into pebbled pools of dark water. As we ride, we follow the path of the sun across the sky—like a yellow bruise it is now, smeared over with cloud—and mark our way by looking at the shape of the trees.

"They're bent by the wind, see?" Cenry says. "And the wind's most often in the east. If the trunk grows moss, there'll be more of it on the sheltered side, and if the day's still, it smells different, too, on the windward side of a tree."

We must trail the Elmet-set as we would a roe deer in the forest, Wulf told us, and so everywhere, I look for signs that folk have passed this way, just as if I were tracking a deer or a boar, even though we ride over wild moorland. It seems hopeless that we'll hunt down so much as our supper out here, let alone a rebel tribe.

"Why don't the Elmet-set settle in one place?" I ask. "What kind of kingdom shifts about all the while, like a flock of wretched geese?" The sun grows hot today, even though the leaves are turning gold, and I feel sweat sliding down my back. Maelan is tired, too. We ought to stop soon and rest the horses.

Cenry leans back in the saddle, sighing. "They're not a kingdom: my grandfather killed their last true king before Da was even born. Elmet's part of Mercia, paying tribute to Granfer. But for the most part, they've British blood, the Elmet-set, not Anglish or Saxon, and they've been Christian since before the folk from Rome left. Elmet's full of rebel chiefs like Orhan who won't pay their tribute to Granfer because he's a heathen and send it to the High King instead. We've been playing cat-and-mouse with them for forty years, Da told me."

How must that be, to live in a kingdom chased about the countryside like a hare hunted at sundown? It can't be too different from ruling the Underworld of Constantinople. What would I do if I were Orhan of Elmet?

I would not ride about the moors, to start with. I rein in Maelan, patting her neck. We're on high ground, a ledge that sweeps down, tumbling toward a line of darker green at the edge of my sight. Woodland.

I swing myself out of the saddle and take a long draft from the water skin hanging over my shoulder. I'm glad to wet my throat, but it's got a dusty, leathery taste.

"Over here, girl." I lead Maelan to a stream singing through the heather, then turn to Cenry. "We should rest the mares. There's no use dithering around this moor for days on end; they're not here."

He raises an eyebrow, following my gaze to the dark line of forest where the land rises up to meet the sky. "I know what you mean." He springs neatly to the ground, and Fleet follows him to the stream, dipping her head beside Maelan. As they drink, we stand gazing out at the moor dropping away beneath us, and the far-off smear of woodland. Cenry turns to me. "They'll see us coming, you know."

I smile at him. "Of course they will, and so they should." We want Orhan's men to think that we don't have a grain of sense; to them, we must seem no more than a pair of green young fools, puffed up with our own worth.

Cenry's dark eyes light up with the kick of it. "You're just as crazed as everyone says. What if they choose to kill us straight off?"

"They won't do that. It'll do them no good to kill outsiders without asking questions first. Anyhow, they've been on the run forty years. Do you really think we could get near an Elmet-set camp without them knowing? They've more than likely spotted us already."

The Elmet-set have seen us now. I know it.

The wood shore has risen up to meet us; trees nibble at the fringe of the moor. I'm glad of the shade, for the sun's high and it's hot. Far above us a lone bird circles, drifting, calling mournfully.

"A curlew," Cenry says, handing me his water skin. I drink. "How many men watch us, do you think?"

He hears sharp, does Cenry, but not so keen as me. I close my eyes. It's easier when I can't see. There's the curlew again, keening her sorrow. I hear the rubbing chatter of the little many-legged creatures in the grass, the hissing soar of the wind that scatters white puffs of cloud about the sky like sea foam, and the water song rising from the stream at our backs.

I hear my heartbeat, and Cenry's. I hear Maelan's — deeper, slower — and Fleet's. There's a jumble of others. It's like when the village folk drum at the time of apple harvest, calling to their old gods, and Leofric the priest can only sulk in his church.

"Three." I spur Maelan on. "Three men. None on horseback. Two behind us, in that jumble of rocks, I think, and one somewhere near that mere. All archers, too, I'd wager."

Cenry grins, glancing over at the brownish smear of water to our right. It's flanked by gorse. "Do you know," he says, "I think I feel a yen for a swim, so hot it is."

I laugh. "Come, they're not fools. They'll know we're playing with them if we do that. Let's go and have done with it." The last time I was tricked, I finished a slave. I'd be lying if I said I was glad at walking into another trap.

They follow us all the way to the wood shore, and I've rarely seen such skill. Nearly as sneaksome as I am. How easy will it be to fox them? We pause just as the trees thicken. The wood's too quiet; all the sound has drained away, just as it does when I hunt deer. They are all around us. I can hear the soft rush of their breath, the beating of their hearts, though not a leaf stirs. Oho, they are good, these Elmet-set rebels. Very good. Cenry hears it, too; he grips Fleet's reins a mite tighter, and the lines of his face grow harsher, the color draining away, leaving him a shade paler, his dark freckles standing out clear. I love this: I love the thrill of playing out a trick, of reining in my fear.

Every shred of flesh and bone in my body screams at me to turn Maelan and ride out of this cursed wood as if the devil himself were at our backs.

But I don't.

Cenry glances my way, his face bright with a great, wicked smile. He leans back in the saddle as though he hasn't a care, and starts to sing that north-country song of Edge's: "Oh, I forbid you, maidens all, that wear gold in your hair, to come or go by the western wood, for young Tam Lin is there—"

With a sudden rush I feel a jab of pain in my arm, and I know Cenry has it, too, for I hear him hiss, "Jesu, we're elf-shot, Cai. This is no work of man."

Head swimming, I look down and see a thumbnail-size iron arrowhead bedded deep in my flesh just below the elbow, dark blood seeping all around it. And I think how crazed these Anglish are, with their ungodly beliefs in the elvish kind, but my thoughts spin around in my head, and

I keep no hold on them, and everything is going black, just as it did when Thales the Knife caught me.

I have really done it now.

Ah, Christ, but my head aches. It feels as though my skull is being slowly crushed, but when I cry out and put up my hands, there's nothing there to fend off. I'm lying on my back in a dark place. It smells of wood, and wood smoke, like every Anglish hall I've been in, but there's a clean, clear edge to the air. A silvery line of light streams from a gap in the wall, most of it covered by what looks like an old blanket, nailed across it. I turn my head to the right, biting down so I don't cry out in pain, and see Cenry lying beside me, flat out as though he's been smacked in the face with the anvil in Garric's smithy. He's breathing, though. I haven't killed the heir of Mercia, thank God. I wish Wulf had sent me away with Edge instead — less of a fuss — but that wouldn't help, now that I think on it, since Edge is the heir to all Britain. I laugh, even though the ache in my head's making my guts churn. Another crazed-up mess you're in, Ghost.

I lift my right arm, wanting to look at the wound, but my left comes with it. My hands are tied at the wrist. Oh, I love this. Even so, I can see my elbow still. The arrowhead's gone, whatever it was, and there's a strip of linen bound around my arm, stained dark with blood. Say what you will, Cenry, but I'd wager that the elf-kind do not bind up the wounds of their mortal victims.

My throat is dry with thirst, and I'm burning with the need to piss. I haul myself up onto my knees, turning toward the rush of cool air. There's a door in the wall behind me, just another gap really, tacked over with a heavy woolen blanket, like the window. With a sigh, I lean next to it, elbowing the blanket out of my way.

Mary, Mother of God. The Elmet-set do not build their halls like anyone else, that's sure enough. I'm fairly sure no other folk have them up in trees, to start with. The forest floor falls away beneath me, a blur of leaf mold and bracken far below. Leaning out a touch, I see the trunk of a great oak, wrinkled and ridged with age. Ripple-edged leaves fan out all around me, shaken by the wind, as though I stand in a shower of green rain. I can just make out another shack like this one, cloaked in the branches of an old elm.

I do not know why, but it makes me smile. It's just what I would have done, were I the king of a rebel tribe. It's the way of the Ghost.

It's cursed hard to piss with both hands tied together, but I do it, anyhow.

I lie back down on the thin blanket, my head throbbing as the song of the forest whispers all around. It sings me back to sleep.

Twelve pairs of eyes fix us hard. I kneel, keeping my own eyes on the floor. There is a hole the size of a coin in the boards, and I can see the blur of the forest floor far below.

Too high up to easily escape. They take no chances, these Elmet-set.

"So." The girl's voice is hard, light, and dry, like wood washed up on the beach, scorched by salt and sun. "What do you come here for?" She speaks Anglish but with a strange, rushing edge that reminds me of water falling over rocks. It's odd, but the men all keep their tongues, letting the girl do the talking. They are a lean, sun-browned folk, dark-haired, rust-tinged, and every last one of them black-eyed like Cenry and me. All the Elmet-set have strange, swirling patterns graven on their faces, a blue-gray color, like the sea on a hot day. Wynn's old mother has these marks, too, and Cam's uncle, but I've never seen so many marked folk in one place. It gives them an otherworldly look. It was hard not to stare, at first.

"We come here to see Orhan, your chief." Cenry speaks western British, like his mother, and it's like hearing someone talk underwater, so thick and strange it sounds.

From beneath my lashes, I watch the girl's face change. The slight, mocking smile slips from her lips, but her brow lifts very slightly in surprise. She's only about the same age as Edge. Her thin brown fingers lie still in her lap. "Much chance you have of that," she replies in British.

Just hearing the rushing, songlike words reminds me sharply of Tasik. Cenry opens his mouth to speak again — *fool*. Sometimes it is best to let others do the talking.

But the girl slips in before him: "Orhan is beyond your reach now, whoever you may be. My father is in the ground a moon and more, and his soul with Christ, God keep him."

I look up, and quick. It's as well. They would grow uneasy if we let such news wash over us. She is telling the truth. There is no shadow of a lie about the girl, and I should know. Cenry bows his head low, and I follow him. I wonder what took Orhan to the grave: fever or wound? It is strange that a king may be laid low just as surely as the merest thief.

"My lady," Cenry says, "take our sorrow, and the sorrow of my father and his also."

The girl lifts her shoulders a touch, a faint smile playing around her mouth.

The faces of the eleven men sitting around us do not change; they are hard, like old gray rock. But the air's alive now, thrumming: Cenry's got them on a hook.

"I thank you," she replies, her words laced with mockery. "But tell me, who might your father be, and your grandfather, and why should I care for their sorrow?"

Cenry looks up, treating her to one of the finest smiles in all his great armory — eyes warm, a great spoonful of grievous pity. *Not bad, my friend, not bad at all. Even I could not do better than that.* "My grandfather," he says, "is Penda, King of Mercia, and I come here with my foster brother to drink the age-old pledge of honor between Mercia and the Elmet-set. Only now, of course, I see that it is with you, my lady, that we must raise a cup, given that noble Orhan is dead. May I have the honor of your name? Mine is Cenred, House of Mercia."

"Of all the brazen insolence. You cannot let this pass, Llineth." It's one of the younger men who speaks, more of a boy, really — senseless. A deep, wine-red flush floods his face all the way down to his neck, but he fixes his gaze somewhere on the wall facing him, just as the others do.

No one moves, but the air thickens like porridge left too long over the fire.

For all the girl's cool edge, she's riled now, I can see it: her pupils widen and she taps one finger against her leg very slowly. "Where are your manners, Yfelys?" She smiles faintly, turning back to Cenry. "Now that you have been given a gift of my name, we shall drink to the memory of my father, and I will think on this age-old pledge you speak of."

I'll leave that to Cenry. I know my errand here, and now who to chase it with: Yfelys, the foolish kinsman of Llineth, queen of the Elmet-set.

Though we go everywhere blindfolded, I counted the steps from the bottom of that cursed rope ladder that bucks and swings as you climb down, and I know we walked southerly a score of paces through thick, clinging undergrowth before we came here. I heard the heartbeats of gathered horses, too, and smelled their sweet, warm breath drifting on the night air from the east. They must keep their horses corralled somewhere near here — Fleet and Maelan, too, I'm sure.

The noise of folk talking and laughing grew louder till it rang in my ears, and when I could smell their closeness, the sweat of close-packed bodies and cooked meat and honey wine, I reached out swiftly with one hand and felt my fingers trail over a flap of tanned leather as we passed from the night's chill into warmth and light. So they live in tents, as well as high up in the trees, these folk. When they took off our blindfolds, I saw that word must have gotten around, for no one stared as Llineth and her men bore us off to sit on a spread of skins and bolsters piled about the embers of a fire.

Now I sit listening, blank-faced, as Cenry talks sweetly to Llineth and her men about Orhan's great loyalty to Mercia and King Godsway's hardheaded foolery.

"Orhan," Cenry says, smiling, "had the sense to know that while Godsway is High King in name, my grandfather — and Mercia — truly holds the reins of power on this island. Who can deny it?"

Llineth smiles, too, her eyes cast down. "Whoever did would be a fool." But I know she is afraid, and most likely longing to prove herself against this new threat. I can feel the unease drifting from her men, too. It is not good: folk do foolish things in haste, like take hostages. Or lives.

Wulf told me we should get out the moment I felt this way. But if we did, everyone would say that Cenry and I were afraid.

Either way, my place is not here sitting among Llineth's men, watching her spar with Cenry. He does well enough by himself. They barely pay any heed as I slip away.

I see Yfelys, standing in the shadows, alone at the far end of the tent. I am a sparrow hawk with her prey in sight; I am a hound with the blood-thirst for deer. I am by his side in a moment, moving swiftly and quietly through the throng. Yfelys does not see me straightaway; I did not want him to. I need the gift of his surprise. I stand right at his side without his even knowing. I can do anything; I am the Ghost. I feel my own power, my own strength running hot through my veins. I wait a moment before speaking. "Your uncle must have held her in high esteem." I glance at Llineth. "Most would say ruling's better work for a man. Some other of Orhan's kin would have done as well, surely."

To his worth, Yfelys hides his shock well. And he's not fool enough to pretend that I don't speak of him. "What concern is it of yours, Mercian?"

I shrug and turn to him, giving him the full force of my gaze. I'm such a hopeless sinner to enjoy this so much. "None, but I'm no Mercian."

Yfelys turns and looks at me truly for the first time, his eyes settling on the fine-wrought gold brooch holding together my cloak. "What? You come here with a Mercian atheling; you wear the mark of the boar at your throat." He gives me a sarcastic smile. "I take it you're from Kent."

"No. Northumbria." I look away, taking a long draft of the thin, warm ale in my cup. "I am a hostage." Now I've got him. I feel the quiver of interest. But a few hours since, Yfelys made a fool of himself before his cousin and all her men. I'm giving him the chance to rebuild his honor. Well,

I'm not really. I'm selling him down the river, but he need not know as much yet.

"A most trusted hostage," Yfelys says, lifting one eyebrow. "And one that speaks British, too."

"Most trusted," I repeat. I fix my eyes on Yfelys's: his are the smooth brown of a hazelnut shell, flecked with green lights. I have him. I feel a smile slide across my face, slippery as warm oil. "My lord Wulfhere is a fool — a fool to let his addlepated old father spar with the High King, and a fool to fight the north."

"They — they say there'll be a battle between Mercia and Northumbria before the year's done."

"Ay, there will be," I whisper, "and we shall take the wind from Mercia's sails then, shall we not?"

I could finish Cenry now. It would be easy to kill him here. Llineth has half a mind to serve us an ill turn as it is. And if Cenry were dead, Thorn would never be his. The thought jerks across my mind quicker than a spider.

Yfelys forgotten, I glance across the tent at my foster brother, sitting among Llineth's men. I just see him through the fug of thick wood smoke, the press of folk. His head is thrown back in laughter, his face flushed by the fire.

He is my friend. Sometimes I frighten myself. Why do such wicked ideas come to me so easily?

"My uncle waited years for the chance to cut loose from Penda." The sound of Yfelys's voice tugs me back to the smoke-skeined warmth of the tent. There's a glimmer of a fire at the backs of his eyes now. "Llineth may be above herself for a wench, but at least she has the sense to send word to Northumbria. The High King has only to raise his finger, and we'll ride to his banner when the time comes for a fight."

Oh, I do thank you, Yfelys, from the lowest reaches of my heart, for I know all I need to.

We are back in the treetop house, and I thank Christ that Cenry knows how to hold his drink. He has downed cups and cups of wine with Llineth and her men, but from the look of him, he may just as well have been on his knees at prayer in the god house. I squeeze his shoulder, and he sits up, pushing back his hair. The amber beads hanging around his neck glitter quietly in the moonlight. We exchange a glance. All is quiet. Holding a finger to my lips, I lean across and peer out of the door, down to the dark forest floor below.

They have not set a guard at the bottom of the ladder, but there shall be someone on watch; I would bet my immortal soul on it. But there is no choice. We must get out of here: Cenry doesn't think Llineth will have us killed, but we're both agreed she's not above selling us to Northumbria. Saying nothing, I gather my saddlebag and strap it around my waist; Cenry does the same. He grins at me, eyes glinting in the darkness, and I close my fingers around his wrist, tight, mouthing, *Follow.*

I feel naked climbing down the rope ladder; every speck of my skin prickles with unease. The ladder swings, sways. I move as fast as I can. I do not like this, but there is no other way of doing it. I thought of leaping to the big elm next to the oak and then on, and on again, just as I used to flit between rooftops in Constantinople. Although I grew up among sun-baked buildings and dark, vine-choked alleyways, I could just about trust myself not to rustle a sheaf of leaves or crack a branch. But not Cenry. He's good at hunting, at trailing, but not so good as me. I hear the heartbeats of the men they've got on guard now, no more than thirty paces away, I'd bet anyone a bag of coin. I think of nothing: I am not here. But all they must do is look around and they'll see Cenry.

I've done it: I'm on the ground. Quickly, quietly, I step back to let Cenry down. Good, good, he doesn't make a sound, and he has the sense to breathe slowly, too. I know he's behind me; without looking back I run, streaking through the trees, my heart singing with the thrill of it, listening with every shred of my body for the sound of an iron dart slicing through the air or another set of footfalls.

They've got a man watching the horses. I see them in the clearing ahead, Maelan and Fleet among the Elmet-set horses — roans and dappled grays, slim, fast-looking beasts, each one. Most are sleeping. The horse guard sits with his back to us, leaning against the trunk of a great pine tree. I turn to look at Cenry. His eyes are wide.

We hadn't thought of this: a brainless mistake. Of course the Elmet-set lay a watch to their horses by night. Cenry closes his fingers around the dagger at his belt and starts moving forward. Jesu, he's the child of the Devil's Cub, all right. I grab his arm again, shaking my head. We don't need to slit the poor fellow's throat, and God knows it would make the devil of a racket. Cenry's never killed anyone before, and Thales the Knife always said it took rare skill to finish a man quietly. Cenry raises his eyebrows, shrugging: *What else are we meant to do?* I hear the thought as clear as if he'd spoken it aloud.

I hold up my hand: *Wait here.*

I am not here; I am nothing. You cannot hear me, guardman. Closer, closer, I creep. Maybe it would be kinder to kill him, but I don't have time for kindness. I squat in front of the guard — a man in his middle years, with a lean, dark face, thinning hair, eyelids drooping with tiredness. He wears a silver bead strung through one earlobe.

Good evening, my lord. His eyes flash open, wide with shock; his hand flies to the knife at his belt. But I have him. *What do you start for, friend? You do but sleep. You do but dream.* He slumps against the tree, and I'm alive with the burning brightness of my own power.

No one can stop me; the Ghost walks once more.

I turn and beckon to Cenry. It is long since time that we were away from here.

Three days later:
The Wolf Folk

T HIN, SWIRLING mist rises from the ground, shrouding the trees, hiding the bracken, twisting around Fleet's mud-spattered legs. Pale light lances down through the shifting golden leaves woven high above our heads. It'll be warm later, but when Cenry speaks, his breath hangs on the air, a silvery cloud. "Back in time to break our fast," he says, grinning at me. "I want fried pig meat and a cup of cider, and hot bread."

"I'd rather feel my legs again."

"Well, you've never ridden bareback before. You did quite well at it." He laughs. "Da's going to drop down in a fit when he finds out we left the saddles."

"What choice did we have, fool?" Never mind the horse gear. What's Wulf going to say when we tell him the Elmet-set are ready to betray him at any moment and that we left their queen alive? It would have been no use to kill Llineth, though. Kings and queens are like weeds: no sooner is one cut down than another springs up in its place. Better to leave Llineth alive, wondering just what Cenry is going to tell his father, than dead with a hot-blooded princeling in her place thirsty for a taste of revenge.

"I've no stomach for killing womenfolk, anyhow," Cenry says cheerfully. "Or not young, fair ones, at least. Look — we're close. Last one into the yard's a milksop."

"You're on." And we race, flashing fast through the greenwood, riding hard for home.

I feel it when we're close enough to see the great soaring roof of the hall, the new thatch glowing gold in the early-morning sun — a sudden, deep chill that grips me from within.

Something is wrong; something has happened. I tug on Maelan's mane, slowing her, and call to Cenry, but he's too far to hear or is not listening to me, and he's out of my sight now, riding over the bridge by the sound of it, Fleet's hoofs drumming against the wood.

Jesu. *Go on, girl. One last gallop and we're home.* I dig my heels into Maelan's flanks, keeping a strong leg on her, and we surge forward, the wind rushing past, freezing the bones of my face as the mist begins to lift. I do not like this; I don't know what manner of mess we shall find at the hall, but the fear of it chills me to the core.

By the time I reach the yard, Cenry's alone there, sliding off Fleet's back, leading her to the duck pond in the shade of the great ash tree. I dismount, wincing at the fiery ache in my thighs, patting Maelan's neck, letting her dip her head down to the still, greenish water for a drink.

"Where is everyone?" Cenry asks, looking like a child who's just lost a simnel cake.

"Hush." I hold up one hand. They are singing matins in the god house; the rise and fall of the chant rushes over me like water. Why must Leofric preach in Latin when not a man or woman here understands a word he says? God must seem a strange, faraway father to the Anglish. At home, we always had preaching in Greek, and the word of Christ was among us all.

Cenry turns to me, bemusement all over his face. "What are they doing in the god house? Granfer will kick up the devil of a storm."

Maybe Penda has gone, the heathen old snake, and that's why they're all in church again. Maybe he's dead.

"Come on." I grab Cenry's arm. We leave the horses drinking and hobble across the yard to the god house. I'm never riding bareback again, not for a dragon's hoard.

Cenry shoves the rickety wooden door and as it swings open, creaking on its hinges, everyone inside turns to stare. The god house is crammed to the rafters, and I see strange faces among the villagers. Who are these people? Up on the pulpit, Leofric's pressing ahead with the sermon, but no one pays him the slightest heed. They're all staring at Cenry and me as if we have just come back from the dead.

"My rangers!" The crowd parts to let Wulf and Anwen by; Wulf crushes the pair of us in a hug, laughing and messing up our hair. There's a warm note of relief in his voice, but when he pulls away, I see that shadow at the back of his eyes again, that unease.

Well, his son and heir has returned. What has my dear and only lord got to fear now? Anwen has her arms around Cenry; he pushes her away, grinning. *Can he not feel there's something wrong?*

Who is that man standing by the pulpit dressed up richer than a cockerel, his fleshy face flushed with his own worth? "Well, Wulfhere," says the stranger, "which of these fine young men is to have my goddaughter, then?"

Suddenly, everyone seems to draw back against the walls, leaving a hollow space in the middle of the church. Everyone is staring, even Leofric, who hates being stopped when he's in the middle of damning us all to the deepest pit of hell.

Beside me, Cenry goes whiter than new milk. Wulf lays a hand on his shoulder.

"You're back!" It's Thorn, stepping forward, bright-eyed with joy. She's hand in hand with a woman I've never laid eyes on till now.

I have seen that face before, though, every line and curve of it, every shadow. She is tall and lean, with high, arched cheekbones and long eyes. A strand of fiery hair hangs loose from her linen veil.

Tasik.

"Well," the woman says, never taking her eyes off me, "why has no one told me of this? I do not think I am mistaken."

Wulf is talking, but I can't untangle the words. I can't breathe. The air quivers. I hear the bees humming in the orchard outside, the song of the river, one of the cattle lowing down in the flood meadow.

My heart is pounding. Can they not all hear it?

"Cai —" Wulf begins.

The woman speaks again, paying him no heed: "More than ten years it has been since I laid eyes on my child and his wife, with no manner of knowing if they even still lived —"

"Come, come, Elfgift, my dear," says the cockerel man, "now is not the moment for such talk."

It is as if he has not even spoken. "And now I see that Essa has brought a child of his own into this world, and no one has told me of it." The woman pauses, drawing in a breath. "Where is my son?" Her voice is colder than the bottom of a well. "Why is this boy here, in a Mercian court, when I know that his mother and father sailed for the east?"

She is my grandmother. She is Tasik's mother. Thorn's guardian.

She is here to see Thorn given away to Cenry.

I turn to Wulf, and the words fly from my lips. "Why didn't you tell me? I hate you!"

A few people gasp. Thorn presses her hands to her mouth, and I hear Edge mutter, "Oh, Jesus Christ."

I have broken another of those grim, unspoken Anglish rules: I have spoken out of turn to my lord, in full hearing

246

of a church packed with people, and nothing else matters. I might have laid the head of the High King himself at Wulf's feet and yet I would still be in the wrong.

I can't stand it. I must get out of here, away. I sprint for the door, my head spinning. The brightness of the yard stuns me, and someone pulls me up by the back of my tunic, jerking me around to face them. It's Wulf, and I have never seen him look so angry. *"Never speak to me like that again."* He slaps me hard across the face, and it feels like a splash of boiling water.

I'm so shocked I can't breathe. How has everything gone so wrong so quickly?

"You are an atheling," Wulf says in a low, angry voice. "I don't wish to remind you again to behave like one. I will speak to you of this later. Go and stable your horses."

He doesn't even want to know what happened in Elmet. My heart's racing. I feel as if the blood has turned to dark cold water in my veins. I can charm secrets from the lips of princes; I can go anywhere without being seen. If it were not for me, Wulf's dearest son would most likely be buried among the trees in the Elmet-set forest or sold to the High King as a hostage.

I hate this place; I hate these people.

I bow my head. "As you wish, my lord." *You cannot see me anymore, Wulfhere of the Mercians.* I step away, fading from Wulf's sight, and the glimmer of fear in his eyes brings me joy — but with a bitter taste, a sorry taste.

"Jesu take me," he mutters, and turns sharply, stalking back into the god house.

I lie belly-down on the branch, watching a tree-rat streak across the ground, barely seeming to touch the carpet of this year's leaves, beech mast, and old twigs. Angry thoughts boil in my head: I'll be damned if I'm going back to the village, either to help with the threshing in the barn or to share false honey talk with my grandmother — but I can't help wondering what she's like. My *grandmother*. Even the word sounds strange; I have never had one before, or never known one, at least. Her face haunts me; it merges in my mind with Tasik's. I almost hear his voice, his lazy laughter as I lie gazing down at the forest floor: *A right foolish mess you've wrought for yourself now, hothead.*

I've always known that Thorn is to marry Cenry, binding the Wolf Folk tighter to Mercia, but it's been a fuzzy, far-off threat. Wulf can't have known that the Wolf Folk were coming so soon or he would have told Cenry and me before we left. But now I hate him and I can't stop myself. My face still burns. How can I forget that manner of insult? And he keeps my ring, the only link I have to my family. He uses me to spy on the Elmet-set and now he treats me like a child.

You were not angry with Wulf at first, though. You were angry because Thorn's people have come to see her married to Cenry, and you don't want her to be. You blamed Wulf for it.

It's true, but I can't think about that. I can't.

I damned nearly had my throat cut for Wulf's sake, and I am used to better payment than this for my skills. I am the Ghost; there is nothing I cannot do once I choose to, and I will not suffer such treatment. I think of the hot power that surged through me when I drew the truth from Yfelys, when all I had to do was look at the Elmet horse guard to suck the senses clean out of his mind.

I have been a fool to stay here, a weak, senseless fool. How easily they drew me in, Wulf and Anwen, with their warm, crowded hall, their tales by the fireside, their careless kindness. But wait —

Someone is coming: I hear light footfalls, a heartbeat, too, and that of a hound, a twig cracking, dried leaves crunching. If they've been sent to find me, they'll look a long while. My belly is empty, and I'm so tired, I could sleep for two days, but I'm going nowhere. Whoever it might be, this unseen walker, they come closer.

It's Penda.

He lopes along, wolflike, hunched in a dark green cloak, wiry gray hair loose around his shoulders. It's thinning on top, and I see the pale skin of his scalp spattered with dark, liver-brown speckles. Age melts the beauty of kings just as it does everyone, but, my God, I bet having the ruling of all men makes up for it. I'd wager no one has ever dared slap Penda in the face. Ren follows at his heels.

I have been frittering away my loyalty and obedience on the wrong man. After all, why serve a prince when you can serve a king? For the first time since I set foot back in

Repedune, I smile, then I drop from the branch, landing in a crouch at Penda's feet.

I'll say this for the old snake: he doesn't scare quickly. He just raises one gray, straggly eyebrow, placing a warning hand on Ren's neck as I bow down, resting my forehead on the ground. "Quiet, you foolish hound." Penda treats me to one of his thin, bloodless smiles. "So, boy, I see you left the Elmet-set with your hide in one piece. Rise, and tell me how it went and what you are doing here, when the rest are all on their knees before that sap-headed fool Leofric. Did you not see fit to thank your God for a safe return?" He laughs. "Or make yourself known to your grandmother, at least?"

I get to my feet, head still bowed. Penda is cut from the same cloth as the Emperor of Thieves, and I know just how to deal with such men. "I saw fit to seek out my king, and give him the news he sent me to find." I look up, fixing him with my eyes. "And, my lord, I'm sad to bring such news."

Penda looks at me, sharp. He's got Wulf's knack of seeing straight through folk, and I don't much like it. "Tell me what happened, and fog me with no pretty words." His voice is cold, like the steel edge of a knife.

So we fall into step together, and I give him the tale: Orhan's death, Llineth's plot to betray Mercia and side with the High King. "We thought it best to leave her alive, my lord, not knowing what's to come from you."

He nods curtly. "You did right. Let the wench stew. But the sooner I ride against Northumbria, the better. Ah, for the love of the Lady, we shall come to rue the day we ever let Christian folk preach on this island."

I feel a deep, bright thrill. I'm sharing private talk with King Penda, most powerful of all men in Britain. "Why should that be, sire?"

He turns and glares at me. "Because time was, boy, when the High King of Britain ruled by the strength of his hand, not for his obedience to some puling wretch of a God. We had our own faith, our own gods, and we trusted in the land."

Who would have thought it? This bloodthirsty king longs for the old ways of this island, the old, dying ways of their wild gods and the elf-kind. "Well, my lord, I beg that if there is any other way I can serve you, you shall let me do it." *There's one in the eye for you, Wulfhere. I don't need you when I have your father.*

Penda smiles. "I shall keep that in my mind. There are not many such as you, who know the secrets of all men and can draw the truth from the lips of liars."

It's good to be priced high by someone, even if it is an ill-tempered old man. If I help him, perhaps he will help me. "My lord," I say, "why don't you let Leofric wet your head, then spread the word that you've become Christian to Wessex, Kernow, and all the rest? They'd crown you High King in a heartbeat, and then we should have none of this bother with Northumbria or Elmet, or anywhere else." Oh, Jesu, I've done it this time. Why can't I learn to keep my mouth shut?

But Penda just looks at me and lets out a cracked, wheezing laugh. "I may be many things, boy, but at least I'm an honest man. When I go to meet my ancestors, I shall go with my head held high. I will feast and hunt for all time, and my body will melt back into the earth and the heat of the sun, and mingle with the waters, riding on the waves of the sea. That is how things used to be, before all this talk of eternal torment."

So every man has his price, even Penda, King of Mercia. I have him now. He seeks mastery not only over the kingdoms of Britain but over God, too, and good luck to him. He knows my skills; he'll use them again. Let the old snake think I am his knife to wield; really, he is mine.

Elfgift and Mildreth

IT IS all such lies.

It sickens me, watching the Wolf King and his men glutting themselves with wine and meat, swapping false honey words with Penda and Wulf. It makes me want to throw something. At least I am not the only one mired in a fit of the dismals: Mildreth is worse than useless with gloom, and I know now why Wynn was giving her seven shades of hell the day Cenry and I rode out to Elmet. The silly girl is with child and will not tell a soul who the father is. All she does is blunder around, weeping fit to flood us. She has already dropped a bowl of blood pudding so that it cracked into splinters, which I had to crawl around after and pick up.

I'm at odds with Edge as well. Only this morning, he caught me as I was crossing the yard with the pruning shears Cam sent me for. "I hope you're proud of thaself," he said, looking at me as if I were a maggot. "Sneaking secrets out of the Elmet-set—more or less betraying your own folk, that is."

"What, because I have British blood as well as Anglish?" I sneered at him. "What do I care for that? And right well I was paid for it, too."

"Wulf paid you for your daft, unbridled tongue," Edge snapped. "And lucky you were it wasn't worse. Anyhow, even a fool could see the half of it was that he feels guilty for not telling Elfgift you were here. He should have sent word to her." I was about to stalk off, but then Edge laid a hand on my arm, speaking kinder than before. "Look, Cai, just take care—that's all."

I walked away to the orchard with the shears, letting them drag and bounce in the dust, feeling even more miserable than before.

Goodlord, the Wolf King, is a fool. He is a great bulk of a man, his face wine-reddened as he sits between Wulf and Penda, getting his meaty shoulders in the way when I lean in to pour more beer.

He lumbers to his feet, nearly squashing me against the wall. He's not the kind to pay much mind to those who serve him. He's drunk. He grips the edge of the table to keep himself from toppling over like a rotten tree in the woods.

Passing by with a jug of wine in her hands, Thorn nudges me in the ribs, rolling her eyes at him. I ignore her and she frowns, looking puzzled. "What's wrong?" she hisses. "Cai, you've been like this for *days*. Can't you just —?"

"Here's to the damnation of Godsway and the Northumbrians!" Goodlord's voice booms out across the hall, and they all raise their cups and cheer like the fools they are, for you can be sure that next harvesttime the Wolf Folk shall be pledging their loyalty to the Kentish against the Mercians, or to Wessex, or probably even to cursed Northumbria.

"He's always been a fool," mutters Thorn, aiming a poisonous look at the back of Goodlord's head. She glances at me. "Oh, suit yourself, Cai."

I ignore her, watching Edge pour beer for Leofric farther down the table, his face blank. How does he stay so calm while this gapeseed damns his father?

It's my grandmother who says it. She's sitting by Leofric, who's awed by her, as any fool can see. How much for her holiness, I wonder, and how much for the fairness of her face? I've seen the men's eyes on her, even though she is old — Thorn told me this last was her forty-first summer.

"How can tha wish damnation on Northumbria, Goodlord, when there's northern folk around this table?" My grandmother is smiling, and others smile and laugh, too, for they all know she was a Northumbrian princess long ago, before she was so holy. I wonder why she chose to give her life to God in East Anglia instead of in her own country.

"Fair play to you, Elfgift. I always tell any woman she knows best," Goodlord says, squashing his bulk back onto the bench. There's more laughter, as if he's told a great joke. Anwen shoots him a pretty sour look, though.

Cenry wanders over, holding a basket of bread. He leans closer, whispering in my ear, "They don't much like each other, do they?" I just shrug, and Cenry sighs. "Look, Cai," he hisses, "haul yourself out of this useless sulk. It takes a lot to rile my da, but if you go on like this, then you'll really know of it."

"What makes you think I care?"

"Fine. You're being a fool, though —"

Wulf turns to look at us, and Cenry falls quiet so fast I nearly laugh. "Go, get your meat before these guests of ours finish the lot," Wulf says. Cenry grins and walks off, but before I can follow him, Wulf grabs my arm. "Wait." He smiles, yet I'll be taken in by his charm no more. "Come on, Cai, haven't we given this enough talk? I was harsher than I ought to have been when you came back from Elmet, and you were cursed rude. I'm grateful you went, and grateful for what you did. I'm right glad you're back in one piece, too. For God's sake, let's have a truce."

A *truce?* Hardly. I've listened; he's spoken. I shrug. "As you will, my lord."

Wulf's eyes narrow. They are dark green, like the mere in shadow. I've taken it too far now. "Be warned, Cai, son of Essa," he says, quietly, "that I grow quickly bored with mannerless ill cheer, and you would be wiser not to bore me."

I grab the beer cup and go without asking my leave. I know I'm earning harsh words, and I do not care. I have to walk by Elfgift to get my meat. I keep my eyes on the floor as I draw near, hoping she won't see me.

"Do you sit down with me, child." My grandmother smiles, and I swallow a blind urge to run. What can I say to her? I have to glance away, for she's too much like Tasik, and I feel an ache in my belly when I look at her. "It's time we had talk," she says. "Tha hast so many chores in this hall, I wonder you get a moment to breathe."

I slide onto the bench, elbowing Leofric aside. At least I'm riling the god man, which is good enough for me.

He gives me one of those looks. "I hope, Cai," he says, "that you will recall your manners."

My grandmother smiles at him, and he looks mazed, as if dazzled by the sun. "Father," she says, honey-sweet, "is it true that you have a splinter of the True Cross set in glass?"

"My dear woman," Leofric says, "allow me to fetch it." He's gone in a heartbeat, and I look on her with new respect.

"Such an odd grasp of the Faith," my grandmother says. "So much fire and punishment that he forgets God loves us. When you are my age, you'll know how to manage such folk."

I grin at her, borne up by the first flash of true cheer I've felt in a while.

"Now, let me hear it from your mouth, child," she says then. "How did you come here?"

I freeze. Elfgift has had this tale already from Wulf. Why does she want to hear again how I failed to save her son? What am I to say?

"It is all right." Her voice is kind. "Wulfhere has told me that you fear your father is dead and think the fault is yours, but he's right: you weren't to blame. All I want is to hear your side of the tale."

So I tell her, although I don't know why she laughs when I reach the part where I made for the wall in our courtyard and Tasik snatched me back. I did not think it so amusing. "He hated me," I finish, staring at her boldly. She wanted my tale, and now she's got it. I won't hide anything; if she wants to despise me, let her. "He hated me because I'm a liar." Then I say it before I can stop myself: "A liar like his own father."

"Where did you hear this?" The words snap sharply out of her mouth. She has a quick temper for a god woman.

"Tasik told me," I say in a rush. "He said that although he'd given me his father's name, he wished I didn't have his skill at deceit."

My grandmother takes a sip of wine. "Yes," she says. "I am sure he did. Well, Cai, you must know that a man can be a liar, and many other things as well. Life is rarely so simple. Look, here comes the good man Leofric with his relic, and I must let him bore me clean out of my skull with the tale of it." She smiles. "Now, be away — I've no wish to see you rush into a mither with my holy friend, for he's told me all about your wickedness. But come to me again before I ride south; you make me laugh, and we must all take our merriment where we find it, in these times."

My grandmother is not like any god woman I've ever met before.

Out in the yard, I nearly break my neck tripping over Mildreth. She's hunched up by the side door of the hall, and what she does there God only knows, but it's cost me my supper, which now lies in the dust with my bowl.

"What's wrong with you, you lump?" I cry, and straightaway feel a fool. Mildreth's with child, and the father has clearly said he'll not own it — nothing to laugh about when there'll be a brat to feed.

Mildreth says nothing, just shakes her head. Her face is wet with tears, and all I can hear above the roar of the feast in the hall is her sobbing. It's a lonely sound. I don't know why I sit down beside her.

"I'm all right," she says, which is a lie, for she can barely cough up the words for puthering out tears. "I'm all right."

If anyone sees me do this, I shall die of shame: I put my arm around Mildreth's heaving shoulders and pat her on the back.

"The children down in the village," Mildreth sobs. "They — they throw things at me when I go by. It shan't be long before their mothers do as well. I wish I could go back and change things. I'm — I'm so afraid of going to hell, even though I know I've earned it."

This is the longest and strangest talk I've ever had with her. We've not gone beyond "Good day" and the weather before, and now we're on to eternal damnation.

"Well," I say, "you can bear me company there, then. You're not so great a sinner as I am."

She laughs then, with a wet, spluttering, unhappy sound, shaking her head.

"Why don't you just tell who it was that did it?" I ask. "You didn't get like this by yourself, did you?"

But Mildreth shakes her head. A tear drips off the end of her nose. "Just leave me," she whispers. As I stand, she looks up, smiling wetly. "Thank you, Cai. I know everyone says you're wicked, but I don't think you are truly. I think you've a kind heart."

I go before she has the chance to say anything even more sickening. Dear Christ, what a night of odd talk this has been, what with my grandmother, and now this. One thing I know: I shall stay away from girl folk as long as I can. Trouble finds me quick enough as it is.

27

A sennight later

Tbey were married this morning, Cenry and
Thorn, hand-fasted together before God, and now
the whole hall is bursting with firelight and song,
and soon they will push back the long tables and dance.
The nights are drawing in, growing chill, but even so, folk
have spilled out into the courtyard, and I hear their chat
and laughter. It sounds far away from the darkness of the
stable.

All I can think of is how to make sure I leave this place
with Penda when he rides out to another of his halls.

I sat alone at the shadowy end of the hall while the rest
of them stuffed roasted meat and new bread and spiced
puddings into their faces, pouring enough Frankish wine
down their throats to flood the valley. When Wulf came, I
was polishing Penda's sword, Darknail, dipping my cloth
into a bowl of linseed oil and working up such a shine that
the blade shone silvery black like the side of a mackerel.

A darker shadow fell across me and when I looked up, there was Wulf. He sat down beside me. "Why do you work when you should be feasting?" he said.

I shrugged and made no answer. Darknail was so bright that I could see my face in her. Wulf reached out and took the cloth from my hands. I stared down at the blade.

"My father is a demanding man," he said, "but even he does not expect work to be done at a time like this. Cenry and Thorn have both been asking for you, and the girls, too."

"I've been given a task," I answered, not looking up, "and I would like to finish it, my lord."

In one swift move, Wulf snatched Darknail from my lap, resheathed her, and leaned the sword belt against the wall. "Come with me."

Out in the yard, Wulf leaned back against the wall, thumbs hooked into his belt, shoulders hunched. He watched me a moment before speaking: I hate it when he looks at me like that, as if he can see inside me, and I can hide nothing.

"Listen," he said. "I've had my fill of this game you play, allying yourself with my father. He may be old, but he's a dangerous man, and if you knew the half of what I do, you'd be glad of your lot and show me some respect instead. Now, will you come inside and have a drink with Thorn and Cenry?"

A wave of misery rolled over me. "No!"

"Fine. Stay out here till your temper grows better." And he went back inside without another word.

So I am out in the stables with no one to talk to but Maelan, annoyed that I feel so guilty. Why should I care if Wulf's got himself all riled up? But someone is coming: I can just hear them walking across the yard through all the chatter and shouting. How can they all be so merry when I feel so wretched?

Oh, no. Whoever it is, they're coming into the stables. I sink lower into my pile of hay, leaning back against the wall. I pray to God it isn't Cenry or Thorn. They won't find me. But it's not. It's Elfgift. What does she want?

She pauses in the doorway, looking swiftly around. Moonlight strikes the linen veil she wears wound around her head. There is something about the upright, proud way she stands that puts me sharply in mind of Elflight.

My sister, I think. *My twin, where are you now?*

My grandmother steps forward, smiling, and I realize with a jerk of horror that she can see me. I should not be surprised: I could never hide from Elflight or Tasik, either, so why should I be able to hide from Elfgift?

"No stomach for a feast?" She sits down beside me.

I shake my head.

"I knew I would find you out here," Elfgift goes on. "You are much more like your grandfather than Essa. Cai often preferred the company of horses to menfolk, and he used to sulk fearsomely, too. With your father, there would just be a great blaze-up, and that was the end of it—but I'm sure you've seen a few of those yourself."

"I'm not sulking."

263

She raises one eyebrow — it's a trick of Tasik's, and it snatches away my breath for a moment. "Yes, you are," she says, "but no matter. I don't mind — there isn't a day that goes by that I don't miss Cai, and so it is good to see him in you. I loved him out of all reason, you know. We ran away together when I was fourteen summers old. I was meant to marry a Pictish chief who was as ancient as I am now, and I had no stomach for *that*. The devil of a lot of fuss we kicked up, your grandfather and I."

I laugh.

Elfgift turns and gives me a bland, innocent smile. "Thorn has always been one for sulking, too. Ever since she was a little girl. I'm glad she's hand-fasted to your foster-brother, for even a fool could see that he's not that way and will always be able to tease her out of a black mood. I think it's best for married folk not to be too alike. Ah well, such talk is not like to interest a lad your age. Come, let's go inside."

She gets up, quick and lissom as a girl, and glides toward the door without looking back. She knows I'm going to follow her.

Well enough, Grandma, my dear. You win. I slide to my feet and go.

Back in the hall, the air's thick with heat and honey wine. I see Penda, leaning back against the wall, watching the riot ebb and flow around him. He watches all from beneath lowered eyelids, always with that thin smile on his face. Everyone else, on the other hand, is in their cups, even Wulf, who can hold his wine better than most. He's mired in chat with that lout King Goodlord, but when he sees me walk by with Elfgift, he reaches out and pulls me over. "Ah, here's my ranger, Goodlord," he says, grubbing up my hair. "The youngest and the best. Am I not lucky to have such a one?"

"I think you are," Elfgift says, rather tart, and she goes to sit with Anwen and Leofric, who is not so holy that he doesn't get stone-blind drunk, I see. "Off you go, Cai. This is a night for you to be with your friends, not your old grandmother."

What a cursedly managing female she is.

Wulf gives me a hug and shoves me away. "Go on. They've been mithering me all night about where you've got to."

For God's sake, why must he make it so hard for me to hate him?

Cenry, Thorn, and Edge are heaped up near the fire with some of the young ones from the village — not Mildreth, though, I see. Poor wench. Thorn runs up, shrieking, and throws her arms around me, forcing a cup of beer into my hands. "Where have you been?"

Edge grins at me, shaking his head. "Never mind where he's been. Sit down, cousin, and have a drink." And I'm grateful to him, for Edge knows what I'm like, that I've been off in a black mood, but he won't let Thorn make me admit it.

Cenry just sits there, sprawled on the pile of skins and blankets, looking at me. I look back at him, fending Thorn away. The dog roses woven in her hair are making me feel drunk, dizzy. "Sorry," I say to Cenry.

He grins, the shadow of Wulf. "Don't be a fool." He hauls me down beside him, and as I sit between Cenry and my cousin—my foster brothers, my friends—I begin to wonder if I've been wise to swear my service to Penda.

I want to stay here. It is my home now, whether I like it or not.

It's growing light outside, and someone has thrown open the great doors when I hear it. Most folk have now gone to sleep behind the drapes, or back to the village. I sit up, knocking over my cup.

"You fool," Edge says, cuffing me. "I'm drenched."

"Stow it!" I hiss.

Thorn's lying with her head in Cenry's lap. "What's wrong?"

"Can't you hear that? There's a horse coming."

Cenry glances at me. "I do." He grins. "But I'm damned if I'm doing aught about it. Have another drink, Cai. It's most likely Hlafy or one of the others coming back."

But this is no ranger, riding closer and closer; I'm sure of it.

If we hadn't all drunk so much, someone would have gotten up. But there is not even anyone at the gate. So the stranger comes in alone, into the hall, into the embers of our feast. He is a tall man, wrapped in a heavy plaid cloak, road-filthy and road-weary, too, by the look of it. Beside me, Edge draws in a deep, hissing breath and his fingers tighten around his cup. The stranger pushes back his hood, and the early sun coming in behind him lights up a head of hair the color of fire.

Tasik —

I feel my heart jump. Edge is gripping my knee so hard that it hurts. It is not Tasik. *It is not him.* This man is younger, and Edge has never seen Tasik before. A great, roiling wave of disappointment rolls over me, stealing the breath from my lungs. No one says a word.

The stranger looks around him, at the table littered with greasy fowl-bones, heels of bread, garlands of bruised dog roses and ivy, and empty cups. An amused smile spreads across his thin lips. "The end of a feast," he says in a dry, mocking voice. "What a foolish moment to arrive."

Wulf's on his feet now, and Anwen emerges from behind the red drape wearing just her shift, a blanket around her shoulders. Penda sits quite still, watching, waiting.

"Whom do I welcome to my hall?" Wulf says, holding out his hand.

The stranger steps forward and clasps it. "Highrule," he says, "nephew of Godsway, High King of Britain, son of Godsrule, who has been dead these last ten years and more."

Beside me, Thorn sits up, clutching my cousin's arm. "*Edge!*" she whispers. But he pays her no heed. The color has drained from his face, and his jaw is set hard. "Well then," Wulf says. "You are very welcome, Highrule. Here is my wife, Anwen, lady of this hall, and here is my father, Penda, king of this country." There is no hint that so much as a drop of wine has passed his lips now, yet he must have put away close on a barrel of the stuff.

Still with that thin, mocking smile, Highrule walks around the table and drops to his knees at Penda's feet.

The silent wait seems to last for days.

At last, Penda says, "Rise, Highrule, and do me the honor of telling me why you have left the side of your uncle and come to the hall of my son. What news do you bring from the north?"

Highrule gets to his feet, the thin smile still drawn across his face. "Well," he says, "I'm not fool enough to fight the losing side in a battle, and so I have come to give you the strength of my sword, Penda, King of Mercia. It's in my mind that you are the rightful High King of Britain, for you hold more land than my uncle, your might is more than twice his, and the men of the north are too foolish to set aside their differences and stand together — all we hear is talk of Deira, Bernicia, never one kingdom of Northumbria. Wilt tha have my sword?"

No one says a word. Anwen moves closer to Wulf. Edge looks sickened, as though he has just stumbled on something dead and rotting, something foul. I can't take my eyes away from him. Is he going to faint — he's pale enough — or do something foolish?

At last, at long last, Penda smiles.

"Well enough, Highrule, son of Godsrule," he says. "You may fight for me when the time comes. Now, I bid you to sit down, and Cai shall bring you meat and wine."

But now Edge is standing—standing and shaking. Anwen opens her mouth to speak, but Edge doesn't give her the chance. "You filthy traitor!" His voice rises to the rafters, jarring in the golden early-morning quiet. He strides toward his cousin, who just stands there with that faint, mocking smile on his face. "You should die here this day. You'll rot in hell for it."

"Edge, be quiet!" Anwen's voice rings out. "Have you forgotten all courtesy?"

"Well," says Highrule, "how goes it, Peaceblade? How tall you've grown, child. But a stripling you were when we brought you here, long ago."

It's as if Edge hasn't even heard. "Dost tha not remember how your mother wept when Penda took tha father's life, Highrule?" he shouts. "May God curse tha children and tha children's children, traitor!"

Beside me, Thorn weeps silently, tears spilling down her cheeks. Her wedding feast is blighted now, spoiled. Cenry grips her hand, squeezing her fingers tight, his face frozen. Edge spits on the ground at Highrule's feet, and Wulf moves at last, his hand crashing down on the table so all the bowls and cups totter in their places.

A thick, horrified quiet settles on us all. I watch a cup jerking, swaying, till it tumbles off the table and cracks into shards on the floor.

"Outside," Wulf says to Edge without raising his voice, "before you let loose any more foolish words. Never have I been so shamed."

Edge stalks away, letting the door swing shut. I scramble to my feet, ready to sprint after him.

"Cai," Wulf says sharply, "bring meat and wine for our guest, as you were asked."

Anwen begins fussing around Highrule, taking his cloak, pouring him a cup of beer, bidding him sit, all as if he were just any traveler who had happened upon our hall and Edge merely said it had rained a lot of late.

It's close on full daylight before I get the chance to slip outside.

I find Edge sitting in a shadowy corner of the barn, pitching stones at the mice that flit from shadow to shadow.

"Cursed hawks don't keep them down," I say, glancing up at the beam where my lord's hooded hunting birds roost.

Edge says nothing. I feel the sorrow burning out of him. He's never been stung by Wulf before, at least not while I've lived here. He's not like me. Worse still, Edge is two summers older than I am. If he were at home in the north, he'd be counted a man by now, wearing a ring for his father as Cenry does for Wulf.

I sit down and pass him the leather cask of wine I hid in my tunic. "Here. Have a draft of this. You need it."

He drinks, taking long gulps, then passes it back. "You ought to go. Get some sleep."

"They won't know I was here," I say. I take a swig myself and hand the cask back.

"I don't know what I'm to do." Edge's voice is on the point of cracking. I've not heard him like this before; he's ever bitter and mocking, and never seems to care much about anything. "I'm Northumbrian, House of the Serpent. I was born to give that kingdom my loyalty till the day I die, yet my father sells me to Penda's son, and now Highrule. And who has looked out for me since I was eight summers old? Wulf, my father's sworn enemy. I can hardly even recall my father's face, Cai."

"Have a drink, you fool," I tell him, and he takes another draft, then lets out a long breath. "Don't fret on what you can't mend; it was your father's choice to send you here. Why should we care what these foolish old men do, anyhow? It's a mess, but it's none of our making."

Edge turns to look at me. "Listen, Cai. You don't know the half of Penda. Have you never heard the tale of how my uncle Godsrule was killed? He was taken in battle with Mercia — I was no more than three summers old. Penda ordered that his corpse be torn limb from limb, his head, his arms, and his legs mounted on poles and stuck along the high road to remind folk thereabouts not to shift their loyalties again from Mercia to the High King, who was their rightful overlord, anyhow."

I feel cold inside.

Edge sighs. "Penda's many things, but he's not foolish, Cai. He's dangerous, and now Highrule has sworn loyalty to him, the man who killed his own father. Jesu, we're in a mess, all right, and it's going to get worse."

"Look, do you really think Highrule's here just to lend his sword to Penda?"

Edge shrugs. "Why else did he come, then? For the fine hunting and the fair women of Repedune?"

"What, like Wynn?" I say, and we both laugh. "Edge, have you no wits in your head at all?" I lower my voice. "I'll lay you my dagger that Highrule's not here to lend Penda his sword but to look out for your safety."

Edge throws a stone, missing a darting mouse by an arm's length. He throws another and hits one, sending it skedaddling across the barn floor. Then he laughs. "I bet he's right glad of the welcome I gave him, then." And he turns to me, his face grave now. "Cai, it's coming soon. There's to be a fight, a great fight, and you and I must keep our wits sharp if we're to come out of it with our skins whole. If Penda orders Wulf to take our lives, he must do it. You know this, don't you?"

"Give me the wine," I say, shoving him. "Don't talk to me of wits after the sport you gave us tonight."

But Edge is right.

I may be a liar and a thief, but I am not normally a fool. Only now I'm sure that swearing myself to Penda was the most foolish mistake I've ever made.

28

A gathering storm

I T BEGAN when I was sitting in the yard beneath the ash tree. Wulf told me once that they used to praise it as a god when he was a boy, before Christianity came to Repedune Hall. I had a stick in my hand and was scratching patterns into the hard-packed dust at my feet. The words alit in my mind like a flock of birds. I was back in the courtyard at Yannis's, unraveling the *Iliad* in the shade of the apricot tree. The stick sprang to life in my hand, and I wrote in the dust of Achilles' great sorrow, of the wine-dark sea lapping at the sands of Troy, shaping the letters that once I hated.

"Cai, what are you doing?" Rhiannfel stood there with her sister and a gaggle of village brats. They stared down at what I had written, fear shadowing their faces. No one writes or reads here, for all Leofric claims he was taught in that Northumbrian god house where he was bred up to plague me. Is it my fault these Anglish deem letters dark magic, fit only for the god men?

"Making a tale," I told her. I do not even know the Anglish word for writing. "Not that it's any concern of yours, wench."

Rhiannfel nodded slowly, kneeling down beside me, her dark hair thick with dust. She must have been in the barn, where they're threshing the wheat. "Show me how to make my name." I scratched out the sounds of Rhiannfel's name in the dirt, and she turned, her freckled face bright with laughter. "Is that really me?"

"More or less. You try," I said.

But the other brats looked edgy now, afraid. They hissed and sighed when Rhiannfel took the stick, ready to copy the letters.

"Don't do it!" someone cried.

"Witch boy, witch boy, he'll curse you!"

"They're fools," Rhiannfel whispered, but it was too late: folk poured out of the barn, dusty with the threshing, coming to see what was amiss, and then I saw Leofric striding across the yard from his god house, dark robes flapping around his scrawny ankles. "He was just showing me, Father," Rhiannfel said. But Leofric paid her no heed. She may be the daughter of his lord, but she is only a girl.

"I'll thank you not to frighten the youngsters with your heathenish tricks, Cai." Leofric dealt me one of his scornful smiles and kicked my work into nothing, leaving no trace as the dust settled again. The children scattered, running toward the safety of the barn, where their folk watched, narrow-eyed.

I don't know what made me do it. Maybe it was the heat of the day; perhaps it was just the feeling of being crushed by this place, overwatched by everyone. "I was only writing in Greek, dear Father," I said, tasting sour delight as the color drained from Leofric's shriveled face and his lips turned white. "If it was good enough for Saint Paul, it shall do well enough for me."

He didn't agree.

So now I am sitting alone in the dark, shadowy god house. I'm meant to be on my knees praying for my soul, as if I'd just committed each of the seven deadly sins. At least if I'd done that, I would have had some sport and cheer. I ought to have kept my mouth shut: Leofric hates being reminded that I know more of the Bible than he does. I've had all the Psalms by heart since I was six summers old, and he can barely read.

I lean back against the wooden wall, watching a spear of butter-yellow light point down from that high window beneath the thatch where swallows nest in spring. The smell of frying pig meat and fresh bread drifts in, and out in the courtyard there's laughter. They've forgotten about the witch boy.

Oh, they like me well enough when I can draw truth from the lips of their enemies, but they're happy to lock me up the moment I scare them. It makes me sick. I long for Tasik, for my own people. I wish my grandmother were still here. I'd give anything now even to see my dagger-tongued wretch of a sister Elflight.

"More cider, my friend?" I hear someone say—Garric, I think—and there's the clink of earthenware cups. They're all sitting out in the yard, toasting the sinking sun and their day's work with that apple wine everyone's so cursed fond of on this island. The brats are at play, too, running and shrieking. They're safe from the witch boy now. I should steal back my ring from Wulf. I should get away from this place before it's too late.

I hear horses, folk calling out greetings, more laughter. Wulf. He's been away with Penda these past few days, off staying in the hall of some border-march lord or other, bound to Mercia with a golden ring. They took that slip-some eel Highrule, too, which I was glad of, because Edge cannot look on him without bristling like a guard hound, no matter how many times I say he's really here to watch for Edge's safety. And here they are, back again. Right grim and cheerless Wulf has been, ever since Highrule rode in that morning. I've had my fill of it. I thought he'd be less uneasy once the Wolf Folk left, but he's worse, if anything.

Something bad is going to befall us all; I know it. How I wish I could shake off this dread, this sense that everything is going to change forever.

How I wish there were a door to the past and I could walk through it.

*　　*　　*

I dream of Asha.

It's hot in the courtyard: the sun's high, streaming down, beating against the white walls. Vine leaves hang, limp, among the green, shadowy tangle. We sit on the rim of the fountain, our legs cool in the dark water. It's good to be here with Asha once more, even though part of me knows this is not real.

She turns to me, her face calm, serious. Her hair is loose down her back, black and shining. *I had my freedom and my family taken from me,* she says. *You have given yours away.*

I wake up breathless. *Why did I do it?* I lie in the dark hall, listening to Edge's slow, steady breathing beside me. *Why did I give up those I love? Why have I fallen out with Wulf, and why did I swear myself to Penda?* First the Emperor of Thieves, now the King of Mercia. What's wrong with me? Am I truly so power-thirsty, so wicked, that I'd cling to the cloak of the devil himself if I thought I'd gain from it?

I dread falling asleep again. I don't mind dreaming of Asha, but I fear the other dream, the one I know will come again tonight, just as it has every night since Cenry and I rode back from Elmet.

But sleep I must. . . .

Fear grips me. I see a white-haired king sitting on a dark throne, and all around him are dead, swollen corpses; there is not one living tree, not one blade of grass. There is but the king sitting alone, lord over a blasted wasteland, never to know the warmth of companionship again.

I draw closer, and I see the lines of sorrow etched on the king's face, the loneliness. And I look at his eyes; they are black and long — the same as mine.

He is what I shall become should I grow too fond of twisting men's thoughts, should I thirst too deeply for the bright, burning power of it: ruler over them all, but alone.

I stand at Garric's shoulder while he works; I need arrowheads, but he won't talk to me till he's ready, and I like watching him. He's making nails, holding a coil of metal in the fire with the tongs. The iron glows red, then gold, then white, and swiftly, smoothly, Garric draws it from the forgefire and hammers it against the anvil to flinders. He scoops them up and drops them into the water trough; there's a white, hissing plume of steam.

I can't get used to the way everything we use at the hall is wrought by hand, from the cloth the girls and women make in the weaving shed to the shoes on our feet. At home, all we needed was to be had for coin from the stalls thronging the Mese.

Finally, Garric turns to me, his broad face glistening with sweat. "Well enough, witch brat, and what can I do for you?" He says nothing about my brangle with Leofric yesterday, and I know he won't. I like Garric. He never mutters about the Halfling Witch, even when he thinks I can't hear; I've never once seen him make the sign against the evil eye as I walk by.

I grin. "I want to go shooting, and I have no arrowheads. You swore you'd make me some."

"And so I did, you grasping wretch. I meant to give you them last night, but you'd gone to sleep when I came. They ought to be on the hall table still. Go on, get out of my way — even if *you* can hie off shooting all day, I've work enough."

I run into the quiet hall, bow bouncing against my shoulders. I can see the leather bag of arrowheads from here, resting on the end of the table. I mean to go after a brace of ducks today, and Wynn shall cook them for us tonight.

"Cai, what are you doing?" It's Wulf, sitting by the fire with Penda.

Oh, no. It's like turning over a rock and finding an adder, fangs waiting and ready to strike. When Anwen came to fetch me from the god house last night, she told me to stay out of Wulf's way, and now I see why: his temper's frayed to shreds, and so would mine be if I'd been riding around for days with no one but Highrule and Penda for company.

"Have you lost the power of speech?" he demands. "Come here."

Where is the old Wulf, the one who was always shouting with laughter and merry as an eel in a barrel of wine? He has changed; these times have washed the cheer from him.

I tuck the bag of arrowheads into my belt and drop to my knees at his feet. "I'm going hunting for ducks." I search his face for a trace of a smile, but there's not a glimmer of one.

"Was the fuss you stirred up yesterday not enough?" Wulf's voice fills the hall right up to the rafters, and I flinch. "You were told to go up to Far Acre and help with the plowing. Why have you not done so?"

He hasn't even asked for my end of the tale. No matter what I'd done, Tasik always heard my side of it. I wish he were here now.

"Because I'm weary of folk staring at me all the while and whispering, that's why!" The words are out before I've the sense to swallow them.

Wulf's eyes narrow, and I've a plunging feeling in my belly, as if I'm falling. I'm going to get it now.

But then Penda holds up one thin, wrinkled hand.

"Wait, Wulfhere," he says. He's smiling, and I shudder. "Perhaps we're well met this morning, Cai." He turns to Wulf. "Might this not be the way to untangle our little problem?"

Wulf looks at him sharply. "Father, I don't want him mired up in it."

"Mired up in what?" Again the words are out before I can stop them.

Penda leans back in his chair and goes on talking as if I haven't even spoken. "No, Wulfhere. Cai chose to disobey your orders this morning, but perhaps it's the working of fate. You must agree that there's no one here could do the job better. Peaceblade trusts him."

What's he talking about Edge for? A chill slides gently down my back.

Penda leans forward. "Come and sit down, boy. Bring up a chair and we shall talk like men, shan't we?"

I glance at Wulf and he nods. After all, what choice do I have? Penda is my king, mine to obey, and I swore my service to him. Moving as if underwater, I get to my feet and reach for a stool. Time was I would have loved this, sitting with my lord Wulf and his father, drawn into their trust. But now I'm wishing myself elsewhere.

"What think you of Highrule, boy?" Penda asks.

I stare at the flames. "He's a traitor, my lord," I lie, for I do not believe he is. I'd swear on my life that Highrule is playing a double game. "But lucky for you — I'd wager you've learned all sorts from him about the Northumbrian fighting men King Godsway has got."

"Well, boy," Penda says, "I do not know if I am lucky or deceived. But you could find it out for me, could you not?"

Oh, no. I don't like the way this is swinging. "My lord —"

"*Quiet!*" Penda's hands grip the arms of his chair, bunching up like dead spiders. "*Do not speak until you are spoken to.* You will find out for me just where Highrule's loyalty lies. But not from him; he's too sharp, even for one with your sneaking skills. Get it from your cousin Peaceblade and come to me with the news. Do you understand? You shall be rewarded."

Penda is asking me to betray Edge.

Long ago, when I was the Ghost of Constantinople, I would have done it. But I think of Asha, and I hear her saying, *You have given away your freedom.* I think of the dark-eyed king who haunts my dreams. I think of Cenry, and the way he looked at me when I used my skills against him. I think of Edge, too — my cousin.

I bow my head and then look up, right into Penda's watery old eyes. "I am sorry, my lord." My voice comes out in a whisper. "But that is something I will not do."

A smile flashes across Wulf's face, quicker than a fish in the shadows.

Penda's voice is cold, deadly. *"What did you say?"*

My heart is hammering and I can scarcely breathe, but I am triumphant. He can do whatever he likes, and I don't care. This time I have chosen to do good, and I shall.

"Father —" Wulf begins.

But Penda pays him no heed. "Wulfhere," he hisses, "I'll have no such disobedience. Take the boy outside and teach him otherwise."

Oh, Jesu. I don't care, though. I still don't care. I bear whip scars on my back that I'll carry to the end of my days. What does Penda think they did to make us row on that slave boat? Give us honey cakes? I can stand another whipping if I must.

But Wulf is shaking his head. "I am sorry, my lord. I can't punish Cai for being honorable."

The silence seems to last a sennight. I can hear the river rushing outside, the women laughing in the weaving hall, the clink and grating of metal coming from Garric in his smithy. But in here, it is as if the world has stopped and we three are frozen around this fire till the end of time.

At last, Penda spits into the flames and gets slowly to his feet, grasping his stick. The old man walks to the door and goes outside without once looking back, and I don't even know why, but I feel tears burn the back of my eyes as I watch him go. He is just an old man, a lonely old man whose world is falling to flinders around him.

Wulf and I sit without saying a word for a long time. At last, he picks up a stray twig and casts it into the fire, turning to me with his crooked, half-crazed smile. And I see the Wulf of years ago, the boy who has finally bested his father.

"He's going to make me pay for this, isn't he?" I wipe my face with my sleeve. "I'm a brainless fool."

Wulf laughs, shaking his head. "Well, I'll not argue with that." He gives me a tired smile and for a moment looks like his old self again.

We stay by the fire, and I wish I'd seen before now what manner of man Wulf is, how much courage he has. I would do anything for him.

I wish I had seen the truth before I bound myself to Penda, for I've made an enemy, the most dangerous one I've ever had, even after Thales the Knife and Achaicus Dassalena. It must be quite a skill of mine. If I don't take care, Penda will finish me.

PART FOUR

Betrayal

Some weeks later:
The month of winter full moon, AD 655

I
T'S DARK in here, dark and cold. The light's gone
from the day already, and the fire kicks out more smoke
than heat, casting long shadows up the walls of the
barn. They look like long, skinny black fingers, clutching us
tight. Edge and I sit side by side, a hand span between us,
leaning against a stack of hay. I feel hollow inside, empty
like an old bone.

Wulf has betrayed us.

They have gone: my lord, Cenry, Highrule, that snake
Penda, and all the rest of his men. Gone to meet the war-
riors of Northumbria on the banks of the river Winwaed,
and I do not know who shall come back, nor when.

My mind's caught on the leather bag Wulf left; Edge said
he'd never touch it, and we made a pact not to, but I can't
help wondering what's inside, our lord's last gifts to us. It
sits on the floor between us, unopened.

They said we were not to have a fire, that it was too great a risk with all the harvest in here, but if they must lock us in the byre like mad dogs what choice do we have? So we lit one, anyway, in a shard of a broken bowl I found in a dark corner. I'm glad no one thought to take Edge's strike-a-light or our knives. He's better at such things as fires. It was so careless of Wulf to let us keep our blades that I can't help thinking there was a message in it: better to die by our own hands than by his. He shut us in here on his father's order; he'll kill us, too, when Penda says it's time.

I don't trust his word. If he truly meant we'd come to no harm, why must we be locked up?

"We cannot do it," Edge whispers, fiddling with the hilt of his knife.

"What choice is there?" It comes out harsher than I meant. "We're trapped in here like goats before the slaughter, and we're finished whichever way the fight goes." It's not true that we're trapped. I could get out of here without even thinking on it, but Edge couldn't and I'm not leaving him.

"If my father's lot wins, Penda must send me back to Northumbria — and you, too."

I laugh, but there's no mirth in it. "You heard what Highrule told us: Penda's got fighting men from the Wolf Folk, Wessex, Powys, the East Saxons — more than three times your father's count. Now they don't care if Penda's a Christian or no; all they want is to be on the winning side. Edge, your father will not win this."

Edge's face twists with misery. "Well enough," he says.

"Well enough. What do I care, anyhow? But if Mercia takes the fight, why does Penda need to kill us?"

"Fool — how can he let us live, a pair of Northumbrian athelings? Edge, why do you think Highrule came in here before they rode out? Why do you think he asked if you recalled the way from the north?"

Edge falls quiet and does not answer. *Twenty days' ride south we rode, when you were but a little brat. Dost tha remember, Peaceblade?* I hear Highrule's words echoing in my mind. *We had the sun at our left shoulders all morning, and at our right all afternoon, and close by the coast we rode, so that the song of the waves kept us on our path.*

He did not have time to say much else before Wulf came in.

"Must I bid farewell to my cousins so soon?" Highrule asked.

Wulf just said, "We go now."

Highrule bowed his head at Edge and me, mocking to the last, and we sat on the floor, not looking at Wulf. I felt hollow, like a dried-out sheep skull left to crumble in the meadow. How could he do this?

"I want you to have this." He knelt and tried to press the leather bag into my hands, but I let it fall.

"We want nothing from you," Edge spat, and then the shouting began outside.

"I don't care who you are; you'll not keep them locked up like beasts." It was Cenry. "They're my friends, my brothers. Does that mean nothing?"

Pride and sadness burst in my heart: that speech to his grandfather would cost Cenry dear and he knew as much, but he made it, anyhow.

"May the Lady Frigya and God keep you," Wulf said then, and if I had not been so full of misery, I would have laughed. Wulf is no Christian, though he stands in Leofric's god house each Holy Day. He must have thought our chances truly hopeless. He got up and strode out quickly, not looking back at us, and his voice was added to the storm of words in the yard, and soon Cenry fell quiet. That was the last we heard of him. Cenry at least was loyal to the end, unlike his father.

"Edge," I say, "if we stay here, it'll be our deaths."

He digs the point of his knife into a floorboard. "All right, then." He speaks so quietly that I can barely hear him. "Give them time to get well away northwest to Winwaed, and then we'll go. Although how we're to get out of here, I know not."

I smile in the flickery, firelit dark. "Don't fret about that," I tell him. "You may leave it to me. Not this night, then, but the one after?"

Edge sighs. "Yes. The one after."

If the wind were in the east, we would not know Mildreth was having her child. But as it is, her cries are borne on the air over the great soaring hump of the hall and the yard, and to here. Poor Mildreth; she has suffered enough already, with all Leofric's sermons about sins of the flesh, and the gibes of the folk down in the village, and the sidelong looks of the women, all of whom you may wager are wondering if it's their man who strayed and cursed Mildreth with this baby. Chances are they're right to be wary. Why does the father hide his part in it unless he belongs already to another woman and has brats of his own to feed?

"Poor sow," Edge says. "A man who does that's a coward, all right."

I watch a mouse streak from one stack to another. Anwen must have gone down to the village with the girls; our food would not have been forgotten otherwise. I could eat my own leg, I'm so hungry, and always I must keep a grip on this darkness in my mind, this crushing horror that comes with being locked up.

Edge puts his hand on my arm. "Cai," he says, "you're shaking."

"I'm afraid," I tell him. "I hate being closed in."

He smiles. "So even you are afraid of something."

"Just this. Just being closed in. Not of anything else."

That's a lie: I'm scared of dying. If I were not, I'd not be talking Edge into getting out of Repedune and riding fast away till it's nothing but a lump on the horizon behind us.

We sit wordless in the dark.

"Cai," Edge says at last, "what was it like on that boat? On the slave boat that brought you here?"

I've not told anyone of this — not Wulf, not Thorn, not even Anwen. No one at all. I do not think I ever shall. A sticky awkwardness grows in the air between us as Edge realizes that I'm not going to tell him. I hear him breathing. I even hear the soft drumbeats of our hearts. There's quiet in the barn and quiet without: Mildreth has stopped her wailing.

"She's had it," I say. "Either the child's born or she's dead, or they both are."

And then, out of the silence, a shrill, high cry pierces the air.

It's thick night now, and still no one has brought our food. The fire has burned down to embers that glow bloodred.

"What's wrong?" Edge asks, shredding a piece of straw. "We've had nothing since just past dawn." He turns and looks at me, his face a pale blur in the shadows. "Cai, do you think they mean to starve us?"

"No. Anwen wouldn't, even if Penda told her to. She and Cenry were the only ones who stood up for us. No, there must be something else."

We fall into quiet again, waiting.

I sit upright, chilly with fear: I hear footsteps moving across the yard. Two sets, light, coming slow. My fingers close around the handle of my knife, and I kick Edge sharply in the leg; he's dozing, his head lolling forward as we slump against the hay. I see his hand go for the hilt of his knife before he even opens his eyes. Twitchy and quick are Edge and I, and who can blame us, locked up in this nest of traitors?

"Who is it?" Edge whispers.

"How should I know?"

The barn door swings open slowly. My hand's sweating into the leather-bound hilt of my blade. I hope it doesn't slip.

It is Anwen and Thorn. I let out a breath and feel my heartbeat slow. But there is something sorely amiss; I can see that now. Even in the gloom, Anwen's face is pinched and pale, and Thorn drags her feet, a strange, glassy look to her eyes, the brightness quite gone from her face. I sense Edge tense at my side: Thorn looks wrong, as though some deep, inner spark is missing. She looks as if she has lost her wits.

"Help me," Anwen whispers. "For the love of God, I can do nothing with her. She'll listen to you two. Just get her to drink a sleeping draft—please do it." She's gripping a small vial in one hand.

We're on our feet in a moment. "She needs to sit, for a start," Edge says in a cold, harsh voice. "What's wrong with her?"

Between the three of us, we get Thorn to sit on the hay. She moves as though asleep, slow and clumsy. Tears slip down her cheeks, leaving tracks that glisten in the shadowy darkness.

"What's wrong?" I hiss at Anwen. I can hardly stand to look at her. I know she spoke for us when Penda said we should be prisoners, but still it burns me to lay my eyes on her: my foster mother turned jailer.

No one had the courage to stand up to Penda in the end, no one save Cenry.

Anwen opens her mouth to speak, but no sound comes out. Thorn is rocking slowly backward and forward, and Anwen puts her hand on her arm, offering the clay bottle, saying, "Oh, darling, I'm so sorry, will you not take aught just to help you sleep?"

But Thorn does not answer and turns her face away, rocking and weeping, rocking and weeping.

"What's amiss?" Edge demands. "Tell us."

Anwen sighs. "Mildreth," she says softly. "The child's father — it's Cenry."

We stare at her, wordless with the shock of it.

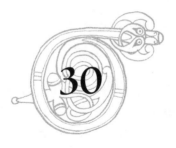

30

N O," EDGE says sharply. "That can't be right. He would never—"

"Well, he did," Anwen replies. "Much though I wish it weren't so, I think it is. Mildreth's ever been a truthful girl."

Their speech fades as I stare at Thorn. I reach out and rest my hand on her shoulder, not knowing what else to do. She looks up at me, and all the light has gone from her face. Her eyes are dead, flat like pebbles on the riverbed.

"Come," I say, keeping my voice low, as if I were speaking to a tricky horse. "Come, you silly wench. You can't let yourself be riled by a great fool like Cenry. You were not even wed to him then, and he's got muck for brains, anyhow—we all know that."

But Thorn just shakes her head, tears slipping unstoppably down her face, and I feel a burning twist of anger unwinding deep within me.

Who do they think they are, this family?

Edge snatches the bottle from Anwen's hands and holds it to Thorn's lips, forcing back her head so she has no choice but to drink.

"Take care!" Anwen cries. "You'll hurt her."

Edge ignores her. "Swallow," he says to Thorn, and she does, even though some of the dark juice trickles from the corner of her mouth like blood from between the lips of someone killed by choking sickness.

I want to speak; I should say something comforting, but I cannot. I feel as though I am on fire, that I burn.

Suddenly Thorn sits up straight and we all jump, as though a corpse has just opened its eyes and stared right at us. She is looking at me. "Cai." Her voice is flat and hollow. "You ought not to pity me. You of all folk should not pity me."

Anwen's hands fly to her mouth. "My honey," she pleads. "Don't say it. How can it help?"

It's as if she has not spoken. Thorn's face twists into a mockery of a smile. "No," she goes on. "The wrong this family has done me is nothing next to what they did to your folk and mine, long ago. Your mother and father told you nothing of it, did they?"

I shake my head, but Thorn did not mean me to answer, anyhow.

"Penda knew your grandfather." She speaks in a dry, rasping voice. "He was a spy, a double dealer. He spied on Mercia for the Wolf Folk, and all the while Penda thought

Cai was *his* man. Cai was just like you: he moved like smoke and they say he could have talked the stars out of the sky had he chosen to. When Penda found out, he swore to take revenge.

"Penda and his men, our dear lord Wulfhere counted among them, they've laid waste to many a village," she goes on, fixing her cold, dead eyes on me. "They've taken the lives of many poor folk who've done nothing but been in the wrong spot when the Devil and his Cub rode through. The day Penda's army killed my mother and father," she says, "was the day they took the lives of all your kin but Elfgift and your parents. Every last one of them: your mother's mother, her brother, and even her grandfather, too. Cai was there — your father's father — and Penda made sure he killed *him* himself, of course."

I'm cold, too cold. It feels as though someone has tipped a hogshead of icy water down my back. I'm back in the hall that night with Elfgift again. *Well, Cai, then you must know that a man can be a liar, and many other things as well.* This is how Penda knew of my skill: I'm not the first to have it. My grandfather died for it.

There are no secrets anymore. I wish there were, though. I wish there were.

"It wasn't like that," Anwen whispers. "Wulf tried. He tried . . ."

The cold's rushed away; I'm aflame. I burn; I cannot be quenched. I feel light, full of power, as though I am formed of naught but fire and air. I hear Edge saying, *"No, Cai, no,"* as if from across a field, but I have not time to heed him. I shrug myself out of his grip and I run, swerving past Anwen, who reaches out to me with a cry. I'm out in the yard, shocked by the chill of the night, the great sweep of stars above me in the blackness. All blurs as I make for the stable, so fast that neither Edge nor Anwen has a hope of catching me. There's warm horse-smell, darkness. I let Maelan out of her stall and leap onto her back, wrapping my legs around her.

We've a run ahead, my dear heart, I think, and I hope she can understand me.

"Stop!" Anwen cries, running across the yard.

I lean forward, gripping hard, clutching tight at Maelan's wiry mane. If she minds being ridden bareback again, she shows no sign of it. She is swift this night, my darling. I hear the hiss and roar of the river, and I wheel about, setting her at it, feeling the strength of her great body as we leap.

I look back over my shoulder at the straggling houses of the village, the river's bend, the bulk of the wood looming up behind it. I will never see this place again.

From Repedune Hall northwest,
into Elmet-marches

WE TEAR through the dark hours of the night, long since out of the land I know from hunting. All I can be sure of is that I'm riding north, for the great star is above me. Bleak country flashes by—flat, sweeping, with crooked trees snatching up at the night. The trees thicken now, drawing in around me, silent, watching.

It has been lit, my slow-burning anger, and I cannot put it out. I am borne up on its wings, swooping so fast that my eyes water. My legs burn from the ride, from the effort of keeping my seat without a saddle, but I do not care.

I am tired, so weary that my head sinks low over Maelan's neck, and I feel she's at the end of her strength, too. Her sweat is soaking through my clouts, and it's cold out here without a cloak. I hear the song of water rushing over rocks; if I must rest till morning, it may as well be here, where I can let Maelan drink.

Stop, my darling, I think, tugging gently on her mane. *Stop now.*

Once she's drunk her fill, I lie down near the stream, so tired that my every move is slow and graceless. I'm hungry, too, but I'll get nothing tonight. The first folk I find I must beg food from, and the way. But where will I find folk, out here in this wildwood? Despite my misery, I can't help laughing at the thought of asking the Elmet-set for help. I draw closer to Maelan's warm bulk, pulling dry leaves over as much of my body as I can. I wish I had a strike-a-light. I wish I had something to eat. I can see the stars through the cross-hatching of twisted branches above my head. Silvery streams of cloud drift across the night; there must be a bright moon somewhere behind all that. It must be nearly full, and I know the fight is to happen the dawn after full moon. I do not have much time. Steam rises from Maelan's heaving flanks, and I throw my arm across her, saying, "I'm sorry you're cold. I'm sorry I brought no blanket for you, nothing to rub you down with. I'm sorry."

My voice sounds starkly alone out here, so I stop talking and listen to the sounds of the darkness instead. I have not been by myself in the wild like this for a long while, not since the last time I ran away, and then I had Thorn with me. Poor Thorn. An owl calls, hunting. Odd shuffling noises rise from the bracken. Shrews, maybe, or mice.

That's all it is.

*   *   *

I wake just before dawn. Maelan breathes slowly and steadily in her sleep, her oyster-shell-gray flank rising and falling gently and evenly. I'm not so cold as I was. The fire crackles low — Jesu! I lit no fire. I sit up, shrugging off the blanket thrown over me, and close my fingers tight around the hilt of my dagger.

"Don't give thaself a fit," Edge says lazily. "You weren't hard to follow." He sits hunched by a small, guttering hump of flames, poking them with a stick. Lightfoot, his horse, is nosing around in the leaf mold a handful of yards off.

It's not a blanket that covers me but my cloak, and I wrap it tightly around my shoulders.

Edge tosses the stick into the flames. "Some messenger came from the Wolf Folk just as I was off, too. Crashed in through the gate like a storm on the wing, he did."

Who was the messenger? Goodlord and his men must be well on their way to the battle place. Why would his court send word to Repedune now? A full night of it they've had, at Repedune Hall, what with Mildreth's brat — *Cenry's child* — and Edge and me leaving, and now a messenger, too. I don't like that at all. What can it mean? Have the Wolf Folk backed out of the fight? Or do they know something that Wulf does not? Maybe the fight place has changed, or it's a trick and Wulf rides into an ambush. But why should I care what happens to him? He betrayed us, Edge and me.

Edge reaches into one of the saddlebags sitting on the ground beside him and tosses me a ring of twice-baked bread and an apple with the skin just beginning to wrinkle. I crunch the hard bread, spraying a cloud of crumbs. Then he throws the leather bag at me, the one Wulf left with us, the one Edge swore he should never lay even so much as a fingertip on.

"Why do you laugh?" I say. "And what did you bring that for? I want nothing from that traitor."

Edge just laughs again. "Open it. Then you'll see."

I wipe breadcrumbs from my face with the back of my hand, tug at the bag's drawstring, and tip its load into my outstretched palm.

It's my ring, my father's ring, and a key with a long handle kinked like a dead adder. Garric made that when he was a young lad, and folk always laughed at him for it. It's the key to the barn.

I pick up my ring and loop it onto the leather string of green glass beads at my throat, then tie it up again. Why am I not glad to have it back after all this time?

I was a fool to use it, that day on the slave boat. I should have kept the cursed thing hidden in my rags, and I would never have delivered myself up to the Devil's Cub. I feel empty, numb, like a crimson-dyed egg with all its insides blown out for an Easter gift. I feel as though I might crumble into nothing.

"Don't you see?" Edge says, grinning. "Wulf didn't betray us after all. He knew it wasn't worth riling Penda, so he just locked us up and gave us the way out."

I shrug, getting to my feet as I bite into the apple. "Maybe Wulf betrayed us," I say, swallowing a sweet mouthful, "and maybe he didn't, but Thorn told no lie. Did you know of this? How Elfgift could sit there among them, I'll never know." And I'll never know, either, how Thorn's borne it, all these years, knowing it was Wulf's army who orphaned her.

"Your grandmother's got her wits about her, that's why," Edge says roughly. "And I did know, if you want the truth, and when I see Thorn again I'll slap the daft girl's face for telling you."

"Was she well, when you left?" I search through Edge's saddlebags. He's brought my bow and a quiver for me, too. He's got some sense, at least. I sling both over my shoulder, then snatch out a bag of oats and shove it under Maelan's nose. She nibbles the edge of the bag first, as she always does, then dips her head, nearly dragging it from my grasp.

Edge looks at me a moment, then sighs, as if he were going to say something but changed his mind. "Asleep. She's trouble, that girl. Cenry was a fool, mucking about with Mildreth when he was betrothed to Thorn. She'll make him pay dear for it, and more times over than he can count. What do you think you're doing?"

"Kicking out the fire—what does it look like? Are you coming, or am I going alone? They're a day and a half ahead of us already."

I have an uneasy feeling that we're being watched—followed, even—but when I listen, I hear only four heartbeats: the horses and ours. So there's no one hidden. But still the back of my neck prickles. A lone oak leaf, fire-colored, falls from a branch high above our heads, and a wren darts off through the thatch of trees. I must get away from here; I must move on.

Edge gets to his feet, shaking his head. "Cai, what do you mean?"

"You've had your fill," I tell Maelan, unhooking the nose bag. I mount in one leap—a year ago I would not have been able to do that. I learned something, after all, living in that nest of liars, killers, and traitors. I learned a few things.

I squint up at the sky through the tangle of branches. It's a drab day, but by the slant of the light, I can put the sun just behind my right shoulder, as Wulf taught me. I know that the chosen place is a few days' ride northwest of Repedune as the crow flies and that both sides shall meet when the moon's full. Sooner or later I'm bound to pass some dwelling, some traveler, and I'll learn the way to Winwaed River.

Edge is at my side; I don't think I've ever seen him move so quickly.

"Wisht, wisht," he says to Maelan, patting her muzzle. "Tha'll go nowhere yet, whatever he may bid you." He looks up at me. "Cai, you aren't thirteen summers old. I'll take tha north to my father's hall, but over my dead body shall you ride to that battle place."

"You'll not take me anywhere," I tell him. I sound chilly and dead, like Thorn did. "I went; you followed me. I did not ask you to. I'll find that battlefield or I'll die trying. You can come with me or you may ride north, for all I care; you choose. Take your hand off Maelan — she's getting edgy."

Edge looks at me hard.

"God take your eyes, Cai," he says. But he mounts up, anyway, and we ride on.

Winwaed River

THIS MORNING we came to the shore of a great stretch of woodland where hazy hills swept out before us: a tumbled mass of green and gray, stretching as far as I could see, shrouded in long curls of mist. A flock of geese soared above, arrowhead-shaped, and I wondered how they knew to fly like that and how they chose who would take the lead and who would follow behind.

"The fells," Edge said. "Ah, but it feels well to be back on high ground. Seven summers, it's been, since I saw hill country."

"The woods are afire," I told him. "Can you not smell it?" The stink of burning wood hung lightly in the air. "Not far from here, either."

Edge shook his head. "Na," he said. "It'll be charcoal burners, most likely. It's too damp for the trees to burn alone.

Come, let's ask if there's one who knows the way to the Winwaed. We can't be far now. Either that or we're lost."

I prayed we were not. If we came but a day too late . . .

We followed the smoke and found the charcoal burner, all right, minding his great heap of wood. The mound was a big one; it would have been higher than my head had I been on foot. There was so much mud plastered over the crisscrossed pile of branches and leaves that it looked like a great upturned clay bowl. The burner was plastering mud over a crack leaking smoke when we came, and at first he did not look around, even when Edge called to him.

"The path to Winwaed River?" he said then, cackling. An old man, he was bent and crabbed with age, with wisps of gray hair flying free from the wool rags bound around his head. His hands were marked with dark, reddish blotches, his fingers thin and fleshless, but his eyes were bright and swift, bluer than the sky above the City of the Rising Moon. "I'll tell you, all right, but you'd as well turn your nags and ride the other way. It's a great fight, that one, and your mothers shall miss you when you're dead, boys." He cackled again and could hardly speak for laughing, though I do not know what he thought so funny. But he told us the way, all right.

"I'd bet you my knife that he was touched in the head," Edge muttered as we rode away.

"Just as long as he gave us the right path, I don't care."

"Cai, you may kill as many Mercians as you please, and it shan't change the past."

I shrugged, saying nothing. Edge does not understand that I cannot help myself. I am alight with rage; it bears me onward, as though a taut rope pulls me faster and faster toward my destiny. I cannot stop now.

I only wish I did not have this sense that someone follows us. When I listen closely, when I let myself become nothing, one with the woods, one with the hills, I hear a pounding of hoofs as though a great drum is beating, sending shudders through the warp and weft of the earth. But always the sound fades, as if it's something I hear in the tatters of a dream on waking.

And if I told Edge that a lone sparrow hawk has flown overhead for three days now, he would laugh at me. *Do not be a fool*, he would say. *It's not the same bird. Hawk-kind never leave their air-marches. Tha does but fancy it.*

In my mind I hear little Aranrhod speaking of the Half-ling Witch that evening after the hunt, when Wulf told tales of him and Tasik: *He spoke to birds, and horses, too.* I remember Anwen, too, saying that the hawk saw her brothers coming and told him. I think, too, of that long-ago day in the City of the Rising Moon, running sweat-soaked through the streets till I came to the harbor, and always the same buzzard circling above. And then Tasik found me.

Don't be a fool, I tell myself. *He's not here. How could he be? Wanting Tasik won't make him come.*

We're in rolling, hilly country, scattered about with gray shoulders of rock. The sky above boils and spits down rain.

The greet sweep of woodland is long left behind; now only a handful of hunched-up trees clutch up at the clouds. I'm glad Edge brought my cloak, but even so, the rain soaks in, dampening my tunic and chilling me all the way through.

Still I see that wretched sparrow hawk. Sometimes I don't spy it for hours, but sure enough, there it is now, making loops in the heavy gray sky above, and the skin on the back of my neck prickles.

Now I hear it: a noise like a thousand silver spoons falling onto a stone floor, a clashing of metal on metal, very faint. There's a low, bloody roaring, too — it sounds like the cry of a huge beast. A deep rumbling shakes up through the ground as though the Great Serpent that binds the world shakes her shining coils, unwinding in her deep, secret place, ready to strike.

I glance across at Edge, who reins in Lightfoot and waits a moment, his face still and quiet, shining with streams of rainwater. The light's fading. There is but a sliver of this day left, and so much will be changed by the end of it, one way or another.

"There," he says at last. "We've found our fight. Ist tha cheerful now?"

So we are not too late, after all. "Come," I tell him. "We've not many hours left, by the look of the sky."

Edge reins in again and reaches out, putting his hand on my arm. "Hear this, Cai. If we come apart, make for the Northumbrian shield-wall and stay behind it. Shoot as many Mercians as you please with your bow, but do nothing foolish. It's not for brats your age to do aught but stick at the back and throw stones. Do you swear?"

He feels guilty for coming with me, for not forcing me somehow to ride safely up to the north. "Well enough," I say. "I swear."

Edge should know better than to make me swear to anything.

I am a liar, after all.

We ride on, picking our way up the hill. On its crest, we look down to see the river Winwaed, swollen and huge, spreading silver across the bottom of the valley, just as the charcoal burner said we would. Willow trees rise up from great swaths of floodwater.

"She's burst her banks," Edge says. Rain drips off the end of his nose. "By Christ, we'll be in mud up to our knees."

I say nothing.

The air beats now with the sound of iron clashing against iron, and the roar of men's voices raised in the fury of the blood-rage that settles like a red mist when men fight. At least that's what they tell of in the songs. To me it sounds more like they cry out in fear, and in pain.

All I care about is that we are not too late.

"It's in the next valley, then," Edge says. He speaks level and calm, as though he talks of a deer we're tracking, not a great battle that might mean the end of us. "Best to stay on the high ground." We stare at the rounded hillside, listening.

This clashing of metal and this bloody screaming is like nothing I've heard before. It's a long way from the dusty knockabouts with wooden swords in the yard at Repedune. It's a long way from drinking cider in the courtyard, throwing spears at old sacks stuffed with straw. No one laughs here. And the smell: the stink of blood and dung nearly makes me choke.

"It's like Blood-month," Edge says quietly, and he's right. It smells as it will in Repedune when a few more weeks have passed and the beasts are killed for winter and the yard runs with blood.

I ride on, and Edge follows me till we are side by side. My heart thunders so loudly I wonder he doesn't hear it; for a moment its beat drowns out the clashing and shouting of the fight, and I wonder that all the men in the field do not hear it, too.

"Don't be afraid," Edge says. I don't know if he means him or me. "These big fights, they're all set out like a game of Fox and Geese. If tha stays at the back, tha shan't come to harm —"

I feel it before I see it. A great, crashing rumbling that runs through every sliver of my blood and bone.

"Edge!" I cry — and here they are, a stream of horsemen rounding the top of the hill, their faces scrawled with swirling blue Briton clan tattoos, bloodstained, their ragged hair streaming behind them, spears flying. One has a sword, which he swings above his head. It shines like the sun on water, and I think how fair it looks.

I hear Edge calling my name, but when I look around, I cannot see him, just this crowd of horsemen streaming over the hilltop. The battle's broken, the shield-walls scattered. It's a raging dogfight now, and I'm in the middle of it. Edge is nowhere. Where has he gone? A throwing-spear flies by, a finger's width from my head. The air's thick with screaming, with battle cries, with the groaning of the fallen.

I crouch low over Maelan's neck, whispering, "Easy, my darling," and her ears are flattened back onto her neck with fear. But there is no time to be afraid. "Come, come," I say to her softly, squeezing with my thighs till we go faster, faster, and we are crashing down the hill at a gallop, and it's all I can do to keep my seat, and I'm cursing myself for not bringing a saddle at least.

The valley boils with men and death. It is like one of Leofric's tales of hell's deepest pit. There are so many fallen, and they are trampled on, dead or alive, by horses and men alike. The darkening sky's thick with arrows; they rain down with the water from the sky and I'm gripped, frozen with fear. I've never seen rain like this: it is as if the heavens have cracked open. I was a fool to have come here, a fool to have dragged Edge into this, and now I have lost him and —

Maelan lets out a shriek — I have never heard her scream before, and the sound freezes my guts, and I'm falling, sliding off her back. I tangle in the shaft of a spear that sticks from her flank and hit the ground with my cloak torn. It is not the earth I lie on but the twisted corpse of a man staring up at me. His eyes are brown like a field in winter. I'm covered in blood, and I leap to my feet. His belly has been torn open, and the air's thick with the scent of human dung and blood. But Maelan, oh, Maelan, she's lying on her side, her eyes wide with fear.

I feel a hand on my shoulder and wheel around, clutching at my dagger. A man with a pockmarked face jams his spear into Maelan's side; it unfolds slowly before me — her flesh half swallows the shaft — the point must be deep in the mud by now. She shudders, and is still.

"What game do you play at, boy?" the man says to me roughly. "Tha should be aback of the shield-wall, whatever side you're on."

"My horse —" I say, foolish with grief for her. She is dead; Maelan is dead and the fault's mine.

He claps me on the shoulder. "Go, boy, get out of it if tha wants to see morning."

"Isn't the shield-wall broken?"

"The Mercian only. If tha's with the Devil and his Cub, pray to God. Godsway's men advance; get up the hill and tha'll meet them."

Wulf, I think, desperate. *Cenry*. But then I hear Thorn's words echo in my mind, and I'm hollow once more. *The day Penda's army killed my mother and father was the day they took the lives of all your kin but Elfgift and your parents. Every last one of them: your mother's mother, her brother, and even her grandfather, too.* Poor Ma. No wonder she never spoke of her life on this island: it is filled with nothing but ghosts.

I have been living in a nest of vipers, and they shall pay.

313

"Have you lost your wits, boy?" the man roars. "Run!"

As he speaks, spear-bearing men seem to rear up on all sides, their faces twisted with battle madness, and he turns with a roar, jabbing-spear held out before him like a claw, shield up.

I reach for my bow, still hanging from my shoulder, but the quiver full of arrows is gone — it must rest now in the mud next to Maelan. I am alone in the midst of a battle, weaponless save for my little dagger. I run blindly, snatching arrows from the mud wherever I find them. I even pull one from a dead man's leg; it makes a sucking, grinding noise as the head comes free from flesh and bone. He makes no sound, so he must be dead. I hope so; I should not like to have done that to a living man.

I'm at the core of it. All around me, men hack and scream at one another. They ram spears, wheeling and jabbing, parrying blows with their shields. It is like a dance. Spearheads smack into shields with dull, wooden thuds. Somewhere, someone blows a horn, a low, mournful note that sings out across this bloody field. Hot liquid splatters my face and I taste blood. Where I tread not on corpses, I'm up to my knees in mud and water. What good shall these arrows be now? They're no use down here; I have nothing but my speed. My shoulder feels strangely hot, and I'm breathless, but on I run, weaving through the throng. A man comes straight for me, his face twisted with rage, hair matted with mud, spear jutting out like a claw. I dodge him. I know not where I go, but a strange calm washes over me.

None of these folk shall touch me. None of them can catch me; they barely see me. I am the Ghost and I am not here. I seek only one man. I seek Penda of Mercia.

The bloody knot of men twists, surges; I hear roaring, I hear men calling out to their God for mercy. One cry rises above the others, and it strikes a note deep within me. *I know that voice.*

I run for higher ground, heart pounding. I turn and look back down the slope at the brawling clash below. Spears fly through the air like darts of lightning, the crash of iron and steel so loud I can scarcely think. A horseman rides hard down the hillside facing me, knocking men out of his way, a tattered black cloak streaming out behind him. Hair flies back from his bare head in fierce-blown flames. He rides like one of the elf-kind come galloping straight out of the spirit world, fast and tight. He wields a shield and a great spear, and I know who he is.

"Tasik!" I shout and shout till my lungs are in rags, but the battle closes around him and I can't see him anymore, just a tangled mess of men, mud, and corpses.

I must have been dreaming. It is like when I used to see Tecca, slipping too near the land of my ancestors, to the world of the dead. Tasik cannot really be here. There is no way.

Perhaps my death is near, hovering close by, and he has come back from that other place to meet me. I don't know. I don't know anymore what is real.

It's growing harder to move; I'm so weary, and my shoulder burns. Where have all the folk gone? I'm nearly up to my waist in floodwater. When I look down, I see fallen men, floating, peaceful, their wounds washed clean. Their hair spreads around them like fish-weed in the river. Their eyes stare up, blank. One has no head. A red cloud blooms from the severed neck; the torn skin is frilled, beautiful, like the petals of a flower. I can sit to rest for a moment, can't I, surely? There's a ridge of higher ground; I stagger toward it. My legs buckle beneath me, and I sink into the mud on my knees, leaning forward, gasping for breath. The last of the light is melting from the glowering, cloud-heavy sky. What's left of it reflects dull yellow off the floodwater. Rain streams down my face. My clothes are soaked, sticking to my body. A rust-brown stain clouds the front of my tunic. It hurts to breathe. When I look down at my hands, they are white and shaking, but I'm not cold.

I see no living man. I do not even hear the cries of the wounded; they drown as they fall. When I look up, I see birds wheeling in the darkening sky. Six of them, arcing in and out of the cloud, blunt-tailed, spread-winged — buzzards.

And now it's as if the clouds press down on the earth and I can hardly see. The birds fade, hidden from me. I hear the hard breathing of a weary horse, the splashing as it moves. The poor beast must be up to its hocks or higher in mud and water. I hear the breathing of a man, too. One man, alone. *Tasik, please let it be you.* I force myself to stand, and then I see it — the blurred outline of a horse and rider. The horse's head hangs low. Her muzzle brushes the water's skin.

The rider's hunched in the saddle, long, straggling hair hanging forward, shoulders hunched, wolfish. I'm walking, walking down the high ground toward them both. My sight is fading and I've been hurt, though I do not know where, for waves of pain wash through my flesh and bone. All I want is to lie down and sleep, but still I walk on. The outline of the horse and rider grows clearer. It's not Tasik—of course it's not; just an old man, some poor old warrior dragged from his woman and his hearth to fight one more battle.

"Who is there?"

It's Penda.

My hand moves unbidden, reaching up to my quiver for an arrow. My fingers close on nothing—I've lost them again. What a fool I am. A dead man floats in the water by my leg; I reach down and tug the arrow from his chest. The arrowhead's still there, and it's sharp, too. Well enough.

"Who is there? Come, Helitha." Penda's voice when he speaks to the mare is gentle. So he is not bone-deep cruel. He is just a man like any other.

Darkness clouds my sight. I draw back my bow. The gut string cuts into my bowfingers and there's a burst of pain in my shoulder so great that I must close my teeth tight together. I step forward.

"You." There's laughter in his voice. "I will not even ask how you came to be here, boy."

I stand there, bow tight; I burn.

Penda smiles, but his smile is twisted, bitter. He's defeated. "Do it, child," he says, "I beg you. My time's gone. The old ways, the bright ways, they fade; my gods are become demons. There's little place for men such as I among all this meekness and talk. Wrought was I to fight, and that is how I shall die, if you will give me the honor." He bows his head slightly, the old snake, but he looks me in the eye to see it coming. "I thank you," he says, and they are the last words he speaks on this earth.

I hear the dull thud as the arrow strikes home, the scream of Penda's mare as he falls, the dead king. He makes no sound, though. All is quiet. I wade closer, closer. If I haven't finished him, this shall be the end of me, but I must know. I must. The mare's bolting, kicking up great sprays of dark water. Penda shall go nowhere, though. Not now. Most feared of all men in Britain, the king of Mercia floats on his back, drawn down into the water by his mail tunic, my arrow poking from his wrinkled neck. His eyes are wide open. There's enough light to see that they're green, just like my lord's, and that the grim, twisted smile on his face is Wulf's, too.

He died well, Penda of Mercia. I have paid him back for what he did, for the lives he took, but he went well into the next world, and I hope his father and his father's father are coming forth to greet him now, the old warrior gone to his last home.

There's no way Tasik would call me a coward now, if he were here; I'd have made him proud at last.

How foolish that the Ghost should come to this: from a thief and a liar to a hero.

It's as well no one shall find out, or I'd never live it down.

My legs barely hold me up as I turn and walk away, stumbling on the tangled limbs of dead men sleeping in the arms of the Winwaed. It's harder than ever to walk. I cannot do it anymore. I am tired.

I must rest; I feel the waters close over my aching body, the night air chill against my face. It is done. I have done it. I sink into the mud; it clags my hair, dribbling into my ears. I gaze up at the skeins of fog silvered by the moon. It is full, round, and cold, so huge and far away, like a great silver dish. What a price she'd fetch if she were plucked from the night and sold. It is the same moon that shone on me when I was lord of the thieves, lord over the City of the Rising Moon. But I am a thief no longer.

I'm not afraid; I'll follow Tecca. I'll become the night, the falling leaf of an oak, the white crest of the wave. I'll be free.

If this is my end, it is a good one.

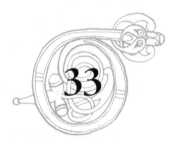

33

I T GROWS LIGHT, then dark. I am riven with pain.
I am hot; I cannot breathe with the heat of it — but
a moment ago I was cold. Someone cries out, and I
can't unravel the sense of the words. I'm cold again, so
cold.

Leofric said I was hell-bound, and I am sure he'd be glad
to know he was right.

Something hot and scratchy covers me and I cry out,
fighting to push it away, but I can barely move. I burn all
over. Devils prick at my skin. I see them; I see their laughing faces, their bulging eyes.

But who speaks?

"Come; be easy." I know this voice but not where it's
coming from. It sounds as though the speaker is at the far
end of a long meadow. I wish it were Anwen, or Wulf, yet it
is not. I will never lay eyes on either of them again.

I hear the voice again, the voice I know, but I cannot make out the words, for they are too far away.

So. I am not in hell, or at least not yet. This place is warm and dry. The floodwaters have gone. I'm lying on something that brushes my arm when I move, something with a faint smoky stink to it. It's a deerskin, the pelt of a roe. I see pale fingerprints against the rustiness of it. Wulf told me once that the gods left these marks when they made roe deer because they had drunk too deeply of honey wine. Blankets are piled on me, three of them. My head rests on another, rolled up, with a white linen tunic wrapped around it. The linen has a smell I know, a salty warmth I can't place.

Where's Edge? Sick guilt rushes through me. If he didn't come out of that fight alive, the fault's mine. I led him to it. I want Wulf to be here, and Cenry. But I've done something they can never forgive.

I killed an old man, an old, helpless man. I shot him down.

This place is full of light, so much of it that my eyes are flooded and I must half close them. It's a tent. Sailcloth sweeps up; there's a pole in the middle. There is no one here but me. The tent flap has been pulled back, leaving an arrowhead-shaped hole where light and air rush in. I wish I knew where Edge has gotten to, what befell him after we lost sight of each other. Dear God, let him not be lying there beneath those still waters, his hair floating like river weed.

Folk speak outside.

"Tha'll be glad on it, my lad!" someone says, and laughs. Northumbrians. I must be behind Godsway's lines, which is just as well, given that I killed Penda. King Godsway, Edge's father, won the fight. Penda can't have, after all, because he is dead.

I hear footfalls, and it grows dark of a sudden. Someone's here, blocking the light.

He stoops to come in and straightens up, so tall that he can barely stand in this tent. His hair's shorter, hanging loose around his shoulders, and he's wiry, leaner than ever. He's filthy, too, covered in muck up to the knees, up to the elbows. He must have been helping to bury the dead. Is that how he found me? He does not know that I'm watching him; he thinks I am still asleep. A strange, tugging pain grips my chest.

He turns suddenly and crouches down beside me with the swiftness of a cat. "Are you awake?" he says — foolishly, for am I not looking dead at him?

He is really here.

I nod.

Tears stream down his face, leaving pale tracks in the grime. I have never seen him cry before. He lets out a long breath, raking both hands through his hair, which falls through his mud-smirched fingers like flames. Then he laughs. "Cai, if you ever lead me such a chase again, I swear to God I'll skin you alive." And Tasik reaches out to grasp my hand, holding it tight. Our fingers twine together. He is real. He is here with me at last. Oh, he's got a few things to tell me, all right. My witch father.

My shoulder burns with pain. I can't think straight. I feel as though I've drunk too much wine. But I don't care. How did he get here? How did he find me? "You've still got muck for brains," I say at last. "I didn't ask to be made a slave." Does he think I wanted to be carried half across the known world and sold as a hostage to the Devil's Cub?

It doesn't matter, though, because now he's here.

Tasik lifts one eyebrow, and my spirit sings to see him do it. "And you're still a gabby wretch. I thank Christ your mother never saw the mess you were in when I found you, puthering out blood like it was water. She'd have fainted clean away."

Ma. It hurts to think of her. "Where is she?" I force out the words. "And Elflight and Asha?" I can't stand to hear it. I can't stand it if they're dead and it's my fault, my fault again.

Tasik glances down at the ground, squeezing my fingers. "I had to leave your mother and the girls behind. It was Fausta — she had them bundled into a cart and taken to Saint Agatha's — your mother was too weak to ride. It's a god house, a nunnery, up in the mountains, far from Constantinople. No one but Fausta knows where they are — not even Constans, the filthy coward, if Fausta kept her word."

So they are half a world away. But they live. They live. Relief washes over me like a bucket of warm water, followed by the old darkness that trails me everywhere. All of this is my doing: from the moment I left my grieving mother to riot through the streets of Constantinople to the firing of the arrow that killed Penda. I will never forgive myself. I'm wicked to the bone, and there's nothing I can do to change it. My grandfather's blood flows strong and deep through my veins; I am like him. I am the liar, the cheat, the great deceiver, and now I am a killer, too.

I want Tasik to know the worst I've done, and then if he leaves me here alone, so be it. The words spew out, hot and bitter: "I killed Penda, Tasik. I shot him and he died."

Tasik looks at me awhile before speaking. I can't read his face. Is he pleased or not? "I know, you little fool," he says at last. "You shouted it often enough in your sleep. You choose your enemies ill, don't you?"

"I thought you'd be glad." Fresh misery wells up inside me. So even that sin is worthless: I've taken a man's life, and all for nothing. "I did it for you. Why didn't you tell me anything?" I can't stop thinking of Wulf. What will he say when he hears it was me who killed Penda, if he's even still alive?

Tasik sighs. Not for the first time, I sense that he looks at me but sees another, long ago. I remember that hot afternoon by the palace harbor: *I may have named you after my father, but by Christ I wish you did not have his talent for deception.* "I wanted to keep you safe." He smiles at the look on my face. "I was once told the same, many years since, and it cut no ice with me, either. But I'm glad you killed Penda. I'm glad he's dead. You did well."

There's a start. I never thought I'd hear as much from him.

I want him to know I've changed, that I'm not a liar and a thief and a coward anymore. "Tasik," I say, "I'm going to do right now, I swear. I'll do everything you tell me."

He stares as if I have just sprouted wings or grown another head, then lets out a great wild burst of laughter. "Don't you dare. I should get so bored. For God's sake, Cai, don't be such a fool."

I grin at him. We are all right now, my crazed witch father and I. "See, you've laid me a challenge."

He grips my hand again. "Na, give me a rest of at least a sennight before you do aught that'll boil my blood. Are you hungry? They make a broth each night in the camp."

I shake my head. I don't want him to go anywhere just yet. I want him to stay with me. "Tas, can we go and fetch Ma and the girls?" I do not know how long it will take, and I care even less. "We've got to find them."

"We will." My father smiles at me. "And then we'll go home. Wherever that is."

And I'm glad, for I am the Ghost, and I have been gone too long.

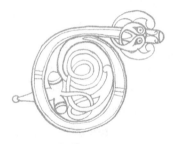

Epilogue:
Hall of the High King,
Northumbria, Yule AD 656

IT'S FILThY DARK out here, and cold, too, but Tasik does not seem to feel it. The great wooden door closes gently behind us. I'm glad I greased the hinges. It cost me a morning's hawking, but oh, it was worth it.

Edge knew. "Not coming, witch brat?" he asked when we'd broken our fast.

And I said, "No. Not this day."

Edge reached out and we clasped hands. "Farewell, then, cousin."

"Good hunting," I said.

"You, too, my friend." He smiled and walked off to join his father in the yard. Edge won't say anything. He's my friend, my brother.

I shall probably never see him again.

Moving almost as one, Tasik and I slip silently across the shadowy courtyard.

We come to a low, slumped building, and I slide my dagger from its sheath. Softly, softly, I take the heavy lock in my hands. It is iron-cold and rusty, but it's no bother to the Ghost. Here she comes: open.

"They used to keep hounds in here, long ago," Tasik says, and I hold a finger to my lips. Jesu, he'd be no use as a thief. The lock clicks free, and holding on to it, I sheathe my dagger and push open the door. We're in.

Wulf sits in the corner, alone, shoulders hunched, long legs sprawling out before him.

Edge's father is a merciful High King, but even he is not fool enough to lock up Wulfhere of Mercia with the rest of his kind. When the Mercian prisoners were brought here last night, a straggling line of weary men, I thought they'd all be put to the sword. But the High King is a Christian, and he has sworn to spare them. Cenry was not among them, and he was not found with the dead, either. The word is he got away — took up his grandfather's torn standard and rode deep into Mercia with those of his people still standing. I wish it may be true, and that Cenry is not dead in some unmarked grave, unrecognized, unknown.

How dare they keep Wulf trapped in here, though, shut in this dark, shadowy dog-byre? I feel Tasik's hand rest lightly on my shoulder — we must be quick. In moments, we're crouching before him. Wulf's wrists are bound, and I feel that flicker of anger again. *How dare they?* I take out my dagger and saw through the knots, just as Tasik leans forward and hisses, "*Wulf!*"

Wulf sits up, eyes open, reaching straightaway to his belt for a knife that isn't there. The High King allows his prisoners no weapons, of course. Then Wulf laughs, leaning back against the damp wall.

He and Tasik look at each other for what seems a long while, as if they speak without framing any words.

"Come, you fool," Tasik says then, "do you want them to find us?" He speaks as if no more than an afternoon has passed since they last saw each other, and not the whole of my life.

Wulf shakes his head. "Not a drop of sense between you." And then he grins, and my heart lifts to see it again, that flashing, half-crazed smile. I know now that Cenry must be alive and Wulf's sure of it. If he were not, it would show in his face. "Well enough," he says. "Where are the horses? I trust you've thought of that?"

"On the hillside." Tasik gets to his feet, moving toward the door. "Quick!"

In answer, Wulf follows me, loping across the dark dog-byre, grinning all over his face like a boy. I shut the lock again as we close the door behind us — that should fool them for a while. Not long, though. We run: me, Tasik, and Wulf.

It's a long ride, and a long journey ahead, but it has started well.

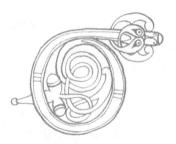

Historical note

B LOODLINE RISING is just a story, but a fair few of the people and places in it creep into the history books, some casting a greater shadow than others. Constantinople in the seventh century was the last bastion of the Roman Empire, which had by this time split itself in two parts, eastern and western, and claimed the already ancient city of Byzantium as capital of the Eastern Roman Empire. Its citizens renamed it in honor of their emperor, Constantine. More than a hundred years later, when *Bloodline Rising* is set, the people of Constantinople were speaking Greek rather than Latin but still saw themselves as citizens of a great Roman civilization, albeit one that was in reality no longer a world power.

Although there is barely thirteen years between *Bloodline* and *Bloodline Rising*, change was gathering pace in Britain, too. By this time, Christianity had taken hold of the island again and the Church was growing in power. The old ways were changing, slipping away, but the many different kingdoms still fought for supremacy. It would be another couple of hundred years before England emerged as a nation, north and south, east and west, bound in an uneasy peace.

There are places in Cai's story that you can visit even now. The great dome of Saint Sophia still dominates the skyline of Constantinople — now Istanbul, in Turkey — a city with one foot in Europe and the other in Asia. Now a museum, Saint Sophia is over fifteen hundred years old, and in her great lifetime she has been both church and mosque. Anyone lucky enough to visit Istanbul can also take a trip to the Basilica Cistern, a vast underground palace, forested with ancient stone pillars, awash with water where blind fish swim.

As for Britain, its history during this period is hard to pin down. Hardly anyone could write, so it's difficult to know what really happened and when, but according to the tales that have survived, after the battle of Winwaed River, and the death of King Penda, Mercia was subdued at last — but not for long. A few years later, in 658, the Mercians rebelled against their Northumbrian overlords and chose a king from their own ranks. Wulfhere of Mercia ruled with great skill — and some of his father's ruthlessness — for the next seventeen years. Wulfhere was finally defeated by the new young king of Northumbria: Egfrith, son of Oswiu. In *Bloodline Rising*, I translated the names of these forgotten kings (probably without much accuracy, I'm afraid to say) from Egfrith to Peaceblade, or Edge, and from Oswiu to Godsway. Whether Wulfhere led his men away from that last battle or was captured by the Northumbrians only to be spared, no one knows, but he did survive it, despite being defeated. And the story goes, of course, that as a young man Egfrith, or Edge of Northumbria, was held hostage in a Mercian court.

Acknowledgments

Thanks very much to Catherine Clarke, Denise Johnstone-Burt, Chris Kloet, Ellen Holgate, and Nic Knight for all their help while I wrote this book. It wouldn't be here without them.

I also owe thanks to a whole host of other people who very kindly lent me their time and expert knowledge of all sorts of different things. They are:

David Hill, John Julius Norwich, and Chris West, who read the book checking for historical accuracy. Any mistakes left behind are most definitely my fault.

Clare Purcell, who shared her knowledge of horses with me again, even though she was busy looking after young Harlan.

Edge Llewellyn, whose name I borrowed without asking. I did mean to, but kept forgetting. Sorry, Edge — hope you don't mind.

Will Llewellyn, Martin Llewellyn, and Alec Birkbeck, who built the shed where I wrote most of this book. Extra thanks to Will, who knows everything there is to know about boats and ships, to Martin for making a flower bed for me to gaze at, and Alec for buying copies of *Bloodline* and getting everyone he knows to read it!

I'd also like to thank Philip Reeve for his support. The man is a complete genius, and if you haven't already, you should read his books: the Mortal Engines quartet, *Here Lies Arthur*, the whole lot.